Alexander [illegible] H. W. Smith [illegible]

Yrs. as ever
E. Stuart Phelps

THE

LAST LEAF FROM SUNNY SIDE.

BY

H. TRUSTA,

AUTHOR OF "PEEP AT NUMBER FIVE," "TELL-TALE,"
"SUNNY-SIDE," ETC., ETC.

WITH

A MEMORIAL OF THE AUTHOR,

BY

AUSTIN PHELPS.

TENTH THOUSAND.

BOSTON:
PHILLIPS, SAMPSON, AND COMPANY.
1853.

ANDOVER: J. D. FLAGG,
Stereotyper and Printer.

CONTENTS.

MEMORIAL.

It is related of an eminent Puritan Divine, that, but a few hours before his death, he called for a large collection of manuscripts, containing the most valuable records of his life, and directed that they should be burned in his presence. The Christian world have sympathized with his biographer in lamenting the irreparable loss. Yet, upon second thought, we cannot but revere his memory the more for that single act. We can scarcely say that we would part with it, even for the recovery of the lost treasure. It is the very nature of some of the most noble virtues, to seek concealment. They cannot but choose to be unseen. They come not into the world conscious of the high mission they fulfil; they come among us, simply to exist. They ask but the privilege of *being*. They perform their mission in ignorance of its import. They are all unconscious of the bland enchantment which they breathe around them — with which the very atmosphere of their presence is laden. When their charm is felt, and the world throngs around them, as it will, to make obeisance to them, they hide themselves beneath the drooping wings of evening, and look with an eye of maidenly reproach, on him who would bring them forth to the broad day to be seen of men.

Such virtues formed in part the character of her of whose life it is proposed here to give a simple narrative — and they have laid restraint upon the effort. Her strictly private journal, in which she had recorded the details of her religious history for the last twenty years of her life, she committed in her last hours to the writer of these pages, in solemn trust that he should give it to the flames without inspection of its contents by any human eye. The most valuable records for the present purpose are thus removed beyond our reach. The spirit of that trust has been extended also to many fragmentary records that remained. It is necessarily, therefore, but a broken narrative that is here offered as a memorial of her.

Mrs. Elizabeth Stuart Phelps was born in Andover, Massachusetts, on the thirteenth of August, 1815. She was the fifth child of Professor Moses Stuart, and the eldest of his daughters, with the exception of one who died in childhood. Her ancestry in the maternal line, she was accustomed with pleasure to trace back to the family of

"Old Governor Winthrop." The chief peculiarities of her natural temperament she inherited from her father, whom in many other respects she strongly resembled. His character could hardly fail to exercise a formative influence on that of a child even less positively disposed than she to sympathize with it. Among her earliest recollections were those of her father's severe self-discipline. In a paper found among her manuscripts since her decease, in which she had recorded some reminiscences of her childhood, the first record is the following: "One thing made a powerful impression on me; it was my waking early on cold winter mornings, and looking from my western window into the wood-house chamber. There was father, sawing wood by the dim light of his lantern. I used to wonder, as I lay snug in bed, dreading to hear 'the first bell,' how father *could* force himself out *so* early when it was *so* cold and *so* dark, to *saw wood.* When I grew older, and learned that he often did this after a wakeful night full of tossings to and fro, with snatches of unquiet and dreamy sleep, and when I saw him coming in to the breakfast-table exhausted and nervous, it taught me how high a price he set upon those golden morning hours."

The scene from that 'western window,' with many others like it, affected her through life. She learned to cherish a more than filial reverence for her father's character. It roused her; it stimulated her to effort; it gave definiteness to her objects of effort; it sustained the steadiness of her exertions; its influence was exhibited even more distinctly than before, in the last year of her life; and in her last hours, her very features assumed a striking resemblance to his.

The predominance of her nervous system over every other part of her physical nature, gave an early and positive development to all her natural tastes and traits of character. The movements of her mind were naturally rapid, and strongly marked, and yet accompanied with very great and often excessive delicacy of sensibility. Her temperament favored the formation of a vigorous yet feminine character.

Very early in life, she manifested a keen sensitiveness to forms of *beauty*, both in nature and in art. The natural scenery at Andover had no small influence in forming her mental habits. Her letters to her young correspondents abound with enthusiastic expressions of her fondness for the hills and rocks, and "woody by-roads," and "speaking elms," and more than all, the "gorgeous sunsets," in the midst of which her childhood was passed. In one of her little Sabbath school books, she has mirrored forth the feelings of her youthful heart on a survey of Andover Hill after a sleet-storm; when the elm-trees "were cased in thousands of glittering icicles," and "bending beneath the weight of their shining armor, branch bore down upon branch, forming what seemed a solid roof of diamonds over the path." "To her awe-struck mind, it seemed as if God dwelt in that shining roof above her; that she could see Him and hear Him." The setting of the sun associated itself so strongly with her earliest conceptions of the immortality of the soul, that it became her choicest emblem of that truth. She never wearied of watching the infinite diversity of sunset pictures, as seen from her favorite 'western window.'

She possessed, naturally, a passionate taste for painting and statuary. The first of these was her favorite recreation through life; and in her later years, such was the pleasure she derived from it, that it became a part of her daily occupation. The first serious enthusiasm which she felt, as a child, in any plans for mature life, was awakened by the purpose which she at one time entertained, of devoting herself to the labors of this art. She never permitted an opportunity to go by unimproved, of visiting collections of the works of great artists. The occasion of her annual visit to the Gallery of the Boston Athenæum, was for many years one of her happiest anniversaries. She often chose, in preference to all others, that mode of spending the anniversary of her marriage. It was one motive to the fatal exertions she made during the last year of her life, that she might earn with her own pen the means of visiting the repositories of Art in the Old World. Although neither her own proficiency in painting, nor her limited means of gratifying her taste by the labors of others, enabled her to gather around her much that would be valued by a critic, yet the desolateness of the home she has left is relieved by the evidences of her taste, with which it is filled. To the ear of affection, its silent walls are eloquent in the thoughts they breathe of her.

She developed also, in early life, a taste for music; and through life was often dependent on its power to soothe her agitated mind, or to elevate her depressed spirits. Her sensitiveness to it was attested by her speechless struggling with suppressed emotion, and the tears which she could not suppress, when for the first time she listened to the Seventh Symphony of Beethoven. Her imagination often disturbed her sleep with *dreams* of harmony, from which she would awake in tears, and which she could not describe but in terms of rapture. So lasting were the impressions of some of these dreams, that they would not leave her until she had committed a record of them to paper.

Her taste for the fine arts, even before she seemed to herself to possess any religious principle, had mellowed and refined her character; and it is the more interesting to her friends in their remembrances of her, because of its association with certain passages in her religious experience, which will be noticed in the sequel. Very closely allied with it in her nature, was her nice sense of *honor*. She manifested this early and always. Without a knowledge of her sensitiveness in this respect, a person could not understand her character. By nature, her *conscience* found its most frequent, if not its strongest, development, in a regard for the honorable and magnanimous. Her sense of right appeared to be blended with her sense of the noble. Her most intimate friends find it most difficult to conceive of her as cherishing a *mean* sentiment. The chosen friend of her childhood writes: "I cannot remember a single instance in which I thought she ever intended to deceive; and she never said or did a thing for display." Her contempt of dishonorable conduct in others was prompt and keen, and fearless in expression. Yet it was one of the singular evidences of the nobleness of her own nature, that she was never quick to discern this defect in the conduct of others. It was often fascinating to observe the childlike artlessness, with which she would attribute to others honorable motives, of actions the interpretation of which, as the world would give it, she seemed unable to understand.

As respects severe studies, her early tastes inclined to the study of mental philosophy and the mathematics. Her love of natural objects does not seem to have produced any fondness for natural science. Singular as it may appear, she had none of her father's predilection for the study of languages; it was rather disagreeable to her. Her favorite department in childhood was that of the "belles lettres;" and in this, her childhood was marked by uncommon mental activity. She very early exhibited a desire to originate trains of thought, rather than to accumulate the treasures of others; and this was characteristic of her mental habits to the end of life.

As early as at the age of ten years, she developed a *tact* in narrative composition. She was accustomed at that period, to amuse the domestics of the family and their friends, with her extemporaneous stories; and among the relics of her writings at that time, are found little volumes of narratives which she composed for the entertainment of her younger sisters. Her own earliest recollections of her mental history, were those of the tales she wrote, or of the materials for them which she was constantly inventing and arranging in her mind.

Her natural temperament was not well fitted to produce a life of equable enjoyment. Even in childhood, she seems to have been subject to fluctuations of hope and despondency. She did not herself regard her youth as the happiest portion of her life. It was not, all things considered, an *un*happy period; it could not well have been so, in the midst of such a home as it was her privilege to enjoy. She often referred to it in later life, with enthusiastic gratitude for the parental influences which were at once so vigorous and yet so genial. The affections of her childhood never decayed; they rather grew with her growth and strengthened with her strength. Still, such was the quickness and power of her sensibilities, that whatever moved her, stirred the depths of her soul. She lived in a world of emotion. Any occasion of despondency took a strong hold upon her. She describes herself, in a letter to a friend, as having been by nature wild and wayward and impetuous in her feelings, yet too sensitive to utter them often to any human being. An instinct which she could not resist impelled her to hold herself in reserve from her nearest friends. So far as concerns *expression* of her inner life, she passed the early periods of her youth in a solitude which is not very common even to sensitive natures. This she afterwards regarded as a great misfortune. Especially in its effects upon her subsequent religious experience, it seemed to her the occasion of irreparable evils. In a letter written a few years ago, to a young friend who was meditating a public profession of religion, she remarks, with a severity in her judgment of herself which at that time had long been habitual with her: "I wish I could say anything to make you see how deeply I regret having indulged my natural reserve on religious subjects earlier in life. It has made my Christian character one-sided, and shut me out from many avenues of influence. Do not start in *your* Christian course with *reserve* and half-revealings. *Speak* — speak out, openly, fully, honestly. Let it be called enthusiasm, or cant, or what it may. I wish you could feel the importance of this, as I do." "You love the Saviour, and why should you hesitate to speak of Him?"

It was indeed unfortunate, that a mind so active as hers, should, from the very first of its earnest workings, have been so constantly introverted upon itself. As might have been expected, her early habits of religious feeling became morbid, and tended strongly to bind her thoughts to some *one* narrow circle. The central object in that circle was, Death. Her own record on this point will best explain it. On a stray leaf found among her papers, she has written as follows: "All my early religious emotions were concentrated on the one thought of death. I used to think much about it. It gave a melancholy direction to all my childish feelings. It was a naked sword ever hanging over me by a hair. My nurse used to take me to almost all the funerals that took place in the village, and at last I was fond of going to them; not because death had become any less terrible, but because there was something in the exciting stir of so strong an emotion as deep grief, which suited my nature. I loved to have my feelings powerfully worked upon; and in that still village no agent could do this like death." "I can remember, as far back as when I was but three years old, and from that time onward, having again and again cried myself to sleep, because I must some time or other see my mother die." The death of her mother was *the* affliction which, in the prospect, often clouded her path, but from which God took her away. Indeed, the invalid life of her mother, who for many years was supposed to be on the borders of the grave, was probably the chief, if not the only, original cause of the fascination which death acquired in the mind of the daughter.

The morbid association of her childish feelings with death, was never wholly broken up. In mature life, she often could not withstand the gloom with which thoughts of death oppressed her. Long after she had learned to think and speak of her own death with a calm hopefulness, she could not meet with composure the death of friends. Their lifeless remains — the bier — the pall — the tolling bell — the slow procession — the *grave* — each, and all, were intensely painful to her. They seemed to realize the idea of death to her physical senses. They formed permanent scenes in her mind's eye, remaining sometimes for weeks, and even months. She has often refrained from sleeping for many hours of a night, because her imagination was so much more painfully active in the creation of such scenes in her dreams, than in her waking thoughts.

Her early experience in this respect, was one of the occasions of her subsequent interest in the composition of books for children. It was her conviction, that much of our Sabbath School literature gives an unnatural prominence to the single idea of human mortality. This appeared to her to be too often the *only* impressive thought, which a book was designed to convey; and in many instances, she thought the legitimate effect of much that was written for the instruction of children, was to associate in their minds early piety with the necessity of an early death. She believed this to be unnatural. Yet, her own experience in the composition of books for the young, taught her how easily a writer may be tempted into this error by the prospect of artistic effect. She gave to this subject much thought, and has recorded briefly the result, in her own conviction that "there is something wrong — morbidly precocious, in the mind of that child whose thoughts are *all* colored by the idea of dying." "The strongest appeals to the hearts of the young," she adds, "cannot be made by trying to force constantly upon them the thought that they are mortal. You cannot produce thus, more than a momentary good impression; it is crossing nature." She did not believe any such "crossing" of "nature" to be necessary to an impression of religious truth on young minds. She has frequently spoken of the abundance of materials for impression, which are furnished by the simple facts of Scriptural truth, and which, as a whole, are eminently cheering in their influence. The vigorous system of religious doctrine with which she sympathized, left no apology, as she thought, for an unnatural *protrusion* of the image of death, in the representations of religion which are made to children. This view led her to propose to herself as the object of all that she wrote for Sabbath Schools, the simple and natural portraiture of religious principle as it is in *life*, rather than as it is in death.

At the age of sixteen, she left her father's house to enter the Mount Vernon school, an institution then existing in Boston, under the care of Rev. Jacob Abbott, in whose family she resided for the greater part of two years. This period was exceedingly fruitful of events which affected her whole character. The secluded life she had previously led, rendered her transition to a large city a great event. New scenes, the formation of new acquaintances, and subjection to a new discipline, could not but impress a nature so susceptible as hers. She ever afterwards cherished a grateful recollection of the skill and vigilance, with which Mr. Abbott at once checked and stimulated the development of her hitherto unformed character. Her mind now unfolded itself rapidly, and with increased vigor of tone; her tastes matured; and especially did her predilection for narrative writing derive advantage, from her intercourse with one who was himself a writer of such rare excellence in that style of composition. It was under his direction, that her first attempts were made in writing for the press. They were in the form of brief articles for a Religious Magazine of which he was at that time the Editor. Those of her companions at the Mt. Vernon School who still survive, will remember some of the contributions which she made to their amusement, under the signature of "H. Trusta,"—the same that she appended, twenty years later, to "The Sunny Side." Her highest and almost only ambition in her first efforts, was to write something that should attract the notice of her father. It is doubtful whether any subsequent success ever gave her keener pleasure, than she felt when she first received from his lips the hearty "Well done," after the publication of one of her simple stories. But a few weeks before she went to join him in Heaven, she recalled with filial pride, the occasion, the hour, the trepidation she felt, the quick look of surprise followed by the smile on her father's face, when she put into his hands the few small bills she had just received as a remuneration for her first toils of authorship; and the playful indignation with 'which he tossed them back to her over the dinner table, saying, "I want none of that."' "Her heart," she said, in speaking of the occurrence, "was as full as it could hold; she was happier than a queen." The narration of this little incident brought back the life to her pale cheek, as the four hundred thousand readers of one of her late productions could not do it.

During this period of her first residence in Boston, she made many trials of her skill in writing for publication, in some of which she was successful, in others, not. One of her fugitive pieces, published while she was a member of the Mt. Vernon School, was very extensively circulated in various forms, being republished in England and returned to this country accredited to an English authoress, and afterwards published also in France. For many years it was a standard article in reading-books for children, and it still reappears, occasionally, among the selections in the 'Children's Department' of our religious newspapers. Little instances of success of this kind, were not fitted to induce the youthful authoress to lay aside her pen. Indeed, from that time it was never idle, till, at Death's bidding, it was laid down forever. Her letters, written during that period, indicate the germinating of a sense of religious responsibility for any power she might possess or acquire, to influence others. She seems to have directed her attention with earnestness, to a study of human character as it is seen in common life. To a young companion, after expressing a trembling sense of the responsibility of those who may have *influence* within their reach, she writes: "We must not be idle — we must work, *studying human nature*, that we may find the hidden springs and touch them to any chord we please." "It is no trifle to hold even a silken thread around one heart."

The period of her residence in Mr. Abbott's family, is marked by the development of her first effectual convictions on the subject of religion. Up to this time, her religious opinions do not appear to have been the subject of much reflection; nor does she seem to have experienced anything unusual to children who have been religiously educated. Indeed, the fidelity of Christian parents appears not to have produced in her case so great distinctness of religious convictions, as that which commonly results from such fidelity. The exclusiveness with which the idea of Death possessed her childish experience on the subject of religion, shut out, apparently, much of the more valuable reflection which the children of Christian parents often have in early life. In the fragmentary record she has left, of the fascination with which funerals affected her, she thus speaks: "The deep solemnity which such seasons left upon my mind, was the result of fear, and of that indefinable awe with which a child looks over beyond the grave. I used at such times to go often to meetings. I would pray much, that I might be forgiven and accepted for Christ's sake. But I had no definite ideas of *what it was*, for which I must be forgiven. I read a great deal about dying, and about the soothing presence of Christ with his followers in their dying hour. When my fears were wide awake, as they used most often to be at night, I used to repeat before going to sleep,

> 'Jesus can make a dying bed
> Feel soft as downy pillows are, etc.'"

She elsewhere speaks of having been often anxiously interested in the salvation of her soul, and she adds respecting these occasions, "They were mostly at times of unusual excitement, caused by some *sudden death*, or by a protracted meeting. I particularly remember a visit of Doctor Nettleton's at Andover, and his 'inquiry-meetings,' all of which I faithfully attended. None of these impressions, however, were lasting; they died away with the exciting cause." This last remark must be understood as true, only so far as concerns the event of her immediate conversion, which is the main subject of the sketch. In a letter to a friend, written not long before this, she speaks of Doctor Nettleton's visit to Andover, thus: "I remember once at an inquiry-meeting, I could not speak to him. He seemed to read my face without words.

Then, in a low tone, — I can hear it now, — he said to me 'Keep near to God — keep near to God.'" This single remark, dropped in the stillness of a solemn hour, never left her. It often recurred to her mind afterwards — even in the last year of her life she spoke of it — and she distinctly associated it with her hopeful conversion, which took place several years after the occasion on which the remark was uttered. She says of it, to one of her correspondents, "It was the first still small voice of peace and holy joy that made itself *felt* to me."

The more general sketch above referred to, proceeds with an account of the manner in which her mind was again engaged in religious inquiries. It is interesting as an illustration of the diversity of God's ways. It shows how He adapts His grace to idiosyncrasies of temperament in those whom he purposes to save. He leads them 'by a way which they knew not.' They 'hear a word *behind*' them, saying, 'This is the way.' Often, silence is made more eloquent than speech.

The narrative of the 'great change' is continued. — "The course which Mr. Abbott adopted, was entirely the reverse of that to which I had been accustomed, and which I expected. Instead of urging God's claims upon me, as others had often done, he preserved an unbroken silence on the subject of personal religion. This surprised me, and after awhile made me uneasy. I brought myself at length to ask him for the cause of his silence towards me on that subject. He told me that he considered the circumstances under which I had been brought up to have been such, that every motive which could influence me had been already urged, and that I had deliberately made my choice; and therefore that it remained for him only to fit me for happiness as far as it could be had in this world. This startled me, and led me to look more earnestly into my heart. From this beginning, I was led on gradually, and to myself almost imperceptibly, until I began to dare to hope that I had become a child of God, and to wish to take upon myself the name of Christ. I was conscious of a great change in me. Thoughts of God no longer filled me with horror; but a view of His holiness and purity was granted to me, which filled me with inexpressible joy. I felt that *life* was an 'unspeakable gift,' *because there was a God.* I desired most earnestly to approach as near to His holiness as I was able, but many struggles taught me how strong a hold sin had in this heart. Here, the atonement of Christ first met me with power. I felt driven to it; and in view of it, even such a sinning heart still dared to look up and struggle on, feeling that its heaviest burden Christ himself bore.

I began to desire to give myself wholly to *God in Christ.* I wished to live and die for Him. I longed to lose myself in Him. I wished to indulge no plans, nor purposes, nor feelings, nor thoughts, of which love to Him was not the guiding spring. To live for His glory, seemed all that rendered life worth possessing. If I must cease to do this, I would also cease to live. This was a great change from my former self, and I have dared to hope that it was God's own work."

The 'gradual,' and to herself 'almost imperceptible,' process of which she speaks, as having preceded the dawn of Christian hope in her heart, was protracted through a period of nearly two years. Her susceptible nature could not but be stirred to its very depths by earnest religious inquiry. Her experience was rendered the more tumultuous in its character, by the fact that this inquiry was awakened just at the time when her whole intellectual being was opening itself to new influences, and approaching the maturity of womanhood. The great thoughts of Life, and Death, and Destiny, and God, swayed her feelings impetuously to and fro. Often, for long periods, her soul was too powerfully agitated to admit of her resting in calm hope.

At least, such was the character of her experience, as it seemed to develop itself to her own consciousness, and as she recalled it in subsequent years. Yet, even at that early period, she had acquired a strength of character which prevented any such tumultuous *exhibition* of her feelings to others. The impression which others received of the workings of her mind, may be best inferred from the judgment expressed by Mr. Abbott, who writes with regard to that passage in her history, "My impression is, decidedly, that her religious experience, in all its stages, though connected with *deep feeling within*, was very calm, quiet, and gentle, in all the external manifestations of it. I do not think there were any great fluctuations of feeling. There always seemed to me to be a certain principle of *momentum*, so to speak, in Elizabeth's mind, which gave great steadiness to all its action."

It was with the utmost difficulty that she brought herself to communicate her feelings on the subject of religion, even with the pen, and to those who possessed her entire confidence. The inquiry which opened her intercourse with Mr. Abbott on the subject, cost her a severe struggle; and so sensitive was she to the sound of her own voice in the utterance of religious feeling, that to the very last of her conferences with her instructor respecting her Christian hopes, she often preferred that her pen should speak for her, although she was an inmate of his family.

From this excessive sensibility in respect to an expression of religious experience, she never wholly recovered. She mourned over it, weeping in secret places; and it was the occasion of many struggles. The brief record given above of her early experience on the subject of religion, was prepared many years afterwards, at the request of a Committee of a Church with which she was about to connect herself, — and this mode of communication was adopted, because, after many fruitless efforts, she found herself unable to appear before them and *speak* of that which God had done for her soul.

Yet, this very delicacy of her too sensitive heart gave a depth of tenderness to her 'first love' of her Saviour. That love was mingled with a feeling of self-reproach, as if she wronged him by being a *mute* friend. It was one of the burdens of her daily supplication, that her tongue might be unloosed, to praise Him. To one who knows the earnestness of her soul's desire in this respect, there is a tearful pathos in her appeal to her young friend, after an humble confession of her own infirmity: "You love the Saviour, and why should you hesitate to *speak* of Him?" Many of her letters, written at about the time when she first indulged Christian hope, breathe the same spirit. Her most importunate desires appear to have been excited for the salvation of her companions. The love of Christ was the unfailing theme of her correspondence with them. She could not 'speak of Him,' but she could enter into her closet, and having shut to the door, under the Eye that seeth in secret, she could pour forth her very soul, in written expostulations with her young friends. The delicacy of her own feelings about these unstudied effusions of her heart, forbids the transfer of them to these pages; but a glimpse of the genial spirit that pervades them, may be caught from a transcript of a single scene in one of the little volumes which she has herself given to the world. It is the scene in the "Peep at Number Five," in which she records an interview between Grace Webster and the Pastor. Of all the characters in that volume, Grace Webster was her favorite; and to one who knew her early history, this was not surprising. That character, rather than others which are more fully delineated, drew her to itself by a secret cord of which she was almost wholly unconscious. Without intending to do so, she has in reality depicted herself in the following scene, so far as concerns her early experience of love to Christ.

"Grace Webster was very engaging in her appearance; her manners were gentle, and she was as timid as a fawn. Mr. Holbrook was at once much interested in her; he tried to converse with her, but could induce her to say but little. Her mother, who had been watching her with intense feeling, at length spoke of the recent interest manifested in the church meetings, and of the seriousness of many of the young people, — 'and our Grace,' added she, with a faltering voice and a burst of tears, 'and our Grace wants to talk with you.' Upon this she rose, and immediately left the room. Old Mr. Webster seemed to understand what was going on, for he resumed his seat by the window, and his newspaper. He was very deaf, and Grace was now alone with her minister, who at once understood and entered into all her feelings. He seemed to know just what she wished to say. Step by step he gently led her on to breathe out that confession, which, as yet, she had dared only to whisper in her closet to God. Her color came and went, — her breathing was rapid, — her heart beat quickly, — and her deep blue eye dilated with intense feeling when the young hope, just born in her heart, found a voice; when she ventured to speak of it to her minister, and say that she hoped she had been forgiven, that her name was enrolled in the 'Lamb's book of life.' From that moment new ties bound her to him. Her fears vanished, and, looking up into his face with her earnest, tearful eyes, as a daughter looks to her father, she opened to him all her heart. She told him of 'her joy, now that she had found her Saviour; how much she had pined for just such a friend, and that she now found in Him all and more than all she had been seeking, — perfect fulness of sympathy and love. Was it not kind in Him, to come and thus fill her heart? — she asked, was ever love like His? — how had she lived so long without Him? And yet,' said she, 'I think I should have been without Him now, had it not been for you. I was interested in you, and I believed every word you said. When you preached so much and prayed so much about the Saviour, and about trusting Him, I could not forget it. On Sundays and on week days I thought of it, —I knew that I was not loving Him, and I had no peace until I began to pray to Him, and I did pray until I found Him — no, until He found *me.*' * * * * *

"Mr. Holbrook rose and took his leave, and Grace slipped away to her own room, and locked her door, that she might be alone with her Saviour."

THUS genially, after a long and cloudy night, did the daystar arise in the heart of the young disciple. One might have hoped that it should be the harbinger of a calm summer day. But such was not, in all its parts, her Christian life. The elements of a vigorous and yet sensitive character are not often adjusted well to each other, without many secret conflicts. Those conflicts are the more severe, when such a character goes through the formative process under the influence of a bold, *positive* system of religious faith. A gifted soul, under such a system, strikes deep down, in search of foundations for its rest. It builds not on sands. In the case of the subject of this sketch, religious character was developed under infirmities of physical constitution, and these were aggravated by positive disease. The period she had spent in the Mt. Vernon school, had been one of untiring industry. Her studies had been pursued with indomitable purpose. She felt that much was expected from her, and her spirit was too lofty to permit her to do less than seemed to be due to the expectations of her friends. She exerted herself beyond her strength. She concealed the first indications of disease. Her studies were pursued with unremitting ardor long after she should have been under the care of a physician. She was compelled to return to her father's house, in the spring of 1834, bearing with her the germs of the *cerebral* disease, which nearly twenty years afterwards terminated her life. For three or four years after her return to Andover, she was afflicted with severe and frequent headaches, accompanied by partial blindness, and followed by temporary paralysis of portions of her body, and great prostration of the nervous system. These affections seemed at length to reach a crisis in an attack of the typhus fever, under which she sunk so low that her life was despaired of, and her father at one time entered her room to inform her that she was supposed to be dying. She recovered, however, and till near the time of her death, fourteen years afterwards, she enjoyed many periods of comfortable health. But her constitution was broken, and she was not for any long time relieved from morbid affections of the brain.

Under such circumstances as these, it was not to be expected that her religious experience should be as equable in its character as, even with her variable temperament, it might otherwise have been. It is true, her outward life was subjected to but few disturbing influences; the lines seemed to fall to her in pleasant places; and to the majority of those who knew her, it was not manifest that her life was one of any unusual trial. But the few friends who were familiar with the habits of her mind, think of her now as having endured a severity of conflict which was fully known only to herself and God. This was especially true of the first few years of her Christian life, in which she was most severely afflicted with disease.

Her public profession of her faith in Christ was an act of great self-denial to her. Under any circumstances, the publicity of it would have been peculiarly painful to her. It was rendered the more so by the fact, that of a large family, she was the first who had been prepared for such a solemnity, and also by the fact that she was called to it at a time when her moral power was weakened by the feebleness of her health. She shrunk from it as from a fiery ordeal. For a long time, she could not bring herself to the point of making the sacrifice, though it does not appear that her Christian hope was at that time clouded. In a letter (already alluded to), addressed to a young friend many years after, she thus refers to this trial of her early faith: —

"I well remember when I stood just where you are, and I should like to tell you briefly where I erred. It required a very great effort for *me* to break the ice and come forward first in the family, and make a profession of religion by joining the Chapel Church. I shrunk from it more than I can describe; and just as long as I did so, I was unhappy. I think the determining to do that thing, and the *doing* of it, cost me more of real effort than any other one thing I ever did. And yet I would not, for anything I can now conceive of, have had the trial less. My love to Christ needed just that test, and through his mercy I bore it. Now I want you to feel just this — that you are to profess your faith in Christ because it is *His* command, and that you *will* do it, though all the world condemn you. It is a matter between your own soul and God, with which a stranger intermeddleth not. The solemnity is so full of intense interest that, you may depend on it, you will forget that you are in the presence of any one but God and holy angels. God bless you."

She became a member of the church of the Theological Seminary in Andover, in the month of July, 1834. Soon after this, the increasing violence of the disease which had fastened itself upon her constitution, caused her much physical suffering, and plunged her into great despondency. Her way seemed to lie before her in deep shadow. Her mind was tempted to swing loose from the faith to which her childhood had been trained. She saw little to cheer her in this world, and, often, as little in the world to come. Those were years which in after life, she sometimes recalled with misgivings, lest the cloud which overshadowed them should gather again. She learned to regard them, however, as having subjected her character to a discipline which it needed. They were the season of her trial, preparatory to the usefulness and peace which were afterwards to be given her. They were necessary to subdue her wayward sensibilities, to strengthen her judgment, to rectify errors of opinion, and to give definiteness to views of truth which she had held obscurely. They enlarged and invigorated her character, in every way. It is doubtful whether she could at that time have borne with safety, a more gentle experience. Such an experience could scarcely have resulted in that intelligence and that depth of religious convictions, which were needed for the best development of a nature so vigorous and impulsive as hers. The truthfulness of this view will be evident from a glance at one or two phases of her life at this time. They are interesting, not only as preliminaries to *her* subsequent usefulness, but as illustrations of the ways in which physical suffering is often made the instrument of mental and religious growth.

The discipline to which she was at this period subjected, led, among other things, to a revision of some of her views as to the nature of a religious life. The first workings of religious principle in her mind had given her, as she afterwards thought, a *theory* of practical religion which was not symmetrical in its character, and therefore not healthful in its operation. Her own experience under it, first directed her attention to its incompleteness. She suffered for the want of occupations which it did not allow to her. The difficulty which she had specially to encounter, was that her conscientious scruples did not for a long time justify the indulgence of those refined tastes, which were so prominent a feature in the make of her being. They were less obviously practical than some others. She could not find a place for them in the routine of a religious life. A suppression of them seemed to her inevitable. Life was to her eye, a passage through a great *emergency.* It should admit only the useful in action and the resolute in mental habit. It should leave no *heart* for the enjoyment of images of beauty or sounds of sweet melody. Such was the language of the first rude instinct of her religious nature. She has left on record a brief account of this passage in her history. The record was made in an attempt, some years afterwards, to aid the efforts of a young friend who was struggling with similar affliction.

"Some five or six years ago," she writes, "when I first began to feel the power of religious obligation, I became an absolute utilitarian. I thought I had no right to employ my time or my talents in anything that was not obviously *useful*—of some

solid, and visible, and tangible value to myself or to others. What good did painting do? or music? or poetry? or a thousand things I loved? None, that I could see. So I condemned them all. I took up Philosophy, and studied, and wrote prose, and sewed, and what not. My days were all given up to the 'solid and useful,' as the world would say. I felt, as every one feels, a sort of happiness in making a sacrifice with a good motive. This sustained me at times; and the regularity of my employments did more. *Yet, I was not happy.* My soul did thirst for the beautiful and the true. Suppressed longings, and unsatisfied tastes, and despised capacities, at length took their revenge. They fretted, and chafed, and wore upon the delicate frame-work that enclosed them, until it gave way. Then followed four long, dreary years. * * * * * *
If I was a Christian then, I certainly was not a happy one, I was a burden to myself and others. My mind became morbid. * * * It was a long process, and a troubled one; but I learned at last to be happy as God would have me be. I found out, that He who made me knew better than I, what He made me for; and that He had not given me tastes, and inclinations, and talents, all in themselves innocent, to be suppres-

sed, and to have others substituted for them. I 'turned over a new leaf;' I did it with trembling; but I did it. And now, I follow all my natural tastes, so far as they are in themselves harmless. I do not hesitate to gratify them, so far as I can, aiming only at a right regulation of them by the principles of the Gospel, and trying to feel that they and I *belong* to Him who gave them. If the bringing to perfection the nature which He gave me, does not sooner or later fit me for my highest usefulness to others, it must be because I am not sincere in my entire consecration of it to Him. Well, what is the result? Why, from the very first half hour in which I broke down the barriers of my old system, and took up my pencil, I said, 'Good bye to doctors.' I have been happier, I have been better, every way. I can now often bring to the altar — oh, how much oftener than in days of yore — the offering of a grateful, cheerful, satisfied heart. I do not find in the Scriptures any jarring with my present view of my duties in life. And I am taught by the beauty of morning and evening clouds, by the sunshine, and the rainbow, and the singing of birds, and the sweet breath of flowers, that a cultivation of our tastes for the beautiful in *His* works and ways, sweetens life and refines the heart, and makes it easier for us to be holy. You will find some goodness in the hovel where there are flower vines at the window. * * * But it is time my strain was over."

The infirmity here disclosed, is no uncommon one in the early religious life of cultivated minds. The two processes of intellectual and of religious cultivation, do not always, in *fact*, run parallel with each other. The adjustment of them, in its perfection, is the result of time and growth, often of mistakes and conflicts. If the subject of this narrative suffered more than others from this cause, it was in part the consequence of her natural strength of character. If she held an opinion, she held it positively; if she felt a conviction, she felt it deeply; if she formed a purpose, she clung to it long — it was so in everything. Besides, her first experience of vital religion occurred during the most romantic period of her youth, and as has been already observed, was simultaneous also with the attacks of severe bodily disease. It is not singular that the revision, of her theory of religion should have cost her some struggles with herself.

She was much assisted in this process of adjustment between her natural tastes and the claims of conscience, by a peculiarity which she adopted in her mode of studying the Scriptures.

It was her practice to observe in her reading of the Bible, all those historical scenes which seemed to her to be good subjects for representation on the canvas. She thus associated her taste for the arts with her love of God's Word, and rendered each in turn the handmaid of the other. Among her papers are found fragmentary criticisms, expressing hints of her ideas of many scriptural scenes, which had thus been made the themes of her study. A single specimen of these may be given here, not for any artistic merit (which it may or may not have), but merely to illustrate the original mode which she adopted for the discipline of her own mind, in respect to the tastes which had caused her so much trouble.

"Matt. 14: 25. 'And in the fourth watch of the night, Jesus went unto them walking on the sea.' This is a very difficult scene, and has been often attempted; but, so far as I have seen, with not much success. The ship tossed with the waves, could be finely represented. There should be a *spirited*, not a *tame* storm. The artist should learn whether there are any appearances peculiar to a storm on the sea of Gallilee. In the dimness, a few anxious faces from among the fishermen should be partially visible. The confusion on board should be in keeping with the storm. Then, in a line of light — on a pathway calm as if oil had stilled the angry foam — the figure of the Saviour should be seen. In all scriptural scenes, I would have our Lord's *face* partly concealed. In this instance, a mantle should envelop it. The calm majesty of his figure, and the firmness of his tread, should be such as to give us the idea of the supernatural. Opposed to this, should be Peter, — the boldness of his face fading away as a huge wave comes rolling up, and the one beneath him sinks. It seems to me, this point in the scene would be the finest, because it would give us at a glance the full moral of it, — the Divinity of Jesus, and the unsteady boldness of Peter. This, if the night and storm were well done, would be a most thrilling picture."

By such studies as this, did the troubled spirit, in its humble way, strive to solve for itself the problem which so many gifted minds have cast from them with disdain, — of reconciling Duty in a world of sin, with the aspirations of Genius.

While these changes in her views of practical life were in progress, another process was going on, of equal importance in its effects upon her character. Those 'dreary four years,' together with several that followed them, were marked by many temptations to doubt the truth of the theological system under which she had been educated. Her earlier inquiries on the subject of religion do not appear to have raised any doubts in her mind. She had received without question the faith of her fathers. She had felt little interest in theological speculations. The Being of God, her own sinfulness, and the Atonement by Christ, seem to have been almost the only points of religious doctrine which her own experience heretofore had rendered necessary to her. And these she had received, because she had for the time *felt* them to be true. When disease and suffering forced upon her a frequent suspension of this *experience* of truth, they forced upon her also the necessity of reëxamining her faith even to its groundwork. This was a kind of effort to which her mind had never accustomed itself. She seems to have engaged in it, for a long time, fitfully, and without much satisfaction. The personal independence which was innate in her, sometimes inclined her to question proudly what others believed. Her wayward spirits, now more frequently depressed than otherwise, gave a magnitude to objections which in later life she smiled at. The Old Testament Scriptures perplexed her. She even admitted at times questionings of the Being of a God. It is not probable that any of these difficulties would have taken the painful form they sometimes assumed, if disease had not so sorely oppressed her. Sooner or later, however, a mind like hers must have encountered them. Perhaps, for thoroughness of discipline, it was better that they came when and as they did. One or two extracts from her papers, will exhibit the most truthful view of the *unsettled* state into which her mind sometimes fell, and of the rebound of her soul, after all, to its early faith, which it would not let go.

In a letter to a friend, written on a Saturday night, she writes: "I am startled to see how many atheistical thoughts I have had this week. I am reading in course the Old Testament. I cannot, at some *moments*, resist the feeling, that if it were not hallowed as God's Word, we should reject it with contempt. Then I put down the feeling, and think that, as the rude ancients would have laughed to scorn the idea that the sun stood still and the earth was in motion, so it may be that in a region of clearer light, all these dark places will be illuminated. Then again, the Mosaic account of the creation puzzles me. It seems like the stories by which we attempt to satisfy the curiosity of children. But, be it what it may, Christianity is the only religion on which the soul can rest. A religion it must have; it cannot believe its own mortality. Then on this faith, glorious if it be obscure, I will rest. Here I intrust this soul. If this faith *be* a fiction, it is the only one in which I can live; and as its convert, I am willing to die."

At a somewhat later period, in recording some thoughts suggested by reading the 'Memoirs of Goethe,' she writes as follows: "I have been accustomed to regard everything of a religious nature as sacred; all prayers, by whomever offered, all acts of worship, all good books, as above all criticism and cavil. Even on the border-land of Eden, Reason should fold her wings, and retire into the background. It may be that this is the safer and happier course: but for a long time it has not satisfied me. The hitherto calm surface has been ruffled by doubts, curiosity, inquiry. I believe the *foundations* of my faith are immovable as the pillars of the universe, but in its superstructure I find a host of difficulties. This book has affected me powerfully, — I do not know that I can add, happily. It has given shape and coloring to many vague sentiments which I have had, but dared not express, — particularly this one, that religion has not a distinct character of its own; that it is not always recognizable; that it is cameleon-like, and assumes the color of the heart where it dwells. Every one frames a Deity for himself, and offers a worship peculiar to himself. No two individuals worship the same God. How is it possible, then, to have any test or standard of piety? How unlike is the piety of Professor ——, and that of old Mrs. ——! How unlike their respective Deities! How unlike their interpretations of the Bible! Where are the points of resemblance to prove that if one is a Christian, so is the other? 'Why, each one acts according to the light he has.' Granted; then religion is no definite kind of feeling and conduct; it is the peculiar development of each heart in its attempts to obey its own ideas of right. Then, how liberal ought we to be!—why not see good Christians everywhere?

"After writing this, I went out in the evening to a lecture on Hindostan. The absurdity, wickedness, and vileness of the Hindoo religion, fill me with horror. But here is a religion of man's own imagination. They follow the "devices of their own hearts." They obey their voice of right. True religion surely is something more than *this*."

In another connection she expresses briefly and more generally the restless state of her mind during this period. She writes: "I seem to live in another world. It is difficult sometimes, with everything around me that heart could wish, to live in this world at all. There are but few hours in which my nature rests satisfied. I get impatient and homesick for heaven. I feel like a wanderer — I am seeking, seeking, seeking, ever like a child lost in the forests." No words could form a more significant epitome of her mental experience for many years after her profession of Christian faith, than these — "seeking, seeking, seeking."

This period of her life should not be regarded, however, as strictly a period of religious scepticism, or of even an inclination to such a state. She did not herself so regard it, in looking back to it, after her opinions and character had been matured. The foundations of her faith were never really shaken. Her confidence in the religious system which she had been taught in childhood, was never really suspended. The perplexities she experienced were those to which every inquiring mind that has been religiously cultivated in childhood, is liable, when it comes to the process of examining for itself the creed it has been taught to believe. The inheritance from its fathers is to be now vested in its own right, and it scrutinizes with new solicitude the validity of the title. In the case of her to whom the tribute of these pages is rendered, the perplexities of religious inquiry were rendered more painful than they would otherwise have been, by the disturbing and depressing influence of physical suffering. The earnestness of her soul under this discipline, is evident in all the records that remain of her experience during this period. They are remarkable for the exhibition they make of the struggles of a tempted spirit. "Lord, I believe — help thou mine unbelief," is the prayer they seem to breathe. Rarely is an expression of doubt or of perplexity recorded, which is not immediately followed by a more positive expression of faith.

The confirmation of her religious opinions was by a very gradual process, and it appears to have advanced nearly in proportion with the improvement of her health. Yet, some more direct means were of great advantage to her. Of these, the study of the Scriptures was, doubtless, the most important. They were her daily companions. She commenced the practice, which she continued at intervals, to the end of her life, of employing her *pen* as an accompaniment of her Biblical studies. An abstract of a scriptural passage was first recorded, and then followed the difficulties she experienced in understanding it, or the inquiries which it raised in her mind, together with the best answers that occurred to her; or if no answer satisfied her, the almost never failing expression of the faith of her *heart*, which no "obstinate questionings" could destroy. She derived much benefit from the study, in this way, of her father's Commentaries. She read them all with pen in hand, except that on the Apocalypse. Upon this she was engaged during the last year of her life, and had nearly finished it when she was called away. There was something in her father's direct and manly mode of treating the difficulties of truth, which charmed her.

Another method which she appears to have adopted, of fortifying her mind against the perplexities that disturbed her peace, was that of recording, in a manuscript volume, the religious convictions expressed by the most distinguished Christian minds. This volume she specially valued. She preserved it for many years after she had ceased to feel the need of its contents. She regarded it as a representation in miniature, of the features of her own mind during a perilous period of its history. A single circumstance is worthy of notice in the construction of this little volume — it is indicative of the whole working of her mind on religious subjects. She has gathered together in it such expressions as she had met with in her reading, of the religious opinions of the world's great thinkers — ranging from Socrates down to Edmund Burke, — and then she has summed up, apparently, the 'conclusion of the whole matter,' by transcribing copious extracts from the address of JEHOVAH, as recorded near the close of the Book of Job. 'Gird up now thy loins like a man, for *I* will demand of *thee*, and *answer thou me*,' etc. Thus earnestly did her mind strive to throw itself back upon the spirit of that faith to which human skepticism and human authority are alike vain.

A very important influence in effecting her deliverance from wavering of religious convictions, arose from her study at this time, of the doctrine of the 'Divine Decrees.' A series of discourses preached in the Seminary Chapel on this subject, was the 'word in season' to one that was 'weary.' Her views of this doctrine before this time, seem to have had little of positive influence upon her character — none, certainly, that *aided* her in her perplexities. It now assumed a richness of value to her which it never afterwards lost. She recorded, at the close of a Sabbath which had been devoted to meditation upon it, her new sense of its importance. The record appears to be in part an abstract of portions of a discourse to which she had that day listened, and in part an expression of its effect upon herself.

"This subject," she writes, "has opened a new world to me. I shall be better for it as long as I live. I am better and happier now, though I went to church with an aching heart." "It is well to loose the spirit from its earthly ties, and suffer it to soar away to that point in eternity when JEHO-

VAH existed alone. Then were all possible events of time decreed by that mighty Mind. The path of the planets was mapped out, and that of the least grain of sand; and in those same paths must they move with undeviating exactness, as if they had been placed in iron grooves. Not an atom floats in the sunbeam, but that, from all eternity, had its curious revolving and intricate way *fixed.* Not the smallest animalcule upon it, which born at noon perishes before night, but that had from eternity arranged for it by this Infinite mind, the exact way in which its opening mouth should be filled. Not one of us, but that had our memoirs then written in His mighty book. *We* were of consequence enough then to have every plan and event of our lives fixed; the moment of our birth, our names, the day of our death—all, were then fixed. Have we a secret sorrow we would not whisper out—it is not the result of accident. Every tear that chases its fellow tear down the cheek has been counted—just so many shall fall, and *not one more.* Every sigh has been numbered, and just so many shall be sent, and *not one more.* Let us raise our drooping and weary heads and repose them safely on *fixed Eternal Purpose.* Like children in the arms of everlasting Love, let us repose without a fear. We can put on these fire-proof garments, and though the furnace be seven times heated, the smell of fire shall not pass over them.

"I never *could* understand or divine, before, *my* claim upon the Deity's overruling care. Now I do get a glimpse of it — enough to make me feel like an infant in its mother's arms. Every event, of every day, of every hour, is unalterably fixed. Each day is but the turning over a new leaf of my history already written by the finger of God, — every letter of it. Should I wish to rewrite — to alter — one? Oh, No! no!! no!!!"

At about the same time, in another connection, she writes: "I do like John Newton's Letters — the sincere piety — the calm reliance on God, which they breathe. There is something majestic in his views of life, his firm *consciousness* that every event, great and small, is directly ordered and controlled by such a Deity. How beautifully he speaks of affliction and the death of his wife! What a different place such a spirit makes of this world! How I wish I were worthy to possess it!"

The very powerful effect of this doctrine, thus vivified in her mind, was not transitory. The doctrine, with the whole group of truths kindred to it, from that time took a permanent place in her affections. It was 'as an anchor to her soul, sure and steadfast.' It gave her new conceptions of the value of existence. In subsequent years, allusions to it became habitual in her expressions of religious experience. In times of severe affliction especially, her feelings seemed to cluster around it, seeking refuge in its strong holds. Her constitutional despondency rendered it often invaluable to her. To her 'aching heart' it was 'as the shadow of a great rock in a weary land.'

The life which she had thus far led, had been one of comparative seclusion. A quiet country village had been her home. With the single exception of the period she spent in Mr. Abbott's family, she had not been long absent from her father's house. Her mind and heart had been developed in the *thoughtful* atmosphere created by the literary institutions around her. This had been well for her. It had given a strength to her character, which she could scarcely have gained elsewhere. Even the confinement of a sick chamber, and the comparative isolation to which years of convalescence had consigned her, had been not all evil. She had been thrown back from the world upon her own resources of thought. She had been led to sound the depths of her own heart. She had communed much with God. The mysteriousness of God's dealings with her, had led her to think much of the principles of His government.

Her first crude views of a religious life had matured simultaneously with her growth in Christian knowledge; her conscientious mistakes being rectified as she advanced to a more intelligent faith. The discipline had been severe; she had suffered much; the marks of its severity were destined never to be wholly effaced in this world. But, under God, it had made her what she was.

> "*So*, the foundations of [her] mind were laid."

But the time had come for her to go forth into a broader theatre.

She was married to Rev. Austin Phelps, then pastor of the Pine Street Church, Boston, in the Autumn of 1842, and she resided in that city until the Spring of 1848. These five or six years of residence in Boston, she regarded as the happiest, and in some respects, as the most profitable, years of her life. The change affected her character favorably, in part because it *was* a change. It introduced her to new varieties of human nature and to new modes of life. She was brought by it more constantly than before into contact with *life* — with men, women, and children, as they are in a busy, and on the whole a happy, world. It added to the lessons of seclusion, those of society, and to the discipline of study, that of action. It was a change of moral *climate*, which, just at that time, her constitutional temperament greatly needed. She felt it through her whole being, and was happier and better for it. She began soon to be sensible of an increasing sympathy with human life. Even her tastes as respects the fine arts were insensibly modified. A fondness grew upon her for those works of art which represented living *character*, rather than for those which represented only material nature. In a letter written from her birth-place, a few years after her removal to Boston, she writes, "Andover is looking most delightfully. The birds sing, and the cool winds are refreshing, and the eye is filled with beauty. As I looked out last evening on these arching elms lighted up by the moon — forming a bower fit for a poet's home — I could not resist the feeling, that the scene had become to me like only a gorgeous picture. I could appreciate it, I could love it, but there was a *soul wanting*."

Very similar to this, was the effect of the change upon her religious character. The ordinary experience of Christians in the humbler walks of life was new to her, and she became much interested in observing it. She found her own soul insensibly sympathizing with it. She would often speak of its simple-hearted manifestations with a glad surprise, as if in the plain unlettered stranger whose words were of the Saviour, she had suddenly found a friend. "It does me good," she would frequently say, on returning from the weekly church-meeting, " to hear these people talk. They speak so feelingly and so honestly what they think and what they want." Respect for the *common* developments of Christian character and modes of Christian speech, became a very positive feature of her own piety. Few things could rouse her indignation more quickly, than to hear them spoken of slightingly. More than once has her eye lighted up and her cheek glowed with the zeal she felt in vindicating them from undeserved contempt. She made no secret of her own readiness to sit as a learner at the feet of any who seemed to know the love of Christ. So strong did her sympathy with the common Christian mind become, that she acquired an enthusiasm bordering upon reverence, for the work of the Pastoral office. It was a severe trial to her feelings, when her husband exchanged that office for a Professorship at Andover.

Yet she was accustomed to regard herself as a recipient rather than a doer of good, in the position she held as a Pastor's wife. The extreme sensitiveness of her nature rendered it impossible for her to perform some services, which are commonly regarded as the duties of such a position. The infirmity which she had lamented in her earlier Christian life, embarrassed her still. She could not *speak*, directly or indirectly, of her religious experience, except to her most intimate companions; nor, indeed, at all times to them. Any duty which was expressive of personal religious feeling, affected her so painfully as to render naturalness and truthfulness in its performance impracticable. Her physical constitution, and all her early and long-rooted habits of mind were unfavorable to any effort she might make, of such a nature. To these was added the unaffected lowliness of her judgment of her own religious character. She seemed to herself unfit to stand as a guide to others. The humblest of her fellow Christians seemed to her to possess higher qualifications for such a position than she had. She was not accustomed to speak of herself as a Christian. She would sometimes *write* that which implied that she thought herself such, but her nearest friend never heard her *say* it. Her lips refused to utter that which, in her conceptions of it, had a sacred significance. An imperative instinct of her nature bade her to stand aside, and permit others to do what, if she had found it practicable, would have devolved, by right of position, on her. She did not now, any more than in earlier life, regard this peculiarity of her religious temperament with leniency. She was quite severe enough in her judgment of it. In writing about it on one occasion she says, "it seems as if it arose from the very *make* of my mind. Those who would flatter me, would call it sensibility. But it is owing to a *weak faith*, and my slow progress in the Divine life." She did not content herself with a severe judgment of her infirmity — she resolved that it should be overcome. A particular duty, which was the severest test of it that could well be devised, had attracted her attention, her own thoughts having guided her to the conviction that it *was* her duty. After many weeks of secret struggling with herself, she resolved to go and do what God seemed to bid her do. When the dreaded day arrived, she devoted the morning to secret prayer, and without informing any friend of her intention, went out in the afternoon to make trial of her resolution. The occurrences of that afternoon are not known to the writer of these pages. She returned home unable to speak of them, having lost all consciousness of them, through the severity of their effect on her physical system. *Her* duty in respect to that class of religious exercises was done.

There are struggles in the unwritten experience of many a sensitive mind, which are not often appreciated in the estimate men form of them, but which He who 'knoweth our frame,' numbers with the last words of martyrs.

This period of her residence in Boston was

marked by a further development of her tastes and power as a writer. Previously to this time she had written much in the form of articles for newspapers and magazines, and children's books. She had invariably published her writings anonymously; and when they were once published, she thought little more of them. There are scattered through several periodicals, and on the shelves of the American S. School Union, and the Mass. Sab. School Society, many of the productions of her pen, which it is impossible now to identify as hers. She herself was often unable to recognize with confidence her own volumes, after years had passed since she wrote them. She has several times been seen bending over the counter of a bookstore, in perplexity as to the authorship of some little book which she held in her hand, seeming to detect some familiar traces of her former self, and yet unable at last to decide whether she were the author of it or not. Her own account of her earlier writings, as given in subsequent years, renders it probable that not more than one third of the little books she has published, can be now distinguished as hers.

Almost all that she had written before taking up her residence in Boston, had been of an elementary character, for children; and this still continued to be her favorite department of literary effort. But her observation of more mature character gradually led her to write for older readers. Composition had become a daily habit. She became unhappy, and even desponding as to her Christian hope, if her mind were long deprived of its customary gratification at her writing desk. Every new class of minds that were brought under her observation, seemed to suggest to her new themes with which to fill her portfolio. Thus, her intercourse with the people of her husband's charge, interested her in writing upon the Pastoral Relation. Her observation of the poverty of a city, directed her attention to that class of writings which are designed to elevate the poor. The cares of domestic life sprung up around her into homely narratives of the common, but not often *written*, experiences of housekeepers. Her domestics were always objects of great interest to her, and more than one of her little books, she wrote for them. She kept a journal of the infancy of her children, preserving thus all the little incidents which usually form the materials of "Mothers' Stories." Distinct from this was her "Family Journal," consecrated to the more private experiences in which her family shared. This journal was subjected to review on certain choice anniversaries, and in her affections stood next to the Family Bible. If she lost a friend, she loved to express her sense of the affliction by writing something which should portray that friend's character. She tried her skill in several of these modes, without at first entertaining any idea of publishing what she wrote.

The study of human character became more than ever her untiring occupation. She took great delight in her daily rambles through the metropolis. The hours thus spent were her most *studious* hours. She would go out of her way to walk in the thoroughfare, where she could see life in its greatest variety. She would often pause in the street to watch the sports of a group of children. She could draw a picture of the young girl she saw behind the counter, or the trio she met at a confectionery. She could characterize and caricature, with pen or crayon, the motley company she encountered in an omnibus. The busy hum of voices continually dropped something which her quick ear appropriated, storing together the aphorism of gray-haired wisdom with the prattle of a child at a toy-shop window, and the harangue of a truckman to his horses. She would pay a street-beggar for a five minutes' conversation; and a talk with an apple-woman on Boston Common, was a treat for the day. She has been known to sit for hours observing the ways of an emigrant party in the steerage of a steamboat; and on one occasion she became so absorbed by her interest in a little Swiss child, that she could scarcely be dissuaded from making an attempt to obtain leave to adopt it as her own.

She strove to aid still farther the improvement of her own tastes in writing, by the direction she gave to her study of books at this time. Thus, she at one period read largely the works of several popular writers of fiction. She did this with the eye of a critic, intent on discovering where lay the secret of their influence. The results of her criticism, as she has recorded them among her private papers, are exceedingly interesting, as exhibitions of her industry in disciplining her own mind. With the same intent, she devoted much time to the study of the Old English Poets. During one winter, she read with great enthusiasm Spenser's 'Færie Queene'; and displayed daily at her tea-table the gems she had selected during the day from the royal treasury. For several winters in succession she enticed her husband from his study, at least one evening of each week, for the reading of Shakspeare at their fireside. She was commonly the reader on these 'Shakspeare evenings;' and one must have heard the vivacious intonations of her voice, and seen the changes of her speaking countenance, to understand fully the intelligence and sympathy of her communion with the great artist of human character. More than all else, however, she valued as works of art the narrative portions of the Bible. These she often adduced as the most perfect models of narrative composition. Among her manuscripts are found criticisms upon some of these, or rather studies of them, in which she has noted the peculiarities which seemed to her to constitute the charm of scriptural narration. Her own simple Saxon style was derived in part from this source. At the same time, she gathered from her miscellaneous reading all the valuable hints she met with respecting the best modes of writing, and these she recorded also for subsequent reference. Thus laboriously did she strive to form her own tastes, and develop whatever faculty she might possess in the use of her pen.

It was during this period of her residence in Boston, that her *social* character was first fully developed. How can this be portrayed? Yet, it was in truth her crowning excellence. She possessed a rare combination of literary tastes and literary industry, with the more unpretending virtues of a woman. Her attachment to her friends partook of the mingled intensity and endurance which characterized all her sensibilities. The loss of a friend, either by death or otherwise, was to her a life-long affliction. The society of those she loved was as necessary to her as her food. There is not one of the few friends with whom she was *intimate*, to whose influence she has not ascribed some definite and permanent improvement of her own character, for which she felt grateful to them, — so generously had her affections responded to theirs, and so trustfully had her heart opened itself at their gentle bidding. A few names were inscribed on her memory, as a constellation whose genial influence ruled her destiny. Whenever one of these chosen friends passed away, she invariably committed to paper her fresh remembrances of the lost one. Several such tributes to the memory of the departed, are found among her papers, written for no purpose but to give vent to bereaved affection which could not be suppressed. Most touching words, which probably she never summoned courage to speak to them while they lived, she thus breathed forth to their voiceless spirits as they hovered over her.

In the ordinary manifestations of her social character, there was a rare mingling of freedom with reserve, of self-respect with generous trust. None could more successfully than she repel by a look, anything that jarred upon her feelings ; yet none could respond more gracefully to an expression of natural refinement. She was independent in her opinions and made no secret of them ; yet, where she recognized the ability, and therefore the right, to correct her judgment if it were wrong, she was as docile as a child. She considered *pride* as the besetting sin of her nature; yet, she was wont to exhibit the most perfect abandonment of self to the influence of delicate kindness on the part of others. She loved to go among the people of her husband's pastoral charge, as *one of them*, restrained by no 'proprieties of position,' but free to rejoice with them as her prompt sympathies bade her. Their generous attentions were her constant delight. Their gifts she would receive with a child's artlessness in the manifestation of her pleasure. If the gift were but a flower, or a cluster of grapes, she seemed always gladdened by it as much as if it had been gold. She possessed very much of her father's versatility of talent in conversation. She had cultivated her mind in this respect, with great care. When her spirit was fully roused, her words possessed a magnetic power. There was no class of society which she deemed beneath her or above her, and none with which she could not, from the heart sympathize in something, and therefore be at her ease. This apparent 'diversity of gifts' was the charm of her presence. Even the stranger, who partook for but a day of her hospitality, went away to speak, years afterwards, of 'her unaffected grace and dignity and sweetness of manner and pious conversation.' In her own house, she strove to spread around her an atmosphere of cheerful piety. This was an object of much solicitude with her. It was a matter of most sacred principle in her plan of life, to suffer nothing to come between her and her family. "She would be a true wife and mother, if nothing else." Her literary pursuits, and the gratification of her taste for the fine arts, were religiously subordinated to her duties "at home." This was not a mere sentiment in her mind — it was her daily study; it cost her thought and labor, and was achieved only by an indomitable resolution. With her feeble health, to perform with her books and her pen and her pencil, all that was necessary to satisfy her own mind, and yet to preside over the household of a pastor, was not — a pleasant song. She accomplished it by the most rigid systematizing of her duties from morning to night. She remembered the "wood-house chamber" as seen from the "western window" in her father's house. Every hour had its allotted duty, and the duty was *done.* Her plans for weeks in advance were all recorded with her pen. Among her manuscripts are now found, "Memoranda of Housekeeping," in which are written her plans for the work of her servants and for her own — even weekly "bills of fare," in which are arranged the order of every meal for the week. There are found, also, fragments of journals, in which are recorded the history of experiments in housekeeping and their success or failure. That untiring *pen* seems to have performed an almost incredible amount of service. The result was, that she accomplished her design. She for many years could reserve habitually two hours each day — no more, no less — for her writing table, and keep in constant progress her studies and her miscellaneous reading, and find her recreation in her pencil, and yet the order of her house was like clockwork; her children never showed the want of a mother's care; her home was never the less a *home* on account of her passionate attachment to literature and art. The sincerity of the religious convictions which she carried into these household plans, she has undesignedly illustrated in her little New Year's Story — "The Angel over the Right Shoulder," — and her jealous vigilance over her own tastes, lest they should encroach on the comfort of those who were dependent upon her, is intimated by another of her Home-sketches — "The Husband of a Blue."

It was the struggle of her life to control the fickleness of her physical temperament, and rise above despondency. "Nobody knows," she would often say, "how I do struggle for it." It was her habitual fear that her family might suffer for the want of a cheerful, sunny home. This is a disclosure, however, which will surprise the majority of her friends — so vigilant was she in watching her own varying moods, and so successful in breathing the spirit of joy around her. Her presence in any group was almost invariably a guarantee of vivacious and genial conversation. She often concealed physical infirmity, that she might come to her little home circle with a cheerful look. 'With a heavy heart' she would 'sing songs' for them. She bestowed much attention on the celebration of festival days, for her children's sake. By gathering around her whatever could innocently please the eye or the ear, she made the place where *she* was, the abode of all that was attractive to their young hearts.

May the writer who offers this tribute to her worth, be permitted so far to overstep the limits which perhaps ought to restrain him, as to insert here one or two extracts from her papers, which will give a glimpse more truthful than other words can give of her, as she was 'at home.' The first is from a paper addressed to him on the occasion of a family festival, and containing her review of the preceding year. "This past year," she wrote, "has been a most eventful one to me. All at once, from many quarters, I have met with so much new encouragement to write, that it has half-bewitched me. First of all came my * * * story.

I felt about this, that if I could only get it published in the * * * , and read it to you without your knowing that I wrote it, I should feel perfectly happy. I heard nothing from it for several weeks. One evening I took up the * * * carelessly, and saw a notice that it was received and would soon appear. I watched for it for several months, and had almost given it up, when one Saturday evening I stumbled upon it. I did read it to you; you did not know a word about who wrote it; you seemed much interested; you listened to the end without speaking, and then you said, 'Well, somebody wrote that who knew how.' I felt well repaid. I thought I had quite reached the goal of my desires, and now * * *"

The other extract is a narrative criticism of a story written by a popular foreign authoress. The criticism is thrown into the epistolary form and addressed to her. It was originally written with no fictitious design, but for some reason it remained in the writer's hands. It is as follows:—

"Boston, May —, 184–.

"*To Miss Frederika Bremer:*—

"If one had a child in a distant country, a letter, even from a stranger, which told of the child's health and happiness and every-day employments, could not but give pleasure to his parent. I suppose an author looks upon her writings with a parental eye; and though they wander to a new world and put on a strange costume and speak in an unknown tongue, still she cannot forget that they are hers, and it cannot be uninteresting to her to hear how they are received and how they demean themselves. I have written all this in the opening of my letter to Miss Bremer, that it may serve me as an apology for all that I mean to write, and I place it before me as a shield, if my letter should be received as an intruder. It comes simply to tell thee of the pleasure which sprang up around one single fireside far away in a strange land, through the timely introduction of one of these, thy brain-children. 'The Neighbors,' it is called. It chanced to make our acquaintance at a time when it was a most welcome visitor. I say 'our,' for we had started a little home of our own. This home was in the city, and the husband being a professional man, the day was all filled up with professional duties on his part, and with calling and callers, on mine. When the rare treat of an unoccupied evening came, and we had finished the discussion of the day around our tea-table, then we drew up our stand before a bright fire, rolled up the sofa, and lighted the study-lamp. I took my work, and the gentleman took 'The Neighbors,' and read aloud. I should like to have had you see the enthusiasm with which we followed the newly married pair—how readily our sympathies were enlisted for them—how I had half a mind to fall in love with the rough, good-humored Bear—how we laughed till we cried, at the untiring vivacity of his little wife. I would believe that it was all true, and that the little wife had in reality sent us her experience over the waters, that we might look into the future with a calm trust., It must be no common talent that can so accurately describe from observation — rather, it is a high order of instinct. I thank Bear and his wife for their truthful history. 'Ma Chere Mere' is a character which we never meet here; yet some of her wise sayings have already passed into proverbs among 'The Neighbors' friends. There was one thing, however, which our good New-Englanders shake their heads at — it was her fiddling for her servants at a dance on the Sabbath. Our Sundays are sacred days; we keep them as days of rest from all worldly employments, and such recreations are never tolerated. The capricious little Ella we laughed at, and yet we could not help liking her. Serena we thought too good; it seemed as if she belonged to another sphere. Bruno, I could not admire, although in the scene of reconciliation with his mother, I hid my face, for I half thought I was too old to cry over such stories. Yet, elsewhere, I had no sympathy with a character so morbid and passionate. He seemed at a great distance from the *heroes* who walk around me in this Yankee land. There was Hagar, too, — I wished her out of the way entirely. She brought in an element of the tragic, which seemed poorly to suit the healthful object of the tale.

"When we had finished 'The Neighbors,' we felt as if we were parting with a friend, and I could not resist the impulse to return my thanks to the author of so much innocent delight.

"In our good city of Boston, your books are advertised in every bookstore window. They are much read here, and much liked. Miss Mary Howitt has given us in beautiful English, 'The Neighbors,' and 'Home.' These are by far the greatest favorites with us. In the 'H. Family,' and 'The President's Daughters,' there is too much spicing with German Philosophy, and too much obscurity as to the real meaning of the religious creed, to please our more sober thinkers. In these two, also, much more than in the others, the true object of life, and the true preparation for death, are discussed in a way which does not harmonize with the simplicity of our views of the Christian faith.

"Yet, for an exhibition of the social virtues, elevated in their character, free from selfishness, and made attractive to all classes of readers, we have had nothing for a long time that can be compared with Miss Bremer's stories."

The approach of death, even in the distance, seems often to be foreshadowed by an increased *rapidity* in the development of character. So it was, apparently, with her whose life is here sketched. Her friends, in recalling the closing years of her sojourn with them, can see that they were to her years of rapid intellectual and moral growth. There was a quick blossoming of powers which had long been hidden in the bud, and which the approach of her life's autumn as quickly ripened into fruit. Her soul seems to have put forth its strength, and gathered up its immortal possessions, as if the coming summons to depart had been long audible.

She removed from Boston to Andover in the spring of 1848. The change was not an agreeable one to her. It was often an occasion of unhappiness, and at times a positive affliction. Various causes contributed to this result. She had become warmly attached to Boston, to the life of a Pastor's wife, to the church with which she had been there associated, and to personal friends whom she had met there. Her heart was bound there with a strength of tie, of which she was not herself fully aware, till the tie was broken. Her affections, never weak when once called into life, had become *rooted* there. She wished for no change, and saw no inducement to change. Her own convictions and habits of feeling respecting that juncture in her life, are clearly intimated by some of the closing scenes in the "Peep at No. Five." Her health was also more than usually feeble at the time of her removal from Boston, and continued so for a year afterwards. At the same time, affliction fell suddenly upon her father, and also upon her husband. Great uncertainty hung over the future; and that seemed a dark day to her in which she had bidden farewell to the place where she had passed, as she thought, her happiest years. Her associations with *place* were naturally very strong; and it was not strange that a return to her birth-place should, under all the circumstances that attended it, revive in some degree the affliction she had experienced there in former years. Such was the result.

On one occasion she thus writes respecting the effects of her return to Andover, viz: "Many things about this place do oppress me very much. The last years of my life here — years in which I thought and felt the most deeply — *were not happy*. I had a great many hours of suffering which still cling to certain spots and certain states of the weather here, so that many times they roll back over me with a force that is irresistible. I carry about with me a sore and anxious heart so much of the time, that it is almost the habitual state in which I exist. The life that flows from this is not very sunny; I already live in the past."

It was not the past, however, nor any associations with place, that created the chief burden of her spirit at this time. She proceeds to say: "One thing, in particular, hangs over me like a pall, too often oppressing me with its black shadow; it is, the breaking up of my father's family. I do not know that I *can* have strength enough to live here cheerfully, when I have only their graves to visit. I suffer a great deal also from religious depression. There are times when I almost abandon my Christian hope, and feel that I ought not to go again to the communion table. It seems to me I have no such experience as other Christians have."

Until the question of her husband's resignation of his pastoral charge in Boston was decided, she, with her usual generosity, concealed in great measure the foreboding with which she anticipated the change, lest his decision should be unduly influenced by a knowledge of her feelings. When the change was made, it was for a long time the almost hourly struggle of her life to resist the depression that weighed upon her mind. The severity of this struggle can scarcely be appreciated by those who possess a more equable temperament than hers. At times, darkness deepened so oppressively around her soul, that direct intercourse with God was the only source of even temporary relief. Long continued seasons of secret prayer became necessary to preserve a sufficient degree of composure to enable her to discharge her domestic duties. During one of these seasons of extreme dejection, the only instance occurred in which she ever turned away from the offer of that human sympathy on which she had learned to lean. "Not now," said she; "I must go to the Saviour; there is no one else to whom I *can* go now." And she went, and 'drew near to the *thick* darkness where God was.' Yet, a wrong impression would be received from this narrative, if it should be inferred that the trial here referred to, cast *visible* gloom over this period of her life. It was not so. She had become so accustomed to the ruling of her own spirit, that but few even of her personal friends knew the intensity of her trial. She did not withdraw herself from society; she sought incessant occupation; she allowed herself but few hours of solitude; she forced herself into plans of secret usefulness. Hers was by no means the dejection of a prostrate, inactive soul. Such was the readiness of her sympathies, that she did succeed in really enjoying the happiness that she diffused around her. It is doubtless true also, that in the expression of her feelings as recorded above, she has represented her experience as it seemed to her in her hours of solitary reflection. It was probably varied in the reality by her busy and generous life. She had, moreover, a very high standard of Christian cheerfulness in her mind. An ordinary degree of happiness in this life did not content her. So vivid were her conceptions of God, as a God of Love, and so radiant in her view was the light which the work of Christ has thrown over this world, and so intimate was her own heart with Him as with a personal friend, that she experienced a sense of guilt if she did not enjoy life. She reproached herself for variations of feeling about which many would be less scrupulous. "*Rejoice* in the Lord always; and *again* I say, Rejoice," was a command to which she gave heed with uncompromising fidelity.

The conflict with her desponding spirits during the period now under review, was almost entirely successful; and it was the probable occasion of the very rapid development of her character, which soon began to take place, and of which she herself was in some degree sensible. After some years had passed, she was able to write in the following strain: — "There are bright spots on the canvas, after all. I do not see why my working years should not yet come, nor why I should not do my work well. I never can expect always to pitch my tent by the "still waters." But it is cheering to me that I do see much more clearly than I did, what is my duty, and that when I am thrown off the track, I find my way back sooner. All is not 'chaos and old night.' I have a centre to which I can turn in my flight, and where I can rest; so that, in my heart, I am happier than I was."

At a still later date, she writes: — "As to the great point of contentment with life, I really think I have gained upon it. It has been a thing for which I *have* struggled and prayed; and for the most part, my mind *is* at rest, and my heart contented. I *think* I can say this; and what is equally true, a feeling of habitual gratitude has gained ground within me. I do carry about with me, a great deal of the time, a thankful heart. I am so grateful for the bright rallying-points around which my thoughts cluster, I make a great effort to keep them constantly in view. I feel that I should be guilty, not to do so; and month after month, I think I can see that it becomes more and more *natural* to me to look on the bright side of things."

On another occasion, in speaking of her children, she says: — "I do not know how to be grateful enough for them. They have been a God-send to me, — stars in a dark night. I have been so afraid of loving them too much, that I have constantly brought home to my heart the commission, 'Take this child, and nurse him for me.' My strong and habitual feeling is, that they are not *mine*, — they are lent to me. If I can but do my whole duty to them, I shall feel that my life's work is well done. I want a *cheerful* Christian home for them to grow up in. I want them to be happy Christians. I believe that is the best style of piety. I suffer from the want of a cheerful spirit. * * * * Yet, I do think I am enabled to rise above my constitutional gloom better than I once did. I have many happy hours, — sometimes whole days, — sometimes many days together. I somehow am able to feel that much of my despair has arisen from physical derangement. Better health, change of scene, anything that enlivens me, seems to change, as by magic, my spiritual prospects. I have found it so, many times. Now, though I have more doubts and fears than I wish I had, yet for many months I have experienced much enjoyment. Sometimes I think that if I am ever to be saved, I shall not die until my piety, if I have any, has become more mature and symmetrical."

She was nearer the goal of her desires than she supposed. The last of the above extracts was written but a little more than a year before her death. The growing maturity and symmetry of religious character which she was only beginning to hope for, were, in the view of her friends, already hers. They could not but observe the increasing loveliness of her chastened spirit. They saw her growing 'faith and hope and charity.' The change was visible in her softened eye, and in the increasing gentleness of her tones. The doctrines of the Gospel were evidently becoming more precious than ever to her heart. During the last year of her life, she rewrote entirely one of her Sabbath School books, because the story at the first writing had not clearly and precisely shadow-ed forth the views of Regeneration on which she had intended to construct it. Little evidences, which cannot be recorded, disclosed her deepening love to the person of the Saviour. She would often speak of him in terms of personal endearment, and yet with a reverence for His divine nature, which was but feebly expressed by the opinion she held, that no painter should attempt to portray in full that countenance to which, as she thought, no human imagination could do justice. The books she chose for her devotional reading, indicated her sympathy with some of the higher forms of Christian experience. Although she felt little respect for any exclusive model of Christian character, yet she found much to which her heart responded, in the written experiences of Madame Guyon and Catherine Adorna. These, together with 'Bridges' Exposition of the One Hundred and Nineteenth Psalm,' and her long loved favorite — 'Jeremy Taylor's Holy Living and Dying' — were her constant companions.

Her daily effort became more manifest and more successful, to breathe the power of holy principle into every purpose and action of her life. The graces of her natural character blended themselves more and more genially with those that were peculiar to her Christian experience. It was instructive to see her, during one hour of each day, bending with a countenance brilliant with emotion, over a painting which she was executing, — and perhaps the very next hour absorbed with a different and yet not less enthusiasm, in taking notes of her father's Commentary on the Apocalypse. She turned away to conceal her tears at the sight of a painting representing 'the scourging of our Lord,' and for a long time afterwards, was unable to banish the scene from her mind. At the same time, in unconscious imitation of His spirit, she would go far to carry a bundle of clothing to a poor woman's child; and would herself perform some menial service, that her domestics might have an uninterrupted hour for their daily task in learning to read and write. Through all the closing years of her life, she went month by month to a neighboring village, to superintend the interests of a friendless girl from a foreign land, who had been disabled by an accident. She obtained for her employment, and received and disbursed her wages in such manner as to save for her a little fund against a time of need. She had long been accustomed to seek out secret and neglected modes of doing good. On one occasion, a female member of the church had become involved in a difficulty which threatened to subject her to the censure of her brethren. All the ordinary efforts for a happy adjustment of it had failed. One, and another, and another of her friends had withdrawn their sympathy from her. Mrs. Phelps requested at last that she might be permitted to visit the unfortunate woman. It was proposed that she should go as a committee of the church. She promptly refused. "No," said she, "I shall be no committee. Let me go as a woman to her sister." She went. Her woman's instinct and her Christian heart accomplished what a sterner fidelity had not done. A single interview restored the erring one to confidence, and she still lives beloved for her Christian virtues. This was a specimen also of the enlarged charity, which had always been characteristic of Mrs. Phelps's judgment of others, and her appreciation of their difficulties in opinion, or infirmities in temperament.

Yet, in these last years of her life, it was touching to see that, while this magnanimity to others seemed to be almost daily enlarging her heart, the severity of her judgment of herself increased. She struggled long and hard to assure herself that she was honest in her scrutiny of her own heart. She often *wrote* her prayers with reference to certain difficult subjects of meditation, and certain intricate varieties of religious experience, — so solicitous was she to discipline her mind to truthful expression in her devotions. She was so fearful that her private journal would be vitiated by a secret sense on her part, of the possibility of its exposure to other eyes than her own, that whenever in writing it she detected any such thought in her mind, she was accustomed instantly to record some most sacred secret of her experience, which she was *sure* she could not wish to whisper in any human ear. In her intercourse with others, she often did herself injustice, by appearing to be destitute of emotions which were struggling within her, lest she should perhaps express more than she really felt. It pained her that others should think of her more highly than she deserved. The lowliness of her own opinion of her Christian character, could scarcely be exceeded. "I have no reason to think," she writes at one time, "that I ever lived one day so as to wish to live that day over again." "I do not deserve this," was the frequent remark with which she would receive, and sometimes with tears, even the common evidences of God's kindness to her. Her family she would often speak of as undeserved gifts. The inquiry was many times on her lips, "Why have these been given *to me?*" On one occasion, when a favorable opinion had been expressed of one of her little books, she recorded the opinion, and followed it with an expression of the instinctive feeling it excited in her own mind, by inquiring, "Can anything that *I* do, do any good to a child?" One who has been in daily intimacy with her, cannot but remember these tokens of the maturing piety which shed its pure and mellow light over her closing years.

There was also, during these years, an obvious expansion of her *mind.* She engaged with increased zeal and enlarged plans, in writing. She rewrote "The Sunny Side," which had lain neglected in her desk for several years. This volume had been originally written with no distinct intention to publish it, but simply to portray for the gratification of the author, the character of a deceased friend. Several months elapsed after it was completed, before the thought of giving it to the public distinctly occurred to her. It was at different times offered anonymously to five different publishers, and with such modest representations of its value that it was as many times rejected. An edition of but five hundred copies was at length issued by the author's friends. At the present time, less than two years from its first publication, the fortieth thousand have been printed; and it is estimated by those who are most familiar with the channels in which it has been circulated, that its readers number from three to five hundred thousand.

It was in connection with this little work, that she first became known as an authoress. Its unexpected success increased her desire to improve to the utmost whatever talents she might possess, in the preparation of books for the young. She wrote in rapid succession 'The Kitty Brown Series,' for the American Sunday School Union. Her fugitive pieces were scattered through various periodicals. 'The Peep at No. 5,' which she regarded as her best production, she wrote and published but a few months before her death. In less than one year from the time of its publication, it had reached the sale of the twentieth thousand. At the suggestion of an unknown correspondent in Ohio, she gathered and arranged the materials for another narrative, to be entitled the "Minister's Widow." It was designed to be a twin-volume to "The Sunny Side." She had also in mind the materials and plan of a work in similar style, designed for young ladies in the advanced stages of their education. To prepare herself for this latter work, she re-read, critically, the 'Life and Letters of Dr. Arnold,' in order that the theory of education which should pervade her book might breathe his enlarged spirit. Upon these last two works her mind was intent when her failing health obliged her to desist from the use of her pen. It was one of the trials of her long confinement, that she could not commit to paper the characters and scenes which crowded upon her imagination. When a temporary suspension of disease caused her strength to rally a little, she for several days dragged herself to her writing-table for one half-hour each day, that she might finish the revision of a collection of her miscellaneous narratives, which she had promised to the publishers for republication. Her mind seemed to find no rest but in incessant activity.

It had long been her practice to write much, simply for her own gratification or improvement. During the years of her final residence in Andover, she wrote much for her *children*, without any design of publishing what she thus wrote. Such was her solicitude in regard to the earliest impressions made on their minds, that she could not at all times find in the common collections of children's books, just such reading as she wished to put into their hands. Some truth for which their minds seemed to be in waiting, she could not find so stated or so illustrated as to meet her views of their wants. When such was the case, she was accustomed to write books for them, which should realize as far as was in her power, her own idea of what they needed. Several of her published volumes, with much material that is yet in manuscript, were written with this design. She often wrote in the morning, the chapter which was to be their entertainment when they retired for their evening meal, before going to rest. At the hour of twilight, she habitually went with them, and gave them her personal attendance at their bedside. "She did but bathe the weary feet of her little children, but the Angel over the *right shoulder* — wrote it down." "These duties and cares acquired a dignity from the strokes of that golden pen." That hour was as dear to her as a Sabbath hour. It was called in the family dialect, 'The children's hour.' Her own countenance was as radiant as theirs, when their beaming eyes and forgotten meal testified to the interest with which they listened to their mother's stories.

It was one indication of the growth of her mind during the closing years of her life, that she attached less value than she had previously done, to *fiction* as a medium of conveying truth. In her maturest efforts, she drew but little upon the resources of her own invention. Real life became more exclusively her chosen source of materials. Upon principle and by preference, she made real characters the object of her study, and facts the subject of her pen. For this purpose, she kept a distinct diary whenever she went on a journey; and scarcely would she suffer a brief excursion from her home to pass, without some contribution to her stores. She made it a part of her plan of life, to visit once in each year some large city, or some region of the country that was new to her, and to devote several weeks to the opportunities which should thus be afforded, to observe varieties of real life, and to gather truthful materials for her little books. A visit which she thus made, a year before her death, to Niagara and the Heights of Quebec, she regarded as an epoch in her life — so suggestive was it to her mind, of new thoughts, new scenes, new characters, and new stores of illustration for her eager pen. With the same enthusiasm, she anticipated a visit to Europe, as a means of furnishing to her materials for a life's work. But — an unseen Hand was guiding her towards a 'better country.'

It must not be inferred, however, from her enthusiasm in writing and in her plans for the future, that she herself entertained any high opinion of what she had already written. On the contrary, her estimate of her "foolish little stories," as she was accustomed to call them, was not an exalted one. Hers was the modesty of unconscious excellence. She had written rather because she could not refrain from doing so, than because she expected to do any *great* good to others. Unfavorable criticisms upon her productions, she was almost always ready to believe to be well-founded. A singular illustration of her spirit in this respect was afforded in one instance of her early experience as a writer. She had sent a manuscript to a publisher who courteously returned it to her, with the censures of a certain critic upon its literary character. She thought the censures just, and wrote a second time, endeavoring to profit by the advice she had received. Again the manuscript was returned, with further strictures. Her spirit was roused, for she still felt the justice of the criticisms, and she resolved that she would write and rewrite, and write again, until her manuscript should be worthy of publication through *that* channel, and acknowledged to be so by *that* critic. The third effort was successful. Her opinion of "The Sunny Side," before its publication had tested its value, may be gathered from the following extract from a letter addressed to one of the few friends who had seen it in manuscript, and aided in giving it to the public: —

"I have had some troubled feelings at my foolishness in permitting my friends to spend their money so, — but the more I think of it, and the more I sift my motives, the more I think I have a sincere desire to make the most of any talents I may have, in service of the good cause. I love writing; it has become a habit with me; and is it not possible that this taste may yet be turned to some good account? I do not anticipate much, however, from this offering. I am fully convinced that it has found already, its most partial readers.

I do not mean to be disturbed by any fate that may await it. My chief desire is, that I may myself derive some good from the writing of it. But my heart did misgive me last Friday, when I saw a boy crossing over to the bindery with a larger budget of copies than he could well lift. I felt like hiding my head, or putting my veil down."

Even after the very favorable reception of her little book, she could not persuade herself that this argued any considerable merit in the author. She attributed its success to the rare worth of the leading character it portrayed, and that being taken from real life, she did not seem to herself to deserve much credit for her skill in the painting. The large and rapid circulation of this volume and others that followed it, bewildered her. Yet, it is needless to say, that she enjoyed her success — she did so with the same enthusiasm that she felt in everything that fairly enlisted her interest. More than this, — she felt grateful for the opening prospect of usefulness in a way which was so congenial with her tastes. When reports came back to her of the favor with which one after another of her little 'offerings' were received, she would sometimes burst into tears of grateful surprise. She could never be persuaded, however, to append her name to any of her publications. It was painful to her, to learn that her name had become known as that of the authoress of "The Sunny Side." That book would never have been published, if she had anticipated such a result.

A brief extract from her 'Family Journal,' written after her books had begun to attract attention to herself, will illustrate the modesty of her thoughts respecting them. The extract is interesting also, for the shadows which it discloses as appearing to cloud over her vision of the future.

"It has succeeded," she writes, alluding to one of her recent publications, "beyond my most sanguine dreams. It appears to me that the way is now opening for me to write, — a way which I have sighed for, long. I do pray that my fondness for it may not lead me to overrate my ability for it, or its comparative importance. At present, I do not understand either what I can, or precisely what I wish to do in this way. I work in the dark. Everything lies in chaos before me. My life is a riddle to me; the past is all I can read. *I cannot tell a letter of the future.*"

One year from the time when this was written, she was sinking rapidly to her rest. Did the "Angel with mild and loving eyes" hold before her the "Book" whose "golden clasps" were so soon to be closed upon her life's work, that He might kindly hide the future from her hopes?

Death had, from her very childhood, been too familiar to her thoughts, to take her now entirely by surprise. No other single object had gathered around itself so many of her thoughts, fears, struggles, hopes. She had accustomed her imagination to *face* it, in a thousand forms. She had often summoned it from the distance, and looked upon it steadily, till, in magnified stature, and swift-footed, it seemed to stand just before her. She had thus endeavored to try her strength with the great enemy. Among the varieties of the modes of meeting death, of which she had often thought, she had anticipated, years before they came upon her, very nearly the precise circumstances in which she was at last called to die. They impressed her mind so powerfully, that she recorded her feelings under the fiction of a dream. To read it now, it seems to have been almost prophetic. It is as follows, viz.: —

"I have had a dream. I was in a darkened chamber, and there lay before me a pale sufferer. I could see her face distinctly, for above her hovered an angel from whose form light radiated. This, I saw, was the Angel of Death; and yet he was *not* terrible. He looked earnestly with mournful and yet loving eyes, on her pallid countenance, and words seemed to come from him without breath. 'Then, choose, my child; I have here for you a crown. Come with me, and it is surely yours. Your sins are blotted out forever.' One stepped up, and reached to her her first-born. She gazed at it long—she touched its innocent forehead—she looked at the angel—her lips moved, as if she would say, 'What, *alone* in the world?' 'And God tempers the wind to the shorn lamb,' was the reply. Then her dark blue eye turned on one who stood weeping by her side. Her lip quivered; a stern struggle was in her heart. That breathless voice spoke again, 'Life *has* rich gifts of love for you; but sin is here. Will you leave with me for Heaven? Choose, my child.' And the struggle convulsed her frame with mortal agony; then it ceased, and all was calm. Without a tear, her eye turned on death. She placed her hand in his. Music and light, such as angels love, filled the air; and death took his gift. Yet, I saw that he left a form, cold though it was, whose expression was still so radiant with rapture, that as we looked, our hearts were comforted. I awoke in tears, but they were not for the departed; they were for the solitary mourner who was bending over her."

More than fifteen months before her decease, she expressed the conviction that her constitution was failing. The severe illness of one of her children at that time, had greatly exhausted her strength. This was soon followed by the sudden death of her father — an event which shocked her whole system. The foreboding with which for many years she had looked forward to the 'breaking up of her father's family,' seemed about to be fully realized. The affliction sunk deep into her soul. Her father often seemed present with her in physical form. He sat and talked with her in her dreams. Her spirit seemed unwilling to let him depart from her. The cord that had so long bound her life to his, would not break. She suffered too great intensity of feeling for her exhausted body. At her father's funeral she expressed the belief that she should be the first of his family to follow him into eternity. She sought relief in redoubled exertions at her writing table. Within the space of a short time, she wrote and rewrote the "Peep at No. 5." It was an untimely, and — in connection with the events that preceded and followed it — a fatal effort. She passed the ensuing summer in a state of great prostration. The apprehension that she should not recover, often suggested itself to her mind, and she put her house in order, in anticipation of the possible, perhaps probable, event of her speedy departure.

A short time spent at the seaside in July, caused her strength to rally a little. There she enjoyed much in riding several hours daily on the beach, now listening to the reading of some of her favorite authors, and then communing in silence with the sea. She conversed freely respecting herself, recalled many of the most interesting passages in her life, spoke gratefully of those to whom she was indebted for valuable influences upon her character, and expressed many wishes with regard to the training of her children, if she should soon be called to leave them. With the most melting tones of self-humiliation, she expressed her sorrow for the 'waste of years' which, to her severe judgment, seemed to constitute her past life, and for her great unworthiness of the blessings with which God had filled her life up. "And yet," said she, "I have struggled hard to know my duty in life, and to do it. I do not feel as if I had succeeded, but nobody knows how I have struggled to do right. And now, if it is God's will that I should die, I *think* I can say that my mind is at rest in whatever He wills. For myself, I *think* I need not fear, but I do not *see* how my family can spare me yet, nor do I know that I feel ready to leave them. If it comes to that, I think God will prepare me for it."

To one of her old school-companions, whose Christian counsel had for many years been a solace to her, she wrote at this time as follows:— "After all, I have more hope than fear for the result of this sickness, though sometimes I see it just as it is, doubtful. Dear A——, if it comes to the worst, I want to say to you, that from first to last, you have been invaluable to me. If I could ever do for any human being what you have done for me, I should feel that I had not lived in vain. This is all true; and if the great gulf separates us soon, my best love stays with you; and if *I* am fit, I know we shall meet in Heaven. I cannot write much more. You must not infer that I am gloomy — I am not. I dare not say how I should feel with the certainty of death before me; but now, in thinking of it, my mind is at rest. I am willing to leave myself in God's hands. I do *think* that the question of my life or death, and what is more, the salvation of my soul, I am willing to leave there. I have no hope but in my Saviour; and if He has not saved me, then this too I know is just, and God's Decree I would not change."

Thus cautiously, and with severe self-distrust, did she express her Christian hope, though on the verge of Heaven. It was with the same lowly spirit that, eighteen years before, she had "begun to dare to hope that she had become a child of God." To one who knows her habit of using few and measured words in speaking of her own Christian experience, this brief extract speaks volumes.

Especially does its closing declaration reveal one of the deep places in her heart. Her now long-rooted habits of *rest* in God's Decrees, led her to utter the most solemn words that can fall from human lips,—"*If He has not saved me, then this too I know is just, and God's Decree I would not change.*" This was, to her mind, no idle profession, nor had it any vague significance. She knew what she meant by it, and she meant what she said. One who has been familiar with her ways of thinking, and her use of language, can almost imagine her as uttering the same words beyond the confines of this world.

In the month of August, 1852, she gave birth to her third child. For several weeks after this event, her health improved, and her friends began to lose their fears of a fatal termination of her disease. She herself engaged in new plans for the employment of her pen for years to come. Her love of life strengthened as her hope of life brightened. Life never before seemed so desirable to her as now. New ties bound her to this world. During her long illness, two objects seemed to flit before her as emblems of her chief desires for the recovery of her health; one was, her writing-table—and the other, her seat in the little group that had been accustomed to gather around her, at "the children's hour."

In the early part of October, the improvement that had taken place in her condition, seemed to be secretly arrested. The disease of the brain, which had for many years afflicted her at intervals, began to develop itself with increased severity; and it soon became manifest that her whole system was slowly giving way. About the first of November, she was removed to Boston, in the hope that change of scene, and proximity to the sea-coast, and additional medical advice, might be the means of her restoration. It was all in vain; her physicians soon pronounced her case nearly, if not quite, hopeless.

And now commenced one of the most striking exhibitions of her character that her life witnessed. It was, her calm, deliberate, conscientious, determined *struggle for life*. She had scarcely reached life's meridian. Her powers as a writer, after twenty years of faithful discipline, had but just come to their maturity. The judgment of severe critics had assured her, that a sphere of public usefulness was opening before her. She felt eager to enter it, and grateful for the privilege. Her home, too, called loudly for her. She was a wife, and a mother. An infant family seemed to say to her that she *must not* die. She felt — and who of her friends did not? — that she had everything to live for. Yes, 'Life *had* rich gifts of love for her.' She could not *see* — and who of her friends was more discerning? — the reason for this rupture of ties which no human hand had woven. God, in this emergency, seemed to make 'darkness His secret place.' She had no wisdom to interpret His doings; she could hear only the summons of the 'Angel' with 'breathless voice.'

She had long known the power of the mind over the health of the body. The resistance of disease by force of will, had been a habit with her for years. Her resolute purpose and fidelity in self-discipline, had often kept in check the malady which now threatened to lay her in the grave. After meditating long in silence upon the extremity to which she seemed now to be brought, she called her husband to her side — her voice was calm — her whole manner self-possessed — everything betokened the collected purpose of her soul. As nearly as her language can be now recalled, she said, "I do not wish you to speak to me of death, nor tell me of any discouraging changes in my state. Talk to me of God, and give me pleasant thoughts of Heaven, but not as if you expected me to die. Be as hopeful as you can be, and help me to hope. You need not feel anxious about my religious state, nor ask me about it. That is not necessary. I am at rest. * * * * When the time comes for me to go, you shall know it. I shall not die without being able to say to you all that you will wish to hear. God will take care of that, and He will take care of me. If death is before me, I shall be ready to meet it. *Now, my duty is, to live;* and you must help me."

This calm conviction of *duty to live,* from that moment appeared almost incessantly to be active in her mind. She concentrated the whole strength of her being upon the last struggle for life. Never before had she exhibited so noble an effort of Christian principle as now,—through that memorable month of November. She watched in silence the signs of her failing strength, but expressed continually her strong hope that she should yet recover. When temporary improvements took place in her condition, she rallied her spirits, and threw herself back into life, and formed plans, and conversed blithely, and even amused her friends with her wonted pleasantries. When she was wearied with the effort, she would request that a boquet of flowers or a favorite picture should be placed before her, that she might *rest* in the enjoyment it afforded her. If a friend were overcome at the sight of her wasting frame, she would request him to leave her; and when it was suggested that her elder children should once more visit her, she declined the proposal, for "she had no strength to waste" on scenes of pain and parting, and "it was her *duty* to live." Sometimes, for days together, so stern was the conflict, that those she loved best could scarcely catch from her a word, a smile, a look, that betokened her interest in them. They feared that she might pass away in the silence of those dreadful hours, unable to speak her last message. Yet, she seemed constantly more thoughtful of others than of herself. The kindness of friends around her, was often the only thing that could recall a degree of her wonted vivacity. She seemed unable to express adequately her gratitude to her faithful nurse; and to other friends whom she thought God had directly sent to her in her hour of trial, she would indicate in many nameless ways how deeply she felt their unsought beneficence. Her mind associated them with Him who 'went about doing good.' She told them that she understood as she had never done before, why Christ spent so much of his life with the sick and the suffering; that nobody could know the good which was thus achieved, except those who themselves lay on a sick bed. Her silent thoughts of her own family, too, would sometimes break from the restraint she imposed on them. In one instance, when her infant child was taken into her room, it seemed to unloose her imprisoned affections, —her face lighted up with tenderness, her eye assumed that depth of meaning which none but a mother's eye ever has, and for a few moments she poured forth her love in the dialect which only mothers know how to use — then fell back, as if to renew more resolutely the struggle against the disease that consumed her. There were occasions of extreme and immediate peril, when she would herself give directions as to the various remedies she needed, and would mark the time, minute by minute, at which the remedy should be repeated. On such occasions there were moments when, as if to proclaim its own immortality, the soul seemed to come forth from that dimmed eye, and in almost visible presence, to *strike at* the unseen foe. Meanwhile, all that poor human affection could do, was to stand near and give in quick succession the weapons of assault.

For more than thirty days she thus maintained the unequal conflict. At length, her hope began to waver. "If it were not for my children," said she, "I would not struggle any longer." It was not till the evening of the twenty-ninth of November, that she became convinced that the struggle was a hopeless one, and that God was calling her to Himself. She then gave up all, with scarcely a moment's agitation. "Without a tear her eye turned on Death. She placed her hand in his."

The closing scene was just like *her*. Her whole manner was so self-possessed — her words were so truthful — her spirit so self-distrustful, so severe in judgment upon her own infirmities, so penitent, so hopeful, so thoughtful of those whom she was leaving, so full of love to that Saviour who was waiting for her coming — that it did not seem like dying. It was rather, life drawing to its close with a beautiful *naturalness.* She took her husband by the hand, and after speaking of the path they had trod together, as none but she could have spoken, she said, "You must not think I have been unhappy during this sickness — I have not. I have done the best I could do to live, but I have not been unhappy. The Saviour has been around my bed. I do not *know* that I shall be saved, but now I can only *trust.* He gave Himself to die for *sinners*, and why should I *not* trust Him?" After a brief season of exhaustion, her mind seemed to be full of anticipations of Heaven, and it presented itself to her view in the forms of material beauty, which she had always loved. She repeated a line of one of her favorite hymns —

'Sweet fields beyond the swelling floods,'—

then, after a little interval, added, "It is delightful to stand on the banks."

After another interval of silence, in which she appeared to be looking over the cold river to the 'fields beyond,' she collected her strength to express her wishes respecting her family and other friends. Her intellect was clear and definite in its perceptions, her opinions prompt and positive, just as they had always been. She spoke of many minute particulars relating to the education of her children, descending even to an expression of her judgment as to their physical training. She recalled, distinctly, one after another of her friends, and designated the little mementos of her affection which she wished to present to them. Having recounted these, it was just like *her*, that she could not resist the kindly impulse that prompted her for the moment, to bespeak a gentle treatment for a favorite horse, which had been one of God's gifts to her. She repeatedly cautioned her attendants to preserve a composed spirit around her, and seemed to strive to aid them by speaking pleasantly of her emaciated frame, and calmly expressing her wishes as to the place of her burial. Her interest in her writings seemed to be as fresh as ever. She desired that the publication of a little volume which was then in press, should not be delayed on account of her departure; and it pleased her to listen to the request of a distant publisher, which was received that very evening, for another edition of "The Angel over the Right Shoulder." "Let it go," said she, "it will do good." She inquired, also, for the day of the month, and wished to know the precise age of her infant child, and requested that he might be baptized at her funeral. And remembering, doubtless, her own childhood, she said, " Do not let my death throw a gloom over the lives of my children." She gave a pleasing indication of the intimacy with which her refined tastes had become associated in her thoughts with the more common modes of Christian usefulness, by the fact that in the same breath in which she requested that her daughter might be carefully instructed in the fine arts, she requested, also, that her two little boys might be trained for the work of foreign missionaries.

These thoughts of earth appeared to give rest to her weary mind, and enable her again to revert to the eternal prospect before her. She spoke of the friends whom she should soon meet. " There are a great many there," said she, " and you will all come soon, it will be but a little while — Mother will come very soon." This thought of meeting friends in Heaven, however, seemed to be unsatisfactory to her. It instantly suggested her meeting with Christ, and the infinite holiness of His presence appeared to overawe her soul. " I do not feel as if I were fit to go to Heaven," said she; " are you *sure* that He will save *me?*" Her severe fidelity to herself found expression in even stronger language, when she added, "I do not feel as if I were a Christian — but I cannot make myself such. What shall I do if I am selfish in it all? My mind is a little clouded — I am afraid I *am* selfish." Some passages from the Scriptures were repeated to her, which appeared to give her comfort. Among others, the following, viz: 'This is a faithful saying and worthy of all acceptation, that Jesus Christ came into the world to save sinners.' The speaker paused here, and she instantly took up the passage, and added in tones of most touching emphasis, "*of whom I am chief.*" And after a few moments' silence, she continued in the same earnest tones, "I *do* believe;" and again, in answer to the inquiry, "You *know* that you love the Saviour, do you not?" she replied, "I *do* love Him. I do trust in his atoning blood, and in *nothing* else. I give myself to Him." As one after another of the Scriptural assurances of God's faithfulness to His children were repeated to her, a tremulous pressure of the hand that held hers told how precious they were to her. After some hours had passed, her physical distress led her to ask for some anodyne that should give her relief; but when it was prepared, she refused to take it until she was assured that it could not obscure the clearness of her mind. As life ebbed fast away, the thought of the holiness of Heaven again oppressed her, and doubts clouded the prospect. " Are you *sure* He will fit *me* for heaven?" she asked; and nothing seemed to satisfy her longing for a full assurance, but the very words of God, 'He is able to save unto the uttermost, seeing that He ever liveth to intercede.' 'He that cometh unto me, I will in no wise cast out.' 'Let not your heart be troubled, neither let it be afraid.' 'I go to prepare mansions for you.' 'I will not leave you comfortless.' 'I will come again and receive you unto myself.' 'This day shalt thou be with me in Paradise.' These, and many others of like character, buoyed up her fainting spirit. For several hours before she vanished out of our sight, not a cloud rested upon her vision. She desired to depart. Her last intelligible words were, "How long?—how long?"

It was on the morning of the last day of Autumn, after a still and cloudless night, that she 'fell asleep.' "Music and light, such as angels love, filled the air, and death took his gift. Yet I saw that he left a form, cold though it was, whose expression was so" peaceful, "that as we looked, our hearts were comforted."

Her funeral was solemnized at her late residence in Andover, in the afternoon of the third day of December, 1852. We sung her favorite hymns* — one of which had been in her dying thoughts, and the other she had, in her last sickness, pronounced the "most beautiful in the language." In accordance with her request, the rite of Baptism was administered to her infant child. We could not but be grateful for such a privilege, at such an hour; and when we learned that at that hour the western sun had stolen into that darkened room, and sought out no object there but *her* portrait which was looking down upon us, we could not but be reminded that she *had* indeed smiled upon the scene. She had always been grateful if the winds were hushed, and the skies radiant, and the atmosphere bland, when she followed a friend to the burial, — and such was the hour in which we followed her. Autumn, with thoughtful kindness, had lingered for us; loving spirits seemed to move around us in the serene air; the 'speaking elms,' now shorn of their verdure, sighed in gentle sympathy with our woe; and as we bore her along the path which she had so often trodden with us to the house of God, the setting sun — her own chosen emblem of immortality — paused on the horizon, to proclaim once more the assu-

* The first was the five hundred and tenth, and the second was the three hundred and eighty-fourth Hymn of the collection of "Psalms and Hymns" prepared under the direction of the General Association of Connecticut.

rance to our souls. The tolling bell seemed friendly to us, now that it no more struck terror to her heart; we were glad when we thought that it was *not* 'beyond the stars heard.' It was a comfort to us, that her little ones mourned not, but followed her trustfully. It helped to soothe us as we drew near to the narrow house, that we could lay her down to rest in that consecrated spot, where are few, if any, for whom men have mourned as those that had no hope; and where so many repose who were 'chosen vessels' unto God. We felt that we brought her to join an illustrious company. We thought, how peacefully she would rest by the side of her father whom her soul loved. 'With kings and counsellors of the earth,'—and more, with 'kings and priests unto God,'—we left her. And there, she sleeps to-day. Yet, not there. We have sought her diligently, and we could not find her there. We have called to her; and she would have wakened at our voice, if she had slumbered there; but the winds answered us hoarsely. We have lifted the cold mantle which we tried to think winter had thrown kindly over her; and she would have reached forth her hand to greet us, if she had been hidden there; but we grasped only the dull, frozen earth. Then suddenly the grave grew deeper, and the darkness thickened over it whenever we sought her there; and the stars seemed to draw lovingly towards us, and we heard a voice from Heaven saying, "What do ye here? Why seek ye the *living* among the dead?" And so we turned away. We sought her among the "living," and our eyes were opened to behold her. In visions of the night, she sought out us, and we took sweet counsel with her. She told us that she had been changed, in a moment, in the twinkling of an eye. She had been carried away to a holy city that came down from God. It had no need of the sun, neither of the moon, to shine in it, yet there was no night there. She had seen a pure river of water of life, clear as crystal; and the street of the city was pure gold. There, was no more death, neither sorrow, nor crying, nor any more pain, and we *saw* that all tears had been wiped away from *her* eyes. She told us, that through the infinite riches of grace which are in Christ Jesus, she had been welcomed there to a mansion, of which she could only say, that *He* had prepared it for her. Her tongue had been unloosed to *speak* His praise. A harp had been given to her, and her fingers had become skilful on its golden chords. She had been admitted to a choice companionship. She was one of the *swift* messengers. She was of those who mount up on wings as eagles, — and many things had she seen in her flight which it was not lawful for her to utter. But, more than all, she had been with Christ. He who had so gently walked 'around her bed' when she had fallen asleep, had been the first to greet her when she woke. That countenance which she had believed no earthly art could picture, had, with more than its earthly radiance, smiled on her; and she was satisfied now, for she had awaked in His likeness. Then we looked and saw, that His name was written in her forehead. Yes, she *had* been with Christ. *She had seen* —GOD.

We comforted one another with these words. Then we remembered the words which she had spoken while she was yet with us, many years before, and which she had recorded, as if to put us in remembrance of her, when they should have come to pass.

"Once, at the hour of twilight," she had written, "I sat at my western window, and watched the dying out of day. To me, the scene is always suggestive of the fading away of this life. I strained my eyes to catch a glimpse beyond the dark horizon. But the distant mountain and nearer hill and valley faded into the grey twilight, and my thoughts turned from the world without to the world within. All at once, from that spot where the red sun went down, arose a bright cloud like a new sun. Soon I seemed to be bathed in its light. The ebbing and flowing waves bore up before me a shining mirror. I looked upon this mirror, and saw reflected in it my own image. It was a truthful mirror. What a heart it revealed to me! How divided between earth and heaven, between self and God! How feeble its best resolutions! How faint its noblest aspirations! How corrupt a heart it was! I wept, and through my tears I saw that the intellect, too, was fettered by prejudice, enslaved by indolence, diseased by sin. Its enfeebled powers returned no 'usury' to the Giver. I wept more and more at this sight. I bent over the image, as if I would wash it out with my tears. As one struggleth for life, so struggled I for something with which I might blot it out forever.

"Again the sunlight waves ebbed and flowed, and again the shining mirror was before me. Far down in its silvery depths, I now discerned a figure of glorious and yet familiar form and features. No trace of care was on that brow, the eye sparkled with beautiful intelligence, and peaceful beyond description was the smile on the lip. I looked within, — the struggles of that heart had ceased, its warfare ended. Sin no more had dominion there, — and now, like a pent-up fountain suddenly released, its pure affections came gushing forth. They needed a glorified body by which to express themselves. That intellect, freed also from mortal chains, how wondrous were its capacities! It sought out, and grasped, and appropriated to itself, all Truth. Free from doubt, and unerring in its decisions, it seemed like a giant armed. Something whispered to me that this image which I now saw, was also my own. It was the image of that which, when I had passed the dim boundary of this life, I should be—a redeemed soul, with sanctified heart and illuminated mind. I gazed upon it, 'lost in wonder, love, and praise.' I panted to be 'unclothed,' that I might be 'clothed upon.'"

THE PURITAN FAMILY.

THE PURITAN FAMILY.

I.

THE LANDING.

In the early part of September, 164–, occurred one of the great events of those days, to the colony of Massachusetts. It was nothing more nor less than an arrival from Old England of a vessel filled with emigrants who had come, some to seek their fortune, and some to worship God. Boston Harbor bade them welcome, and a crowd was gathered on the wharf to receive them. They were a 'goodlie companie,' and many of them as they leaped ashore threw back their heads and stretched their limbs, and took 'long breaths,' as if the relief they felt from the confinement of forty days on shipboard were heightened by a new sense of civil and religious freedom which expanded their huge frames. A little apart from the crowd stood a small group of three — Mrs. Allerton, Arabella her daughter, and Hetty, a faithful old servant. Mr. Allerton was running hither and thither, collecting their most necessary baggage. It was nearly noon, and the rays of the lingering summer fell hotly upon them, as they stood there unsheltered. Mrs. Allerton had passed the prime of life, but was still attractive in person and manner. Her eye wandered over the embryo city which had nestled down so closely to the sea, and she did so with an anxious expression, for there was to be her new home. Arabella possessed the beauty of the lily,—delicate, almost too delicate, it should seem, to bear transplanting; and she stood with her pensive eye wandering back over the waters, towards the home she had left. Hetty, by no means an unimportant personage in the party, watched with a jealous eye each piece of baggage as it was handed over to a black man, who had offered the services of himself and his cart.

"We can't do without this; we must have that—now that green box a'nt put in; Mrs. Allerton, wont you please say, we *must* have the green box? We shall need it the fust thing."

"Never mind, Hetty," said Mrs. Allerton; "we do not know yet what we want, or where we shall go."

"Not where we shall go? My eyes! a'nt there no hotels in this country? Curious place, I think," continued she—talking now to herself. "Wish ourselves back, I am thinking, Miss Bell; only see, Mr. Allerton don't think of the red trunk, and it has got all your dresses in it, — not fit to be seen, any of us."

"Hush, Hetty," said Mrs. Allerton, turning her face towards the vessel, "they are going to prayer."

A large party of emigrants had crowded together on one part of the deck, around their minister, — and with closed eyes and reverent posture, they united with him in returning thanks to God, for their safe voyage. At the close of this long prayer, they sung a psalm, "O give thanks unto the Lord," etc. Mrs. Allerton joined them with a sweet, rich voice, and as it appeared with her whole heart. Arabella attempted to do the same, but her voice trembled and she turned quite away, to hide her tears. Hetty looked as if she thought the service long, and the sun hot. The captain and crew of the vessel paid little heed to the pious thank offering of their puritan passengers, — for during their long summer voyage, they had become quite accustomed to their strange ways, inasmuch as having two ministers on board, they had had many sermons to beguile the tedious hours.

The news of the arrival of this vessel soon spread; and as the last strain of the chant died away, a gentleman approached, before whom the crowd parted on either side. His countenance was mild and benevolent, — his manners, polished and winning. His beard descended to the ruff, which he wore about his neck, and his dress indicated a person of authority. It was Governor Winthrop.

He was watching the landing of the emigrants, with much interest, when his eye fell upon his old friend, Mr. Allerton. He hastened to him, and grasping him by the hand, gave him a warm welcome. So cordial was the greeting, both to him and his family, that Mrs. Allerton felt as if she had met a brother; and the weary, and somewhat dispirited, party revived under the tones of kindness.

"My house is but a short distance from here, Mrs. Allerton," said the Governor; "you must make it your home for the present, and the sooner you are out of this hot sun, the better. Arabella looks half homesick already; see how she watches the old ship, as if now it were more attractive than our goodly town of Boston. Come and rest, child; then we will show you something better than this wharf. You will love New England, yet." Gov. Winthrop drew Arabella's arm within his, and the fair pilgrim felt somewhat comforted.

Mr. Allerton and Hetty soon overtook them, and the whole party proceeded to Gov. Winthrop's house. It was a low, two-story wooden house, painted with some attention to the ornamental, and furnished with blinds. In the porch, which projected over the front door, stood Mrs. Winthrop; and so heartily did she repeat her husband's welcome, that her visitors felt like expected guests. After stopping a while in the comfortable parlor, they were conducted to their own rooms that they might rest, and prepare for tea.

The chamber over the parlor, with its nice white dimity hangings, was assigned to Mr. and Mrs. Allerton; a small room over the entry, to Arabella; while Hetty took her place in the servants' quarters. Their baggage, as it arrived, was stowed away in a loft in the barn, for the present, excepting the invaluable green box and the red trunk, which Hetty made bold to tell the Governor "they *must* have," and some smaller pieces. She bustled about now, in earnest, and released the ladies' dresses from their long confinement, and wished them to appear in their best at the Governor's table.

"Oh! pray Hetty," said Mrs. Allerton, "fold up those damask dresses, and give us something more simple. What will you wear, Arabella, dear?"

"Anything," said Arabella, looking vacantly out of the window over the water. Mrs. Allerton noticed her absence and dejection, and spoke to her in cheerful tones.

"How pleasant everything is here, daughter,— is it not? These bed-hangings remind me of my own room, and almost carry me back to it, they are so like ours; and I noticed that the window of your little room looks out to the west, just as the one in your study at home does. Then to be received so cordially, to meet such kind friends, and find a home ready for us, and to have had so prosperous a voyage, — why, Bella dear! we have a great deal to be thankful for."

"I think so, too, mother," replied Arabella, "and I shall soon feel cheerful and happy, for though I love Old England, yet I love you and father more; my home is where you are."

"Miss Bell," said Hetty, "pray, let me braid your hair. Your father wont like it at all to see you at the table with it in such a snarl — and the Governor and his lady there too."

"Do what you please, good Hetty," said Arabella, pulling out her comb and letting her dark hair fall down over her shoulders. She looked up to her mother at the same time, and tried to smile in answer to her good cheer. She had a little struggle, but she kept back some truant drops, that otherwise would have dimmed her deep blue eyes. 'Poor little pilgrim!' she yearned for her old home.

II.

NEIGHBORS.

WHILE it was yet early, a little bell, ringing at the foot of the stairs, announced the tea-hour at Gov. Winthrop's. Our travellers, now dressed sufficiently to satisfy Hetty, and being certainly much improved in appearance, joined the Governor and his lady in the parlor, where the table was laid. Gov. Winthrop's son was now presented to the visitors. He was social and courteous, and made an effort to draw out the timid stranger. With her beauty he had become quite well acquainted during the very long blessing which his father, as usual, pronounced.

So many questions were asked and answered, that it was dark when the party rose from the table. The evening was unusually mild, and the elder gentlemen withdrew to the settee on the stoop, to finish their conversation, while the ladies sat back a little in the parlor. Mrs. Winthrop was busy with netting, which, however, did not at all divert her attention from her guests. The younger Winthrop described to Arabella, some of the attractions of Boston. Thus passed our emigrants' first evening in New England. When the large clock in the hall struck the hour of nine, Gov. Winthrop rose,—

"Our habits are very simple here," said he to Mr. Allerton; "it is the hour for family prayer." Mrs. Winthrop called the domestics. The younger Winthrop, by his father's request read the chapter next in course; a psalm was given out in couplets, which the family joined in singing; prayer then followed, and all soon retired to rest.

Arabella accompanied her mother into hei room, and seemed unwilling to separate from her

"A good night's sleep," said her father, "will make Boston another place; come here, Bella; I want to see more color in those cheeks; the sea has paled them. Do not you think you will be happy here?"

"I mean to be happy here, dear father," said Arabella, throwing her arms around him, and fondly caressing him.

"Let us unite in prayer in our own room," said Mr. Allerton, "that we may render thanks unto God for his mercies towards us individually." Saying this, he knelt, with his wife and daughter by his side.

"Now, good-night, my child;" and "good-night" again, from the mother — and with Hetty to attend to all her little wants, the idolized child retired to her room to sleep soundly and sweetly, and wake—for the first time in New England.

A fortnight passed rapidly away, while Mr. Allerton and his family remained the guests of Gov. Winthrop. At the expiration of that time, he had hired a house, — out from the more thickly settled part of the town, with a small farm; hoping that this, together with the remnant of his reduced property, would suffice for the maintenance of his family.

This house, after the fashion of the times, was built two stories in front, and sloped down to one in the rear. The small windows made of diamond-shape glass, set in sashes of lead, opened outward on hinges. A large yard in front, shaded by two venerable elms, gave a pleasant and attractive air to this spot.

"It is everything we could desire," said Mrs. Allerton, as with real pleasure she walked about the premises. "It is far beyond what I supposed we could obtain without waiting to build. Bella, dear, we will put a porch out on this side, and transplant that grape-vine for you, and you will like to sit there in the shade, and read and sew."

"I thought of that myself," said Mr. Allerton. "It could very easily be done; we will attend to it early in the spring."

"You should not think so much of me," said

Arabella. "You must care for your own comfort, dear mother. I am young" — "and strong," she would have added, but checked herself.

"The water is nigh the house, and that is one comfort," said Hetty, "but who are we to have for neighbors, I wonder, in that little brown house there? I hope they are good natur'd, as long as they are so nigh."

"Good day to you, good-man and good-wife, and a welcome to our new country. You are to live here, I suppose?" inquired some one so near that it seemed as if the voice must have come from one of their party. "I am the neighbor whom that woman was just asking for, and I live very nigh you. Shall be glad to help you any about setting to rights, if I can. My name is Mercy Whitman. They call me Mercy, mostly. I am a poor lone widow. My husband — the Lord love him — was shot by the Injins, more than five year ago. 'The Lord gave, and the Lord took away.'"

"Have you children, Mercy?" kindly inquired Mrs. Allerton. Mercy, before replying, climbed over a stone fence, behind which she had been concealed, and approached nearer. She was a short, stout woman, dressed in a blue checked short gown and petticoat, and she wore a very high-crowned cap, which was not altogether as clean as it might have been. Her gray, frizzled hair, escaping from under it, hung about a sallow and wrinkled face, lighted by a pair of keen gray eyes, which had a sinister expression. Hetty declared afterwards that "they made her think of a wolf, or an Injin, or some such cretur."

"Not a living chick in the world," said Mercy, "to call me mother. My boy died the winter after his father, and there he lies under that apple tree in my garden."

Hetty surveyed the new acquaintance from head to foot, and with a secret feeling of dislike to everything about her, walked on rapidly and entered the house.

"Can't I help you any?" said Mercy. "I shall be very glad to. My work is up for to-day."

"No, I thank you," said Mrs. Allerton, stepping past her. "We have not much to do at present. If I should want you at any time, I will call upon you. Good morning."

Mercy saw the unpacked boxes, through the half-open door; and vexed a little that she could not satisfy her curiosity, and yet not daring to press the matter farther with the stranger lady, she returned the salutation, and left them; but slyly went round back of the house to the kitchen, hoping to find more favor with 'the woman.'

Hetty was pulling violently at a cupboard door, which seemed to be glued up.

"Bless ye, let me try," said Mercy, "pull at top and bottom both — here, I'll show ye — I'll have it in a minute."

"No," said Hetty, not very well pleased, "I thank ye; but if I can't open it myself, I'll let it go." Mercy looked on; Hetty tugged, and turned red in the face, and broke her nails. Mercy stood still and laughed. Hetty lost her patience — of which she had not a very large stock.

"You had better be a-doing something else than looking at your neighbors," said she, in a passion.

"O that is it, is it? Well, I'll take myself off, then. It's a pity if folks can't be civil when others come to do them a kindness, I think," said Mercy, reddening in her turn.

Fortunately the door yielded, and Hetty felt better. "There," said she, "if I had taken your advice, Mistress Mercy, I should not have broken my nails; and now if you will draw up a bucket of water for me, I'll do as much for you some time."

Mercy was but half appeased. The first shot had been fired. It was said, many miles around, that Mercy never forgot an injury, and people generally were afraid of her.

III.

WINTER IN THE "WILDERNESSE."

By the first of October, our emigrants were settled in their new home. Elegant it was not; for as the deputy-governor had been censured for wainscoting his house, Mr. Allerton would not venture to offend the prejudices of the good people by any superfluities. Mrs. Allerton and Arabella, though equally considerate, did not hit the line so exactly; for many things which seemed to the settlers as superfluities, were to them but matters of ordinary comfort. Some furniture they had brought with them: a carpet that covered the floor of the room which was to be both parlor and bedroom for guests; some heavy, curiously carved mahogany chairs, standing on lions' claws; a small bookcase; a set of oaken drawers, also curiously wrought. These, with three or four family portraits in rich frames, gave an aristocratic air to the best parlor. The other parlor, being the room in which they chiefly lived, had no carpet. Two heavy mahogany tables stood upon its white sanded floor, and its walls were thickly hung with Arabella's paintings, all of which her father had carefully preserved. Two large, high-backed chairs stood in each corner of the huge fireplace. Back of these two parlors was the kitchen and a small room opening into it, originally intended for a bed room, but now used by Mr. Allerton as a library. Here were collected all the books that he had been able to bring over. Hetty's quarters were quite capacious, and on the whole, convenient. She would sometimes grumble about leaving so many comforts behind in England, — yet, in the main, she found more to praise than to find fault with.

Thus, almost necessarily, their house had an appearance of style which was much beyond that of their neighbors, and which at first made the neighbors a little shy.

But as acquaintance increased, this wore entirely away. Mr. Allerton became very popular, and was esteemed as a kind, charitable, godly man, one whose house and purse were open to relieve the suffering, — a "real New England *Souldier*, whom the Lord Christ having prepared for his work in England, had now sent over to fight his *Battel*."

Mrs. Allerton was courteous and hospitable, with a word of sympathy for all who needed it. They esteemed her as "likewise a godly Woman, indued by Christ with graces fit for a Wildernesse condition, whose courage was exceeding great, and who, with much cheerfulness, did undergoe all difficulties; and who had brought up her child to be an honour to Christ."

They were thus established in their house, and in the affections of the people, when the cold, New England winter found them. It brought with it many hardships.

The change from a condition of ease, plenty, and comfort, to their present one, for Mrs. Allerton and Arabella, was very great. The winter set in suddenly, and with violent snow-storms. They found themselves, one November morning, almost buried in the drifts. Their house was not tightly built, and the bitter cold wind whistled in, all around them. No part of the house was habitable but the sitting-room and kitchen, and these were made so only by enormous fires. Hetty affirmed that "the side of the bed where she did n't lie was covered with snow, and one end of her pillow froze down. Such doings she never heard of afore."

To sit over the fire and make themselves comfortable, was out of question; there was too much to be done. No help could be hired in the region, for love or money, and all the indoor work for the actual support of the family, came upon these three. Poor Hetty, scarcely allowing herself time to eat, worked early and late to save her mistress and Miss Bella; but though she taxed her industry and ingenuity to the utmost, she could not do everything. In this "wildernesse," through such cruel weather, all who lived must work.

This first snow-storm we have noticed, was a fair specimen of the rest of the winter.

"Yes, snowing again to-day, Bella dear," said Mr. Allerton, "but our logs burn cheerfully. Get into the chimney corner, child. You had better move up your stand there and finish that drawing; it is a long time since I have seen you with your pencil. It will amuse you this dull day, darling."

"I wish you would urge her to," said Mrs. Allerton; "she works much beyond her strength; I cannot persuade her to spare herself."

"When you will spare yourself, dear mother, then will I," replied Arabella.

"No need of either of you working, and I tell 'em so every day of their lives, but it don't do no good; they will keep at it," said Hetty, who just entered with an armful of wood. "I wish you would put a stop to it, if you please, sir. Mistress even takes hold of the washing, as if I was not old enough to do a washing. They'll both of 'em kill themselves, and I tell 'em so, but they won't mind me, sir."

"Can't you get any help about the heaviest of the work, Hetty," inquired Mr. Allerton.

"Not a living mortal, sir, except Mercy Whitman, and for my part I'd work till I dropped, afore I'd have her about. I believe she's a witch," mumbled she in an under-tone.

"You work now as long as you can stand, Hetty."

"Not I, mistress; and if I do, it's not because I work hard, or am getting old. It is this villanous country, with its horrid storms. When one's bed clothes freeze to 'em, I do n't know why their bones should n't ache. If we were only back again in old England, we would think twice afore we crossed the ocean, — that's my mind."

"Blessed be the Lord who has gloriously upheld us," said Mr. Allerton; "if this great work of planting here the pure religion of Christ were before me, and ten thousand oceans, I would cross them all to do it."

Mrs. Allerton approached gently, and put her hand upon his shoulder. "Amen," said she, in a deep, earnest voice. "Let us rejoice that we are accounted worthy to suffer for His sake. Not for all England could offer, would I turn back, if"—— the mother's voice trembled, for her moistened eye fell upon her fragile daughter, and the sentence was unfinished. For a moment, faith wavered.

"We will cast all our cares upon the Lord,"

said Mr. Allerton, "and assuredly the wants of this wildernesse will never hurt us."

"I s'pose so," said Hetty, "but pray what are we to do for bread; our last peck of meal is in the oven baking, and we have had nothing to eat this fortnight, but 'mussells and clambanks.' Miss Bell can't eat this corn bread, and the fish does n't suit her. She has n't put enough into her mouth this week, to keep a robin alive."

"You are mistaken, good Hetty," said Bella, smiling. "You forget how much milk I drink. What can be better than such nice fresh milk. I miss our old luxuries much less than mother does."

"Our cattle will die next thing, if we have many more such cold snaps," replied Hetty, quite determined not to be pleased with anything in a country where it snowed every day in the week.

Her remarks were interrupted by a violent rattling at the kitchen door.

"Who can that be at this time of day, I wonder," said she, as she hastened to open it. A strong gust of wind blinded her with the driving snow.

"I ran in to see if your good-man was in want of meal," said Mercy Whitman, pushing her way into the kitchen. "I thought he could n't get to mill this week, and I have more than I need."

"It is very kind in you, Mercy," said Mrs. Allerton, speaking quickly, that she might anticipate Hetty's short answer. "The last we have is now in the oven. We will take it from you gladly."

"Wont you walk in and warm you?"

"Thank you, good-wife, but I can't stop this morning, I'm in a hurry," said Mercy, at the same time coming in. O no, no, child, keep your seat. I've no time to spend warming my old bones; and it's not much matter either; the Lord has 'most done with me for this world; I wait his summons. This is a nice, warm corner, child, and I do not care if I just turn the snow out of my shoes."

Arabella's seat was so comfortable, that Mercy was not very expeditious in clearing her shoes. She had as usual much scandal to tell, and many impertinent questions to ask; our friends, though they treated her kindly, were not sorry to see her at length rise to go.

"I wish you would be quick and shut that door after you," said Hetty to her; "you'll let in more snow than I can get out in a week."

"You may shut your own doors," said Mercy, "if you are a mind to be so crusty as that," — and she left the door wide open.

Hetty bestowed upon her some epithet which, fortunately, the howling wind blew quite out of her hearing.

"They never agree," said Mrs. Allerton, closing the sitting-room door, "and I do not much wonder at it."

"How wonderfully has the Lord provided for us," said Mr. Allerton, who had not noticed this little episode between Hetty and Mercy. "Assuredly, even at the last cast, he is near to those who trust in Him. He put it into her heart to come and offer us her meal, when our stock was gone, and we could see no other way of obtaining it. I believe that Christ would rather rain bread from heaven than that his people should want, while they keep about his work. Let us return thanks unto Him for this seasonable supply."

They knelt around their crackling fire, and enjoyed to the full the expression of the sweet consciousness that God was feeding them; then, they went cheerfully to their day's labors.

Hetty's remarks about the work, however, made a deep impression upon Mr. Allerton. So uncomplainingly and quietly had his wife and daughter performed the hard labor of the family, that the necessary amount of it had not occurred to him until Hetty enlightened him. He saw now, plainly, that they were taxed beyond their strength, and he cast about in his mind to see what could be done to relieve them.

IV.

THE PURITAN HOME.

A DESCRIPTION of one short day, during this long and tedious winter, will answer for many.

Hetty rose at five every morning, and bustled about quickly, to have her fires well burning and a hot breakfast ready for the family at half past six. Often with sighs, and perhaps with tears which she in vain dashed away, she dished up the coarse, and sometimes scanty food, — and yet with a delicate thoughtfulness, she would arrange it on the table as much after the manner to which they had been accustomed as the materials she had, enabled her to do so.

Immediately after breakfast, prayers occupied usually three quarters of an hour. Mr. Allerton read from a commentary, and invariably had a psalm sung. His wife and daughter were sweet singers, and even Hetty could join in this part of family worship. After this exercise, with hearts comforted, and faith strengthened, and hope smiling upon them, they separated about their day's toils.

Their house, like many others built at that time, "faced the south," that the sun might "shine in square at noon," and mark the dinner-hour, which was precisely twelve o'clock. This domestic sundial was very convenient. Mr. Allerton had brought out a valuable time-piece, but it had been so much injured on the passage as to be nearly useless.

At twelve, they refreshed themselves with their frugal dinner. Mrs. Allerton would often force herself to partake of what was far from inviting to her, for her husband's sake; but many articles of diet so evidently disagreed with Arabella, that her mother was not willing to have her use them. Corn bread, in particular, poorly suited her. So, at length, she was reduced almost entirely to milk and the scanty supply of eggs they could procure. Notwithstanding this, their meals were cheerful; they received their food, as it were, directly from the hand of God; and they felt that what He had provided for them, was on the whole the best for them. The very coarseness and scantiness of their food they regarded as trials of their faith and love, and a proof that God had not forgotten them, but chastened them in love. Did they want for bread, they cheerfully fed upon fish, and had heavenly discourse of the provision which Christ had once made for many thousands of his followers in the wilderness. Thus linked to heaven and Christ in heart and purpose, ever struggling upwards, and believing in the rich promises of success, their deprivation and toils shrunk away, and seemed to them but as incidents to a glorious mission.

Their dinner over, a part of the afternoon was occupied in necessary labor. This through, Mrs. Allerton and Arabella dressed, and sat down to their needle. The short twilight was soon gone, and before tea and lights were brought in, Mr. Allerton usually joined them, and drawing around their bright fire, they spent the pleasant hour in social and religious conversation. After tea, Mrs. Allerton resumed her needle, while Mr. Allerton read aloud. Arabella, occupied with coarse woollen knitting, sat far in the chimney corner, often listening to her father, and often looking up through the huge chimney, to far distant, silent stars, — as distant and silent, as the answering voice to thoughts hidden deep in her soul.

Hetty kept still at work. Mr. and Mrs. Allerton often called her to join them, but she had always some excuse, and worked on, until summoned to evening prayers. Then again they joined in a song of thanksgiving for a day's mercies, and retired always at nine o'clock to rest.

Saturday night at sunset, all work was suspended. On the Lord's day, Mr. Allerton, with his family, attended Divine service at the church in

Boston, under the care of Rev. Mr. Wilson. The distance was so great, they rode, and were always invited by the hospitable governor to spend the intermission with him. They also returned to his house, at the close of the afternoon service, and remained there until after family prayers. It was Governor Winthrop's habit to assemble his family, to read to them from the Bible, and then repeat to them the sermons which he had heard through the day. This he did from memory, as he never allowed himself to take notes. He was very constant in this, and required all his family to be present.

Mr. Allerton was much interested in Mr. Wilson's preaching. Governor Winthrop remarked of it, "it was after the primitive fashion. It consisted chiefly of exhortations and admonitions, and good wholesome counsels, which would excite good motions in the minds of his people."

"Yes," replied Mr. Allerton, "and sometimes when I hear him, there is such a spirit in him, I feel almost as if I were listening to an apostle."

Edified and encouraged thus by the godly preaching, and also by the conversation and example of Governor Winthrop, the Lord's day was rich in spiritual enjoyment to Mr. Allerton and his family. They hailed its return with joy, — and with its declining sun they again thanked God that he had brought them where they might worship him in simplicity and truth.

The Sabbath also furnished to Arabella another source of enjoyment. Herself and young Winthrop exchanged books, and in this way provided themselves with reading, through the ensuing week,—each selecting from their father's library. Their little secret arrangement was, that Arabella should leave her's on her seat in the carriage, from whence Deane Winthrop should take it, leaving his in return. This was not absolutely necessary, as Deane most generally found something to call him out to Mr. Allerton's during the week; but as their reading was all of a grave character, it was not unsuitable to their rigid habits in observing the day.

One Sabbath in December, they met the younger Winthrop, governor of Connecticut and New Haven, who was on a visit to his father. Having so delightful a party, they lingered somewhat longer than was their usual custom. Arabella and Deane were speaking, by themselves, of the young governor, whose appearance and manners had so much interested Arabella.

"You must love him very much," said she.

"That I do," replied Deane, quickly, "though he is not my own brother; we have different mothers, but it seems to me that he feels almost as much interested in us as in his own little family. He is very anxious to have us on the right side. To-day, he handed me a letter which my father wrote him some time ago, and requested me to copy it and keep it by me always, and live up to it."

"I should like much to see it, if I may," said Arabella.

"Most assuredly, it will give me much pleasure. I have already taken one copy, which I will place in the book, and beg you will retain."

Arabella thanked him, and found on her return, the following, in Deane's handwriting, with a line or two at the bottom of the page, which was not copied, and which, therefore, we will omit.

There may be young readers at this day, who can look over this old letter of Governor Winthrop, with as much profit as it gave to Deane and Arabella.

LETTER.

"You are the chief of *Two* Families; I had by your Mother *Three Sons* and *Three Daughters*, and I had with her a *Large Portion* of outward Estate. These now are all *gone;* Mother *gone;* Brethren and Sisters *gone;* you only are left to see the vanity of these *Temporal things*, and learn *Wisdom* thereby, which may be of more use to you, through the Lord's Blessing, than all that

Inheritance which might have befallen you: And for which this may stay and quiet your Heart, *That God is able to give you more than this;* and that it hath been spent in the furtherance of *his Work*, which hath here prospered so well, through his Power hitherto, you and yours may *certainly expect a liberal Portion in the Prosperity and Blessing thereof hereafter;* and the rather because it was not *forced* from you by a Father's Power, but freely *resigned* by yourself, out of a loving and Filial Respect unto me, and your own readiness unto the Work itself. From whence as I do often take Occasion to Bless the Lord for you, so do I also Commend you and yours to his *Fatherly Blessing*, for a plentiful Reward to be rendered unto you. And doubt not, my dear son, but let your Faith be built upon his Promise and Faithfulness, that as he has carried you hitherto through many Perils, and provided liberally for you, so he will do for the time to come, and will *never fail you, nor forsake you. My son*, the *Lord knows* how Dear thou art to me, and that my Care hath been more for thee than for myself. But *I know* thy Prosperity depends not on my love, nor on *thine own*, but upon the Blessing of our *Heavenly Father;* neither doth it on the things of this World, but on the *Light of God's Countenance* through the Merit and Mediation of our Lord Jesus Christ. It is *that* only which can give us *Peace of Conscience* with *Contentation*, which can as well make our Lives Happy and Comfortable in a *mean* Estate as in a *great Abundance.* But if you weigh things aright, and sum up all the Turnings of Divine Providence together, you shall find great Advantage. The Lord hath brought us to a *Good Land*, and a Land where we enjoy outward *Peace and Liberty*, and above all, the *Blessings of the Gospel*, without the Burden of *Impositions* in matters of *Religion*. Many thousands there are who would give Great Estates to enjoy our Condition. Labour, therefore, my good Son, to increase our *Thankfulness* to God for all his mercies to thee, especially for that he hath revealed his *Everlasting Good Will* to thee in Jesus Christ, and joined thee to the visible Body of his *Church*, in the Fellowship of his People, and hath saved thee in all thy *Travails* abroad, from being infected with the *Vices* of those Countries where thou hast been (a mercy vouchsafed unto but few young Gentlemen *Travellers*.) Let *him* have the Honour of it, who kept thee. *He* it was who gave thee Favor in the Eyes of all with whom thou hadst to do both by Sea and Land. *He* it was who saved thee in all Perils; and *He* it is who hath given thee a Gift in Understanding and Art; and He it is who hath provided thee a Blessing in Marriage, a Comfortable Help, and many Sweet Children; and hath hitherto provided liberally for you all: And therefore I would have you to *Love* him again, and *Serve* him, and *Trust* him for the time to come. Love and Prize that *Word of Truth*, which only makes known to you the Precious and Eternal Thoughts and Councils of the *Light Inaccessible.* Deny your *own Wisdom*, that you may find his; and esteem it the greatest Honour to lye under the Simplicity of the Gospel of *Christ crucified*, without which you can never enter into the *Secrets of his Tabernacle*, nor enjoy those sweet things which *Eye hath not seen, nor Ear heard, nor can the Heart of man conceive;* but God hath granted unto some few to know them, even in this Life. Study well, my son, the saying of the Apostle, *knowledge puffeth up.* It is a *good Gift of God,* but when it lifts up the mind above the *Cross of Christ,* it is the *Pride of Life,* and the Highway to *Apostasy,* wherein many men of great Learning and Hopes have perished. In all the Exercise of your *Gifts,* and Improvement of your *Talents,* have an Eye to your *Master's End* more than your *own;* and to the *Day of your Account,* that you may then have your *Quietus est,* even *Well Done, Good and Faithful Servant.* But my last and chief Request to you is, that you be careful to have your *Children* brought up in the Knowledge and Fear of God, and in the Faith of our Lord Jesus Christ. *This* will give you the best *Comfort* of them, and keep them sure from any *Want* or *Miscarriage.* And when you part from them, it will be no small joy to your Soul, *that you shall meet them again in Heaven.*"

V.

THE PRAYER OF FAITH.

Mrs. Allerton, about mid-winter, was taken violently ill. She had been enfeebled for some time, looking pale, and making a great effort to perform her usual duties. She found herself at length, one morning, unable to rise, and her illness increased rapidly during the forenoon. Mr. Allerton went into Boston and brought out the physician. He pronounced the disease to be a billious fever, and said that it must "take its time;" ordered some medicines; and prescribed "patience and good nursing." As soon as he had taken leave, Mrs. Allerton sent for Hetty to come to her.

"Hetty," said she, "I am going to be ill for some time; I feel it; and I shall be much worse than I am now. I know very well that there is no one to take a step for me but Miss Bella and you. Now you must go at once over to Mercy Whitman, and say that I should like to have her come and help you, this morning. The bed and hangings must be removed from the front room into the sitting room, as soon as possible, that I may get down there. It will save you much strength in taking care of me."

Mrs. Allerton spoke so positively, that Hetty dared not object. She called upon Mercy very reluctantly; she had said that she would never darken her doors, — but time pressed, her mistress must be moved before night. Mr. Allerton had gone to carry the Doctor home, and Miss Bella sat with her mother. She delivered the message as graciously as she could, and Mercy returned with her.

Mercy had many questions to ask about the curtains, as they took them down, to which Hetty's answers became shorter and shorter — "She neither knew nor cared how much they cost, nor where they came from," she said. In taking down the bedstead, another cause of dispute arose. Mercy insisted upon having her own way, and wrenched the posts in such a manner, that Hetty at length told her, "She was a great fool, and she did n't believe she ever saw a bedstead before."

"I should like to know what you think I lie on?" said she.

"Lie on straw, like the pigs, for all I know or care," said Hetty, as Mercy, in her spite, let a heavy post fall on Hetty's foot. They exchanged high words which were fast waxing into a hot dispute, when Mr. Allerton retarued, and seeing how things were, dismissed Hetty to the chamber, and himself, with Mercy's assistance prepared the room for the invalid.

Mrs. Allerton was exceedingly anxious to make the change before night, thinking she might not be able to do it at all, should it be deferred. With great exertion she came down stairs, and sunk exhausted upon her pillow. The effort, and the cold air of the entries, increased her fever. She tossed all night long under its violence. Mr. Allerton sent Arabella and Hetty to bed, that they might be able to take care of her during the day, and himself sat watching by her side. She seemed so very ill that he went again early in the morning for the physician. The case had assumed a more alarming aspect than the physician had expected; and he remained with her, kind old man, through the day. Still, she became rapidly worse.

The weather was intensely cold, and their provisions had fallen short. Almost everything that was needed for the sick room, they were obliged to obtain in Boston. It was a long, cold ride, and no one but Mr. Allerton could be spared for it, or could, indeed, endure it. Sickness was so abundant around them, that it was impossible to procure any one to assist Hetty. She worked herself almost to a shadow. Arabella was with her mother day and night; and could not be persuaded to leave her. For more than a week she had no rest except such as she could take in her chair, while her mother slept. Pale and anxious, scarcely eating or sleeping, she hung over the precious sufferer, without a thought of her own wasting strength.

Days passed; change was not for the better, but rather for the worse. It was evident now, that Mrs. Allerton was fast failing; and unless the fever soon reached its height, she must sink into the grave. One afternoon, the physician looked unusually grave. Arabella, with her pale, thin lips tightly closed, fixed her deep, earnest eyes upon him as if to watch every thought. He turned slowly from the bed, and drawing Mr. Allerton's arm within his, led him into the parlor and closed the door. For a moment, neither spake. "May God support you, my friend," said he, at length. "And — I —must — lose her?" said Mr. Allerton slowly, as if the thought could not find birth.

"I see no hope — I have done all," was the reply. The doctor pressed his hand kindly, and with tears in his eyes, passed quickly out, and left him alone with God.

What that struggle was, we do not know, — but when he came from that room, it was over; rebellious thoughts were gone — "May God's will be done, and his name glorified, though I suffer," was the feeling of his soul. It seemed as if angels had ministered to him, he returned so calmly to the bed-side of his dying wife.

And Arabella, the gentle, fragile, dependent child, seemed in this hour of sorest need, to be up-held by an unseen hand. After the first gush of overwhelming sorrow, when she found her father had given up hope, she also became calm and submissive. She returned to his side, speaking to him sweetly and affectionately, — restraining all manifestations of grief, for his sake; and even striving to comfort Hetty, whose sorrow was beyond control.

There, on that bed, lay the wife and mother — failing, still failing. On one side stood her husband, about to be left alone in a strange land; in a desert land; on the other side, the only child, a daughter, frail as a trembling reed, to be left motherless; — in the background the faithful old servant, weeping violently — repining that she, whose old life was worth so little, could not have been taken instead. The cold, dreary storm howling without, — the want of the comforts necessary to a sick room,— the secret longing of the sufferer (if, indeed, she still felt a wish), to die among her kindred, and be laid to rest in the old church-yard with her fathers. — Could the dim past start to life, how many such scenes of suffering, among those who prepared the way for us, would it picture to us!

"Father," said Arabella, "if mother should revive so as to be conscious, would it not be a comfort to her to see Mr. Wilson, and have him with her in her last moments?"

Mr. Allerton had the same thought, but it was storming violently; their physician had been called in a different direction, and not a neighbor had been able to come to them through the day. The snow lay in deep drifts, and the road was unbroken; there was no one to undertake the journey but himself, and it would, at the least calculation, take him away from that bedside three or four hours — could that expiring flame flicker on so long? "Do you think she would know him?" he asked Arabella, who was at that moment touching her lips with wine. She appeared to swallow with less difficulty than she had for some time previous.

"Mother," whispered Arabella, "if you would like to see Mr. Wilson, will you press my hand?" She pressed it slightly, and made an effort to raise her eyelids. This decided Mr. Allerton. He came to her; he bent over her; the hot tears fell upon her pale forehead; he knew he might be taking his last farewell. "You know how much I have loved you," he whispered, and without another look, left the room.

During his long ride, he experienced such a sense of God's presence, of His holiness, of His love, as he never had experienced before, and he never forgot it. His whole being seemed elevated, and he informed Mr. Wilson of his errand, without a murmuring word or repining thought.

Mr. Wilson listened in silence, but with great interest, for he knew and justly prized Mrs. Allerton. When he had heard Mr. Allerton through, he told him he would return with him, but not immediately; he had something to do in his study, which he must first attend to. A shade of disappointment was for a moment visible on Mr. Allerton's countenance. Mr. Wilson withdrew, and Mrs. Wilson prepared hastily a hot supper to refresh her guest. In about half an hour, Mr. Wilson came down, his face bright with smiles.

"Mr. Allerton," said he, "I have been praying that God would spare your wife, and I am confident that she *will live;* and now, if you please, we will go to her; but first I have something to show you." He went out and brought in his little daughter, a fair-haired, sweet-looking child.

"We had had no children for many years," said he, "until we came here, and then God sent us this blessing. I call her my '*New England Token.*' You see how he hath provided for us, and thus will he provide for you. The wife of your youth shall yet become the staff of your age, and together shall ye depart to those heavenly regions where you shall see Jesus."

At this time, so much confidence was placed in Mr. Wilson, that his prayers were deemed prophetic. A trembling hope sprang up in Mr. Allerton's heart, which agitated him. Mr. Wilson withdrew to make preparations to return with him. Mrs. Wilson had so strong faith in her husband's impressions, that she became very cheerful. She talked with Mr. Allerton; she sought to divert him, that the necessary delay might not distress him. She related much of their own experience. One little incident particularly had interested her, and she told it to strengthen him.

She had been very unwilling to come to New England, and had returned in great dejection with her husband, when he came over a second time for her. After she had been here a little while, an old kinsman of hers sent her over by a friend, 'a present to console her in the American Desart.' "And this is it," said she, taking three small rolls out of a box. "First he presented me this *Brass Counter;* if I made any show of discontent, he was to take no further notice of me. But I was so much delighted by any remembrance from my old kinsman, that next he gave me this *Silver Crown.* And last of all, this *Gold Jacobus,* and with it, delivered this message: 'That such would be the dispensations of God unto me, and the other good people of New England. If they would be content and thankful with such little things as God at first bestowed upon them, they should in time have silver and gold enough.' This has proved true," said she, "in a great measure; for God has given us since, a Token which is worth more to us than tried gold."

Mr. Wilson's sleigh now drove up; and Mr. Allerton, much more agitated than when he came, took leave. His mind seemed afloat; he had lost his anchor; he could not rest on the Will of God, for *what* this Will was to be, was now uncertain. He eagerly strained his eyes for the first glimpse of home, as if the icy roof could picture to him death or life. It was soon in sight; the doctor's carriage was there again. He feared to advance; he could not recede;—is it life, or death? He drew nearer; the door opened; and as Hetty came out to break the tidings, his heart sank. A little behind her stood Arabella; they were now in the yard; Hetty came tramping through the deep snow to meet him. Mr. Allerton did not raise his eyes. "All doing well, Miss Hetty?" said Mr. Wilson.

"All well, sir; a great change," replied Hetty. Mr. Allerton looked up; there was a peculiar smile on Hetty's face; it was always a good harbinger. He sprang past her, and Arabella received him.

"Dear father," said she, "there is more hope; the crisis is passed.

"All true," said the good doctor, who stood at the half-opened door. "Nothing to do now, but build her up."

"Let us go in and return thanks to God, who has, in His infinite mercy, restored her to us from the brink of the grave," said Mr. Wilson. Such a prayer this family had never before offered. And in those moments of overwhelming gratitude, they renewedly consecrated themselves to God.

It was so. The fever had attained its crisis, and danger was almost over.

Mrs. Allerton knew them all, and from this hour began slowly to recover, under the careful nursing of Arabella and the untiring Hetty.

VI.

MERCY WHITMAN.

EXPOSURE to the intense cold of this severe winter, hard work and poor fare, made sad inroads upon Hetty. She was attacked severely with rheumatism; it became difficult for her to move about; and for a time, she was entirely helpless. These were such days as Arabella had never experienced before. Her father assisted her to the utmost of his ability, and neighbors occasionally offered their services; still she was taxed much beyond her strength. The reed bent almost to the breaking. But she had not a thought for herself. She went from her mother to Hetty, and from Hetty back to her mother, cheering first one and then the other, attending to a little want here, and providing a comfort there, — never complaining, never desponding, never seeming weary. Her father looked upon her with astonishment, to see how suddenly the frail child had become a woman, and how rapidly strength of purpose and mature judgment had developed themselves, to a degree which he had not believed possible. He observed also with inward joy how beautifully her Christian graces were unfolded in this time of trial; particularly, how much *life* there was to her *faith in Jesus;* with what child-like simplicity she trusted in Him. This it was that sustained her, and gave to her, through this season of toil and peril, a serenity which nothing could disturb. Older Christians looked on with silent, self-reproach, feeling that she had risen to a height far beyond them.

Poor Hetty fretted under her affliction; it grieved her so much "to have Miss Bella taking steps for her," or to have her doing any part of the kitchen labor, that it really increased her illness. Mr. Allerton at length removed his books from his little library, and putting a bed in there, removed Hetty to it, so that she could have her door open into the kitchen, and direct about the work. This was some relief to Arabella.

Among the many things reckoned as mercies at this time, was the arrival of a black woman named Rhoda. She had been a servant in a family who, overcome by the hardships of the season, had returned to England. Rhoda, by her own request, had remained with a little annuity, large enough to save her from want; and, about the time that Hetty was taken ill, had hired a room in the vicinity of Mercy Whitman's house.

Rhoda was a great comfort; she used to come three, and sometimes four, days in the week. She was kind and honest, though simple-minded. Hetty felt grateful to her, and treated her with a consideration which very soon won Rhoda's heart.

Mrs. Allerton was beginning to enjoy the luxury of convalescence. Her appetite increased so much, that it became a difficult matter to obtain the proper food to satisfy it. This was a source of great trouble to her friends. Arabella often gave up silently her customary dinner of eggs that they might in some way be served for her mother, — and the unsuitable food which she was forced to take in its place, prepared the way, in part, for new affliction.

Upon what little hooks the happiness of a family sometimes seem to hang! Here, one day, simple, old black Rhoda is very busy at home doing up her washing, and she cannot come in to help them at Mr. Allerton's, when they must have some-one, — for Hetty is helpless in bed, — Mr. Allerton is shut up with a heavy cold, and Miss Arabella laid by for the day with headache, — and the consequences are fatal. Mercy Whitman must be sent for, and Mercy Whitman comes.

"You are to make some broth of that chicken,

for mistress," said Hetty, issuing her orders mixed up with sundry groans, from her bed-room.

"I knew that afore," said Mercy. "Did n't Good-man Allerton just tell me? Bless me, do you take me for an adder?"

"I know what I do take you for," muttered Hetty to herself, under the sheet.

Mercy went about her work, fussing around the kitchen, — putting everything out of place, and grumbling and scolding.

Hetty was tried beyond what she was able to bear, — for there she was, she could not stir hand or foot, and Mercy Whitman was let loose in her kitchen.

"Why do n't you put your broth on?" said she; mistress ought to have had it an hour ago; you never will get it done at this rate."

"Well, why do n't you keep your pots in order?" retorted Mercy. "I can 't find one that is fit to cook in; they do n't look as if they had been washed for a year."

"Wash 'em out, then," said Hetty, biting her lips to cut short the remainder of her sentence, — and bravely covering her head with the bed-clothes, that she might neither see nor hear her tormentor. By a great effort she lay there quite still, until she thought it was time for the broth to be done. She waited then a little longer — much longer, — Mercy was still at work. Then she looked out.

"A'nt that broth done yet?" said she; "we might have sent to England for it before this time."

"I am getting it done fast as I can," said Mercy, "and if you want it done quicker, come and make it yourself." Mercy was standing by it, thickening it with Indian meal, and preparing to put in sliced turnips.

"You great fool," said Hetty, as she saw that their last chicken was now quite lost; "you great fool, you know that mistress can't touch it with meal in it, and I told you so, and you have spoiled it on purpose to get it for yourself, — I do believe you are an imp of Satan —"

Mercy dropped her plate — "An imp of Satan — an imp of Satan!" said she, quite slowly — "may the flesh rot from your bones while the breath is in your body, for abusing a poor, lone, childless widow thus —"

"Childless widow," said Hetty, whose anger now passed all bounds, — "widow," and she laughed sneeringly, — "as much of a widow as I am, I guess, and no more."

In an instant, as if with one spring, Mercy Whitman stood by her bed; her eyes started from their sockets, her lips were livid, she clenched her fists, she shook them in Hetty's face!

"I'll have my revenge," said she — and before Hetty could recover from her amazement, Mercy had gone.

VII

HETTY IN TROUBLE.

THE heavy falls of snow had ceased. Now and then, a mild day brought forth the exclamation, that "the back-bone of winter was broken." March came blustering in — the first Spring-month, and it was gladly welcomed by our emigrants. Mrs. Allerton longed to be able to ride out, both for her own sake and that of her drooping lily. Both herself and Mr. Allerton were anxious to see more color in Bella's cheek, and they felt that mild weather and spring birds and flowers would be the best medicine for her.

One morning the family lingered longer than usual at their breakfast table. It was a delightful morning, — the wind seemed to have exhausted itself the day before.

"I think you can venture to ride, to-day," said Mr. Allerton to his wife; "by eleven o'clock it will be quite warm."

"O yes, dear mother; it seems as if summer had come. The fresh air will do you a world of good. We will wrap you all up, and you shall ride in, and stop and rest at Gov. Winthrop's; can she not, father? I do n't know why it is, but I feel very light-headed to-day, — I should like to sing all the time. Winter is over, and you, mother dear, fast becoming strong, — and good old Hetty getting well, too; you must make room for her, father, can't you? A ride will refresh her so much!"

"Where shall we put you, Bella, if we take her," said her father, patting her affectionately on the head.

"Me! O, I will stay at home and have dinner all ready for you, by the time you return."

"There is no necessity for that, for Rhoda is here to day," said her mother.

"Well, I can ride under the buffalo,—any way, so that Hetty can go."

"If you ride there, you will hardly see the violets you are in such a hurry to pick," said her father.

"I can leave those until we go again," said Bella, laughing; "but we will take all our sick ones, that we may see them grow in this fine air."

"Truly, our cup runneth over," replied Mr. Allerton; "a few weeks ago, and there was scarcely room to hope that our circle could remain unbroken, — yet God hath mercifully spared us to each other, and carried us safely through the trials of this bitter winter. How wonderfully did he help us in our distresses!"

Tears came into Mrs. Allerton's eyes, — they were all the reply she could make.

'To lead the van 'gainst Babylon, doth worthy Winthrop call,
Thy Progeny shall Battell try, when Prelacy shall fall.'—

This couplet, sung in a loud, monotonous tone, interrupted the conversation.

"Rhoda feels in as good spirits as the rest of us, to-day," said Arabella. "Rhoda, wont you tell Hetty not to do anything this morning to tire her, for we are going to take her into Boston, after prayers."

Rhoda opened the door. "Mistress, there be a good many gentlemen coming up the yard."

"What can that mean, at so early an hour," said Mr. Allerton, with some astonishment.

A large party of men and boys, followed by several women, passed the window, and entered the house. Mr. Allerton immediately recognized Judge Hathorn, who stepping forward, saluted him, and informed him that he, with another magistrate, had been sent for before daybreak, to visit a poor woman, named Mercy Whitman, who had fallen into very odd fits, of such a nature that the spectators were forced to believe there was something supernatural about them; and that she called repeatedly for a woman named Hetty, who, it was understood, resided with Mr. Allerton; and that said Hetty was summoned by the magistrate to appear in the presence of the afflicted. Then, boys and women, all talking together, gave a confused and exaggerated account of Mercy's sufferings.

"Mrs. Allerton is still feeble," said Mr. Allerton, addressing the Judge; "and this noise and excitement will do her much injury. If you will dismiss these good people, I will confer with you upon the matter."

Judge Hathorn immediately requested the crowd to disperse. They began to do so, but not much pleased, cast ominous glances at poor Hetty, who sunk, pale and trembling, into a chair.

"Hang her for an old witch, said one. "Hanging is too good for her," said another. "The Lord have mercy upon her soul," said a third. "She will cast an evil eye on us," said a fourth.

Mr. Allerton closed the sitting-room door. "Judge Hathorn," said he, "this is an awful accusation; and I beseech you as you would not have the guilt of shedding innocent blood upon your soul in the day of reckoning, that you stop and consider. This woman has been in my family for many years; I could answer for her as I could for my own soul, that she knows nothing of witchcraft, and has had no dealings with witches. She is a faithful, honest, kind-hearted woman; she would not willingly harm a fly. This Mercy Whitman, who brings this horrible charge, I have seen often, but I have never yet seen any good in her. She is in every respect ugly, and has quarrelled with Hetty, and threatened to have her revenge. Now, Judge, under such circumstances, who do you think must be the innocent person?"

"I do not know," replied the Judge; "but it devolves upon me to discover these abominable witchcrafts which are committed in this country, that we may be rid of them; and the woman, Hetty, must be brought before the afflicted, that we may investigate the case."

"She is too ill," said Mrs. Allerton, "she is too ill. She has not stepped out of the house for weeks. It will be the death of her to walk over there."

"The distance is short, and we have no time to wait," said Judge Hathorn. "Woman, are you ready?"

"Ready!" said Hetty, bursting forth in a violent tone. "Ready! I never will put my foot within her doors, while the breath is in my body. Get me there if you can. I a witch truly! If

Mercy Whitman is not bound over to the Devil, herself, then she ought to be, — that's my mind."

The magistrates exchanged a few words, and, approaching Hetty, signified their intention to take her by force.

"Hetty, dear — dear Hetty," said Bella, "pray do not resist. You must go; and now if you love me, go quietly. I will walk by you; I will hold your hand. Here, wrap this around you. Now we are ready, sir," said she. "Mother, do not be anxious; we shall soon return, and all will be well again."

It was but a few steps to Mercy Whitman's, and the throng about the house made way for Judge Hathorn, who passing through them with one hand upon Hetty's shoulder, entered the hut, and Hetty and Mercy stood face to face. Instantly, Mercy fell down upon the floor, strongly convulsed; her head bent back until it touched her feet; her body writhed like an agonized worm; her tongue was drawn out to an immense length, and so swollen, that it seemed impossible that it should ever find its way back; her eyes sunk so far into her head, that they seemed to disappear. If Hetty raised her eyes, Mercy would be drawn up to the ceiling; if she moved either arm, Mercy complained of pinches, and large black and blue marks were visible.

"Come up and place your hand upon this woman," said Judge Hathorn. Mercy attempted to comply, but was thrown violently down upon the floor, knocking her head in a most cruel manner, and then she could not rise.

Judge Hathorn then held Hetty's hand, that she might no more afflict, and commanded her to fix her eyes upon him. He then requested Mercy Whitman to repeat the Lord's prayer, which she was unable to do, being struck dumb. He then lifted Hetty up, notwithstanding her struggles, and forcibly placed her hand upon Mercy, who immediately recovered the power of speech, came out of her fit, and was pronounced well.

"To prison with her! To prison with her! Hang her! Hang the witch!" shouted the mob.

"She must be committed for safe custody until farther trial," said the Judge.

"Leave her with me; I will answer for it that she appear," said Mr. Allerton.

The Judge hesitated. Mercy, who had until this moment, from the time Hetty touched her, been calm, instantly relapsed into violent convulsions. One or two of the bystanders began to groan and fall down, declaring that they also were afflicted. "To prison with her! To prison with her!" shouted the multitude. "Chain her, or the Devil will be on us all," said a gruff voice.

One of the magistrates put heavy irons of eight pounds weight upon her ankles, and the tumult was somewhat appeased.

"We must take her to Boston prison without delay," said Judge Hathorn.

Arabella disappeared, ran hastily home, procured cloaks and hoods for herself and Hetty, and told her mother that she intended to go into Boston, and if need be, spend the night with Hetty. It was, however, with much difficulty that she obtained permission to accompany the prisoner. Placed in a wagon, ironed like a criminal, taking notice of no one, not even of the compassionate girl by her side, still and pale, as if suddenly stricken by death, the unfortunate Hetty passed her home, and was soon lodged within the damp and gloomy walls.

The lamb-like gentleness of the sunny morning disappeared, and the sky, as if sympathizing with our afflicted family, became overcast, and the blustering winds were again let loose. They pierced through the cracks of Hetty's gloomy chamber, and were merciless to her aching bones as man had been. There was no bed, and there were no comforts about her. Arabella sat down by her, and begged her in this distress to call upon God, who was able to bring her safely through. She also knelt by her, and pleaded so earnestly in her behalf, that Hetty was touched, and tears came to her relief. She wept like an infant, and Arabella rejoiced much to see her come out from her stupor.

The jailer, who was a kind-hearted man, came in at this moment, bringing a feather-bed, warm woollen blankets, and wood to build a fire.

"See, Hetty — look, Hetty, God already answers our prayer," said Arabella, "and He has sent you these as a token of His wonderful love."

"That is right, my daughter," said the well-known voice of Mr. Wilson, who was following the jailer, "and shall we receive good at the hand of the Lord, and shall we not receive evil? Let us trust Him at all times, and all will yet be well. But this is too damp a place for you, my child. Your father is waiting to take you home. Your mother is much troubled for you; you must return to her. I will take charge of Hetty; she shall not want for anything that I can provide. Go now, they will not allow your father to come in."

"Yes, Miss Bella, go back, go back," said Hetty, "to your mother. Perhaps I shall be there to-morrow. Do n't come here any more into this damp hole, with that cough of yours."

Indeed it was too damp there. The cold ride home also, exhausted as Arabella was by the excitement of the day, did "that cough" no good.

Mr. Allerton had enlisted the ministers on his side, and urged an early trial. It was appointed for the next day; so that they with much reason hoped Hetty's confinement would be short. In addition to this, he visited Mercy, he talked long and kindly to her, he privately offered her large bribes; but revenge was sweeter to her than gold.

VIII.

CLOVEN FEET.

HETTY'S case excited great interest. On the morning of the trial, the ministers from Cambridge, Salem, and Dorchester were requested to meet for prayer both for the afflicted and the accused. After this, the magistrates assembled, and Mercy Whitman was early at her post.

Hetty made her appearance, still heavily ironed, her face quite pale, and her dress much disordered. As soon as she entered, Mercy and one or two young girls fell down in a fit. Two old Indians in the crowd, also began to wallow about the floor like swine. The examination commenced. A part of it was as follows: —

Mag. "You, Mehitable Hubbard, are brought before authority upon high suspicion of witchcraft. Now, tell us the truth of this matter."

Hetty. "I am no more of a witch than you are, — and if you say so, you lie."

At this, Mercy appeared to be in great torments. She shrieked violently, and declared that spectres were tormenting her. "Where are they?" asked the magistrate. "There," said Mercy, pointing to a table just before Hetty. Upon this, Judge Hathorn struck the table so violently as to snap his cane in two. A smile of derision passed over the prisoner's face. Mr. Wilson went up to her, and whispered a moment very earnestly in her ear. After this, her answers were much more civil. Mercy declaring herself relieved by the blow, the examination proceeded.

Mag. "Pray what ails this woman, called Mercy Whitman?"

Hetty. "The devil knows, I do n't," muttered Hetty in an under tone.

Mag. "We desire you to speak louder."

Hetty. "She can tell that better than I can. I know nothing about it."

Mag. "Do you think she is bewitched?"

Hetty. No."

Mag. "What are your thoughts about her?"

Hetty. "My thoughts are my own while they are in; when they come out, you may have them."

Mag. "Who do you think is her master?"

Hetty. "If you knew her as well as I, you would n't ask."

Mag. [to Mercy.] "Mercy Whitman, hath this woman hurt you?" Mercy rolled up her sleeves, and showed deep scars, as if of fire. "It is she who did this."

Mag. "Whom else hath she hurt?" Two

girls instantly fell in a fit, crying, "She hurts us; she hurts us."

Mag. "Why do you hurt them? Tell me the truth."

Hetty. "As true as there is a God, I do not hurt them."

At the name of God, the afflicted lay like one dead.

Mag. "Well, what have you done towards this?"

Hetty. "Nothing at all."

Mag. "Why, it is you, or your appearance."

Hetty. "It is neither. I am as innocent of this as the child unborn."

Mag. "Is it not your master? How comes your appearance to hurt them?"

Hetty. "I call no one master, but God."

Mag. "Bring forth the afflicted to touch her." Mercy and the girls approach a few steps and fall down again, violently convulsed. The old Indians roll and tumble in a contrary direction. One of Hetty's hands are let go, and several others are afflicted; she holds her head on one side, — all the afflicted have theirs drawn one side in imitation of her.

Mag. "How doth this agree with what you have said?"

Hetty. "It is she who bears me malice that does this; I am innocent."

The court were alarmed; and judging that they must investigate the matter more closely adjourned to the 25th. Hetty was sent back to her dungeon, and was soon followed by one of the magistrates. He urged her vehemently to confess that she was a witch. He told her the devil was then before her eyes, and he would attempt to beat him away with his hand. Hetty declared she was no witch, and bade him leave her dungeon; and wished to know if she was kept there to be insulted?

"No, no!" said the magistrate, who had not yet passed the period of youth; "but for the sake of your friend, who loves you, Goodman Allerton's daughter, I would have you confess, for if you do not, you will be hanged."

"Ah! that is it, is it?" said Hetty, — casting at the man so keen a look, that he evidently winced under it. "Let me tell you, that neither my master, nor my mistress, nor Miss Arabella would ever receive me again, if I confess to a lie. I will not confess, though I hang for it; and if I do, on your soul lie the murder. I have never covenanted with the devil, neither do I know anything of his temptations, excepting what I see in other folks' actions."

It was all in vain; and Hetty was ordered to be kept in close confinement until more evidence, or a confession from her, could be obtained.

IX.

A HINT.

In the mean time every exertion to save her was made, that could be made. Gov. Winthrop himself, from the interest he felt in Mr. Allerton's family, used his influence in her behalf; Deane Winthrop gave himself up to the matter entirely, and was passing between Mr. Allerton's and the place of Hetty's confinement many times a day, — giving comfort at each end of his journey.

By request, all the ministers in the vicinity were again convened at Boston, and consulted. After much deliberation and prayer, they expressed their minds thus: —

"They were affected by the deplorable state of the afflicted; they were thankful for the diligent care of the rulers to detect the abominable witchcrafts which were being committed in the country, and prayed for a perfect discovery thereof, — but advised to a cautious proceeding, lest evils might ensue; and that tenderness be used towards the accused relating to matters presumptive and convictive, and also, to privacy in examinations.

"Nevertheless (the sum of the matter), they humbly recommend to the government, the speedy and vigorous prosecution of such as have rendered themselves obnoxious, — according to the direction given in the laws of God, and the wholesome statutes of the English nation for the detection of witchcraft."

From a trial which was going on at Salem it was evident, after this recommendation from the clergy, how matters would be managed in Boston. All spectral evidence, and all malicious stories were there received, — and it was easy enough to see that they would be, in Hetty's case, notwithstanding the exertions of powerful friends. Mercy Whitman, — who apart from the pleasure of gratifying her revenge, enjoyed her present notoriety, — did her best to spread the mania, that there might be a large party of tormented ones to cry out against Hetty on the day of her second trial; and she was very successful. It was wonderful how many were tormented by day and night, with Hetty's 'appearance' urging them to sign the black book, and often dragging them about by the hair of their heads if they refused.

Hetty's prospects became darker and still darker; even the sanguine Deane began to tremble.

Mr. Allerton and his family appointed a day of

private fasting and prayer in Hetty's behalf, and requested Mr. Wilson to visit them. He did so.

"How fares it with you, my dear friend?" said he.

"Blessed be God," replied Mr. Allerton, "we enjoy peace with Him, though we are in abundance of affliction."

"It is so," replied Mrs. Allerton. "He hath delivered us out of many troubles; even when all His billows went over us, still, His arm upheld us. We are distressed, but not in despair. We feel that God can turn even this mischievous wickedness to his own glory."

A response of heartfelt trust in God, seemed to be the expression on Arabella's countenance. It was hope smiling through her tears, like the sun shining from behind a vapory cloud. After more religious conversation, which greatly comforted them, Mr. Wilson united with them in a prayer which was earnest and affecting. It closed thus: —

"Lord, wilt thou take away the affectionate servant of these Thy children, who love Thee so much, and serve Thee so faithfully? whom Thou hast already much chastened, until Thou hast brought them to love Thee more than all things else? Do it not, O Lord, but deliver her from the power of the devil, and from the hands of unjust men who would shed her innocent blood, — and to Thy name shall be all the glory."

After prayer, he walked the room a few moments, lost in thought. "I trust she shall yet be saved," said he; "but no trial will save her. Will she confess?"

"Confess," said young Winthrop, who entered at this moment; "not if they roast her alive. She is firm as a rock. 'She will never belie her own soul,' she says."

"How is she to-day?" eagerly asked Arabella.

"Well, in body; the flannel I took over to her yesterday, makes her very comfortable, and she seems more composed in mind. The day of her trial is near, and she has not a doubt but that she shall be cleared. She talks little, and sits and counts the hours which are to bring her release."

"She must not stand that trial," said Mr. Wilson, pausing in his walk and fixing his eyes intently on young Winthrop. "She must not stand that trial, and she *must be saved!*" He drew on his over-coat. No one spoke. He bade the family good-day, — and as he passed out, touched Deane's shoulder, — "The twenty-fifth is near; call on me if you need help."

The idea ran through every mind like an electric shock. There was now but one chance for poor

Hetty, to save her from a disgraceful death — escape! escape! But how and whither?

For the next few days, Arabella, though very far from being well, rode into Boston every morning, in rain or sunshine, and was much alone with Deane Winthrop. If others knew the subject of their consultations, no questions were asked. Poor Hetty! if something could not soon be done for her, she would cease to trouble any one. She had become so poor and haggard in her dungeon, as to be frightfully altered. Mrs. Allerton had not seen her. Indeed, the physician would not allow her to do so, as she was yet feeble.

Days of trial and darkness these, truly; and yet our pilgrims had sources of consolation, which "the world could not take away."

X.

THE ESCAPE.

As we have before mentioned, Hetty's jailer was a kind, considerate man. He allowed her every comfort which he was able to provide, and admitted her friends freely to see her, provided only one or two wished to go in at a time. The ministers, in particular, had free access, that they might attend to her spiritual wants, and if possible, pray her out from the powers of the Evil-One. Good old black Rhoda also came regularly, each morning, with food for Hetty, which Arabella herself prepared. This was permitted on account of the prisoner's illness.

One Monday preceding the twenty-fifth, all the family, excepting Mrs. Allerton, were in Boston, spending the day at Gov. Winthrop's. There was coming and going, and much quiet bustle; and there were whispered consultations and anxious faces. Arabella and Deane were much together. Before daybreak, and while the streets of Boston were yet silent, Deane had stolen down to the wharf, where a ship, ready to sail for England, lay. He had a short consultation with the Captain, handed him a note with the Governor's signature, and gave him gold. The matter, whatever it was, seemed arranged to his satisfaction, for he met Arabella with a glance of intelligent pleasure.

Very quietly, a large box was packed at Gov. Winthrop's that day, and several full letters placed in it. Mr. and Mrs. Wilson often sent to their friends in England; and towards the middle of the afternoon, he was seen at the wharf entrusting the box to the care of the Captain, — who received it as if he understood matters.

The tea hour came; neither Arabella nor Deane were present. Mr. Allerton looked troubled, and Mrs. Winthrop went out and begged Arabella to come in and take some nourishment, for she would need it before the evening was past. She did as she was desired.

After tea, Gov. Winthrop prayed fervently that God would appear for the safe deliverance of all who were unjustly held in bondage; his hearers were comforted and strengthened.

The sun set in clouds, and darkness came suddenly on. The party began to decrease in numbers; soon neither Arabella, nor Deane, nor Rhoda were to be seen.

A knock was heard at the outer prison gate.

"Who's there?" asked the jailer.

"Only I, good Mr. Littlejohn, with

and some medicines for Hetty. You will let us in?"

"I do n't know about that, Miss Allerton, it is long after sundown."

"Only a few minutes, good sir, only a few minutes, for we are in great haste."

"You always get your own way, Miss Bella. I can 't keep locked when you want keys. You 'll make me lose my place, one of these days. Not but a minute now, you hear. If anybody should find me open at this time of night, 't would be as much as my life is worth."

"Only a few minutes, good Mr. Littlejohn; and while I think of it, will you be kind enough to give this warm shawl to your wife, as a present from me, for she has been very kind to Hetty."

"Bless your heart, what a beauty, — why, it will be the making on her. I 'll take it, and thank you too; it 's many a day since she has had a shawl to keep her old bones warm. Hetty, Hetty, wake up, here is something coming to cheer you, — a whole basket full. Now, Miss Bella, I 'll just run in to show my old woman the shawl, and be back directly; you will be ready."

"O yes, Mr. Littlejohn; and while you are about it, ask her if she would choose any other color; if so, I will change it for her."

"Bless your kind heart, I 'll tell her."

The key turned in the door.

"Now, Hetty," said Arabella, calmly but quickly, "there is not a moment to lose. You must black your face, and change dresses with Rhoda, and go out with me."

"Not I, Miss Bella; I'll not sneak out in that way. Them what put me in, may come and take me out."

"They never will take you out but twice more, Hetty, — once to a cruel trial, and once to the gallows."

"I was just thinking as much," said Hetty, "afore you came in, and had pretty much made up my mind to it. I've got to die sometime or other; and I do n't know as it makes much difference whether it is this year or next;" and she sat down on her bed.

"You will die neither, dear Hetty; we cannot spare you. You must live for my mother's sake. A vessel waits for you; you go to England for a few months, and then you can come back again safely. Hark! I hear him! For God's sake, Hetty, do not delay; you will break my heart."

"But will not *she* hang?" asked the relenting Hetty, pointing to Rhoda.

"No, she is perfectly safe."

"Don't mind me," said Rhoda, laughing till she shook her sides. "I should like to see 'em hang me for a witch. Come, now, we'll hide your white skin, — hold still."

It seemed as if it were but a minute, and Hetty's face was so transformed, that Arabella started, as Hetty turned it full upon her.

"Capital! capital!" said she, "now off with the dresses." Life was dear, after all, and liberty sweet. Hetty worked now with willing fingers. Dress and shawl, and hood, and heavy shoes, were already on, when Mr. Littlejohn's step was heard.

"Take the basket, say nothing, and follow me," whispered Arabella.

As the rusty old lock turned, Rhoda blew out the light.

"All ready, Mr. Littlejohn," said Arabella, stepping quickly forward. "How was good-wife Littlejohn pleased? I hope she liked the shawl. Good night, dear Hetty. You will sleep very sweetly on that medicine, and Mr. Littlejohn will let in no more visitors to disturb you till morning."

"Not I," said Mr. Littlejohn, "I disobey orders now."

"You are very kind, Mr. Littlejohn; get yourself a good package of tobacco before I come again;" and she slipped a silver half-dollar into his hand.

He was so full of his thanks, that he took no

particular notice of Rhoda, though he affirmed the next day, that it did occur to him "that the blackee went out taller than she came in."

And now the prisoner was outside the prison walls, and heard the last bolt drawn behind her, and stood once more under the cloudy heavens — free. She paused, as if she wished to collect her thoughts.

"Follow me, Hetty; not a moment to lose, — just round the corner."

They stepped quickly on, — they two alone in the deserted streets, — they turned the corner. Deane met them. Arabella pressed his hand, — "All right. Now, Hetty, get upon this horse. Mr. Deane will see you safe on board ship. Keep close in your berth to-night, and to-morrow ask for your box; everything is there."

Hetty turned abruptly round, and began to walk off rapidly in an opposite direction. Winthrop sprang after her and caught her.

"Are you crazy?" said he.

"No, Mr. Deane," replied Hetty, "but I'll never desert my post; if I must die, I'll die there. I am not going over the ocean to leave them alone in this 'Desart.'"

"Hetty," said Arabella, in a tone of command, "*you must go.* Quick — quick — there is not a moment to lose; they wait for you only till nine, and it wants but three minutes of that, — get on, — get on."

Hetty pressed her young mistress convulsively to her, — Deane almost lifted her upon the pillion, and then sprang into the saddle before her; and putting the horse to the top of his speed, was soon out of sight. They were just in time. She was hurried on board, and before the sun rose, she was beyond the reach of Mercy Whitman, and — the Devil.

Late and dark as it was, Arabella found her way back to Gov. Winthrop's, without molestation. She entered their sitting-room, and joined the group of anxious friends, with a smiling countenance, though she was very pale.

"My dear daughter," said her father, "where is your shawl. Surely you have not been out this cold night, without a shawl?"

Arabella related how she had parted with it, — she did not think she should miss it, but indeed she was chilled through.

It was not long before Deane joined the party, with his good tidings, and then immediately Mr. Allerton prepared to return home, and Arabella could not be persuaded to remain. The long, cold ride, she had occasion to remember.

XI.

LIFE IN DEATH.

It was later than usual the next morning, before Mr. Littlejohn discovered the trick which had been played upon him. At first, he was very angry with Rhoda, but she soon soothed him, by assuring him that no one could blame him; and that she was sure he ought to rejoice that such a good old creature as Hetty had escaped hanging for nothing. If he did not rejoice for her sake, he certainly should for Miss Arabella; for, if they had hung Hetty, it would have killed her outright.

Not very much noise was made about the affair, — and this led some of the people who pretended to know more than their neighbors, to remark, that the governor might tell more than he did, if he chose. Mr. Littlejohn, perceiving that he was not to be brought up, was, in his heart, right glad of the escape.

Mercy Whitman was more disturbed than any one else. She was at first inclined to wreak her vengeance on Rhoda; but finding she could not excite any one to assist her in this, she did not prosecute it long. Rhoda was suffered to return quietly to Mr. Allerton's family, where she now took up her abode. Mercy, having offended a passionate man who lived near her, became frightened at his threats, and this, with some secret reasons, led her to move away one night, and go no one knew and no one cared whither.

April, with its smiles and tears, its snow-drops and showers, found Mr. Allerton's family more quiet than they had been for many months. Mrs. Allerton gained rapidly, and became even stronger than before her illness. Mr. Allerton prospered in his worldly affairs. The spring opened favorably for his farm, and he received a timely legacy from one of his distant relatives in England. Several day-laborers offered their services for the season, and Rhoda did her best to supply Hetty's place in the kitchen. It seemed, for a time, as if their troubles had passed with wintry storms. They had "waited patiently upon the Lord," and he had heard their cry, and twice appeared for them when they were in deep distress.

"He is a faithful God, and he will continue to provide for us," said Mrs. Allerton one day, while her husband, as was his custom, was recounting their many mercies. But God was to provide for them in a way which they knew not. They needed one chastisement more; one idol stood in the way of the perfecting of their love; and one more sorrow was near.

Arabella faded away so gently, and sweetly, and slowly, that spring passed and early June came with its flowers and its balmy breath, before her friends were aware how near she was to her long home, — how far from all hope of rescue. When they awoke to the reality, they endured a long, terrible struggle, to bring themselves to give up their first-born, their only child. Mr. Allerton was first subdued to a perfect resignation to God's will. At length the mother too came one day to her husband, — her pale countenance radiant with its look of peace. "It is over," said she, "I am now willing to give her up. Let us seek to make her comfortable while she lingers with us, and to strengthen her for the great change."

"Blessed be God, the sting of death is passed," replied he. "We trust she is fitted for Christ's presence; we have not an anxious thought for her. As for us, God will keep us by sharp travails, in a faithful, watchful, humble, praying frame."

It was with much joy that Arabella observed the change in her parents. She experienced such clear and delightful views of God's character, — she felt so sweetly resigned to his will, — so willing to lie passive in his hands, — to go or stay, — to suffer much or little, — that it grieved her if they found only "clouds and darkness" around about him. When they emerged from these, and like children received the bitter cup from the hands of a kind Father, the last thorn was taken away; it only remained for her to die in peace.

Arabella had made many friends. Mr. and Mrs. Wilson came often to see her; as did also Gov. Winthrop's family. Deane had been much with her ever since Hetty's escape. That his interest in her was not all unselfish, became very evident; but it was as evident, that for some reason he kept his feelings in constant check. He read to her as long as she was able to hear reading; — and brought to her sick room the choicest flowers of summer. She treated him as a brother. She had many ties to bind her to this world; but Faith, who had been her companion thus far on her pilgrimage, now took her on his tireless wing to the "City of our God," and her soul was filled with its beauty. She seemed to linger here more like an angel, whose message is delivered, — but who, inasmuch as his heart is in it, waiteth yet, ere he bear the record.

Very early one morning, Deane Winthrop came in, apparently much agitated, and requested to see Arabella alone for a few moments. Mrs. Allerton hesitated, for Arabella had had a feeble night, and had been rapidly failing for several days. Unwilling, however, to refuse him, she went to see if her daughter were able to receive him.

"Most certainly, dear mother; I feel easy and quiet now, — let Deane come in."

Mrs. Allerton left them alone; but finding that Deane remained longer than she thought prudent, she gently opened the door. Deane was standing by the window, and there were traces of tears on his cheeks. Arabella lay quite still, with her hands clasped, and her eyes closed as if she were at prayer. Deane stept softly by her and passed out, and Mrs. Allerton remained standing until Arabella opened her eyes.

"Dear mother," said she, with a smile and a slight flush on her pale cheek; "I have something to say to you and father. Will you raise me a little and give me my medicine? Let in a little more light, mother dear, and now call father."

Silently her mother obeyed her.

"What have you to say to us, my daughter?" said Mr. Allerton, — "we know that you are soon to leave us — have you any requests to make?"

"Put your hand under me, mother, — there. What I have to say to you is this: You remember Francis Walton, and you know that we were brought up together, — and I wish to tell you — that we loved each other."

"Do not agitate yourself, dear Bella; mother

can easily understand that." Arabella turned her deep blue eye full on her mother, as if to thank her and went on —

"I think Francis loved the Saviour; I am sure he did; we talked much and often of Him. And Francis would gladly have come with us here, that he might labor for Him — but — "

"His uncle, upon whom he is dependent, utterly refused. I know that, dear Bella, for I had a talk with the old gentleman myself, and I did not think it would be right for Francis to leave his uncle alone in his old age."

"You were right in that, father; and it was my duty to follow you, and so we parted, as we thought — forever."

"My precious child," said her mother, "and have you done all this, so uncomplainingly, for us?"

"For you and for Christ," said Arabella. "I felt that it was my duty, and I have never regretted it; God has made it a burden light to bear. Let me say to you both, that I rejoice and bless God that he put it into your hearts to come over here, and gave me grace to come with you. It is a comfort to me now. It is sweet to die among God's chosen people. I feel it; and I hope you will think of this when I am gone."

"And what of Francis?" inquired Mr. Allerton.

"He is here," said Arabella, gently; "he arrived last night. Deane has seen him. He loves me still — as I do him. He has come to claim me for his bride — "

" There was a long silence —

" And his uncle ? "

" Is dead."

" *To claim me for his bride!* " Death has prior claims, poor youth. Say, dying one ! — doth this last temptation gain the victory over thee ? — Art thou now unwilling to hear thy Lord call ? Not so — not so — " I know in whom I have believed, and nothing is able to separate me from the love of Christ." This was the response of the young pilgrim.

"And what would you wish us to do ? " mournfully asked the mother.

" Send for Mr. Wilson. Francis will be here at noon, by my request. Prepare for me a dress as I wish, dear mother ; and let it be to-day. Time presses, father. I may not see another dawn. I would not leave you childless. God sends an affectionate son, who will comfort you. He will love you for my sake. He will have nothing but you left to love in this world. I would give him a right to be called son, before I die."

At the appointed hour, Francis Walton arrived. Arabella was ready to receive him. She had selected from her wardrobe a plain, white, loose dress.

At her request, her mother had plaited a wreath of white rose-buds in her hair.

"Mother," whispered she, "let this be the last dress which he shall see me wear."

Many tears dropped on that white wreath. The mother decked her child for the bridal, and the grave! Mr. Wilson and Deane Winthrop entered the room at one o'clock, and the sad ceremony took place. Francis supported his bride upon a pillow, which was raised to rest upon his shoulder. Mr. Wilson prayed that God would bless this union, not of the living with the dead, but of a mortal with an angelic being, whose wing was already plumed for flight; and that when she had taken her departure, her partner might, in thought, visit her so much in heaven, that it should be seen and felt by all, that he walked with God.

Mrs. Allerton's fears that the bridal wreath might not fade before being needed again, did not prove true. Arabella seemed to rally, and lingered yet a little longer to comfort and cheer her young husband. Her last hours were sweetened by his presence, and she was much comforted by his fervent and manly piety. She was grateful that God had permitted her to see how he would provide for her parents in their solitude. Thus, full of peace and joy, with every earthly wish gratified — she "fell asleep."

XII.

THE RETROSPECT.

The following is an extract from a letter, addressed by Mr. Allerton, to a friend in England: —

"Mine eyes drop down many tears, when I recall the way in which God has led us, and the mercies which have mingled with all our trials. When my dear wife lay at the point of death, He gave unto us such support that I believe we felt in our souls not a wish to detain her, if it were His will that she should go; and when He had brought us to this frame of mind, then He restored her to us, like one "sent from the dead." At the season of our deep anxiety for our faithful old Hetty, He raised up friends for us; and blessed the means for her escape, and stilled the angry tumult around us, causing even "the wrath of man to praise Him;" — for our tormentor, who had done us this great evil, seemed as if worked upon by her own conscience, to such a degree that she soon left us, and our neighborhood was restored to quiet, and not a complaint has been heard from that day to this. Then came heavier trials, — and larger mercies. Our beloved and tender child sunk under the cruel winter, and fell into a decline. But her Christian graces ripened fast; we saw and felt that she was "of the kingdom of heaven," and God brought both her and her mother, and myself to such a state of heart, that we no longer desired to keep her in this world of sin. We blessed God that He had given us such a daughter; and I trust we cheerfully returned the gift, feeling that we should not be forever separated. She was dismissed from her earthly tabernacle without suffering, and fell asleep in Jesus, as an infant falls asleep, lulled on its mother's breast.

"And now, my dear friend, behold what great care God took of us at this last extremity. He sent us over a most worthy and amiable son, who had long known and loved our dear child; and she was united to him, on her dying bed, that she might give him a right to call us parents; and when she left us, her mind was sweetly at rest concerning us. You know not what a comfort he is; my wife seems to feel for him as for an own child. I trust he will be the stay and comfort of our old age. I have many more mercies to recount, — among others, that Mrs. Allerton and myself have never been in better health than now. Francis, also, is well and cheerful. My farm and merchandize prosper. Good Hetty has returned to us, bringing with her a pleasant niece, who will assist her in her labors. God smiles upon us every way. He 'lifts upon us the light of his countenance,' — and we rejoice.

"I left my native land for 'conscience' sake,' and if God will employ so feeble an instrument in this great work of advancing His kingdom, I will spend and be spent for Him; rejoicing that I may be accounted worthy to build up the holy things of Christ. My angel-child had her heart much in this work; she often told us this in her last sickness; and she hath left us the rich legacy of her spirit. I trust we shall follow her example, until our labor is also done, and we lie down to rest with her."

THE CLOUDY MORNING.

A TALE FOR MOTHERS.

"Beauty, thou art twice blessed. Thou art a precious gift of heaven to those who love, and to those who wish to be loved."

Helen Clay was an uncommonly beautiful infant. Her soft, flaxen ringlets, fell over a neck and brow which were almost as white as alabaster. Her clear, loving, blue eyes, laughed out from under long silken lashes, and two beautiful dimples stood like little cherubs each side of her pretty mouth. "What a beauty!" exclaimed almost every one who looked upon her. Helen did not outgrow the beauty of her baby-hood. Every year seemed to add a fresh grace.

It was far otherwise with her sister Laura. She would have responded to the motto of our story, with deep feeling. Nature, so lavish in her gifts to the younger born, had been very parsimonious to Laura. She was almost ugly in her personal appearance; and yet her face could not, with strict justice, have been called so, — for it was a most expressive face; it was a great tell-tale. A more striking contrast, however, between two sisters, is seldom seen; and this was not confined to personal appearance alone. Helen, butterfly-like, seemed made for sunshine; by a natural instinct, she seemed to find it both within and without. There are some such children. She was a bright, quick, active child, warm-hearted, affectionate in her manners, and noisy in the expression of her love, whether it was for doll, kitten, playmate, or mother. She was ready to love the object nearest her; though it were something new every day, it seemed to matter little. Take away her doll, she would play twice as much with her kitten. Regret would not long overshadow her path. Helen lived in neither the past nor the future, — she was all for the bright sunny present.

Laura was a night-shade. The scenes which she planned and acted in her baby-world, were all tragic. They would be full of accident, and sickness, and death, and funerals. Her intellect was not above mediocrity. She had more imagination than Helen, and a better memory, but her comprehension was much less ready; she had none of Helen's quick tact. In childish temper, also, they were opposite. Helen's would flash up at a little provocation, meteor-like, then all would fall softly as a snow-flake, and be quiet again. Laura's was not easily excited; but once roused, the storm lasted long; and a desperate fit of what her mother called 'the sullens,' ensued. When Laura loved, her words were few; but the last fragment of the doll or toy with which she had long played, was dearer to her than a new one. She was also painfully awkward in expressing her feelings. Helen could throw her arms around her mother's neck, and, almost smothering her with her caresses, talk herself out of breath in telling how much she loved her. Laura sometimes laid her head upon her mother's knee, her little heart swelling with feelings for which she could find no words. She was not easily appreciated or understood by strangers, — neither, alas! by those who should have known her well.

Mr. and Mrs. Clay loved their children, and took good care of them, — that is, attended to all their obvious wants; but they were not *thoughtful* parents. They never dreamed of studying the different natures of their children. Early judicious management might have counteracted the morbid and melancholy tendencies of Laura; but every day brought its cares, every evening its fatigues, and thus the years slipped by, and their child was in one sense a stranger at home. They at length settled into the conviction, that their first-born was rather an unfortunate, strange child, who cared little for any one excepting herself. Yet, she often made an attempt to open her heart to her mother, and tell her the little thoughts which were struggling there; but a careless word, an inattentive look, an inapposite remark, or, worse than all, an ill-timed reproof, blasted in the bud that confidence which it was of the first impor tance to that child to have encouraged. She shrunk away and said to herself, "I *am* a strange child." This grew with her growth. Her active imagination aggravated every defect into a deformity, every mistake into a fault. She early felt that she had nothing in common with other children. She feared observation; she became very often depressed and discouraged. At school, she made no effort to rise to even an equality with her mates, — she felt sure that she should fail, if she did attempt it. A few encouraging words now and then, might have incited her ambition; but how often does it happen in a crowded school-room, that individual peculiarities are known and cared for? Laura was reproved oftener than any one of her companions; this made her reserved and silent, and therefore she was not much loved as a playmate. Because of this reserve, her teacher fell into the same error with her parents. A cross word might be spoken to Helen, and there came a violent flood of tears, which soon washed away the sorrow. Let the same be spoken to Laura, and perhaps the deepened color would be the only evidence of emotion, — while in her heart there was left a sting which she felt many days. She would say nothing; they would call her sullen and obstinate, and sometimes punish her again and more severely, still with as little apparent effect. She acquired at an early age a great power of self-control for a child.

One evening, Laura came to the tea-table with a face unusually bright and animated.

"Father," said she, "may I go to ride with the girls, to-morrow? There is a party going out on horseback, and they are all to stop at Farmer Hill's, and have a treat. May I go, father, to-morrow?"

Mr. Clay had just returned from a long walk, and was tired, and heated. Sometimes, when a person does not feel particularly good-natured, he takes a delight in exercising power in such a way as to give pain. It gives him the consciousness that he *has* the power, and he is not in the mood to think carefully, that he is making others unhappy. This was not Mr. Clay's mood.

"To ride?" said he. "It seems to me that you

are always having some foolish thing going on. I think the girls had all better stay at home and mind their books."

"But, father, to-morrow is Saturday."

"Well, what of that? Who, pray, is going?"

"O, four of us, father."

"Foolish plan enough, I think. Some of you will get your necks broken."

"Do, father," said Helen, "let her go. I went last time."

"Well, what of that?"

"I think, Mr. Clay, she may as well go," said her mother, "our horse is very gentle."

He made no reply, but held out his tumbler for some water. Laura filled the glass too full; it spilled over upon his dinner plate, and ran down into his sleeve. What a little thing will turn the scale of an ill-balanced temper. "Look out, Laura, you careless child! You never poured out a glass of water in your life, without spilling it. If you can't learn to be less awkward, I wish you would keep away from the table till you can. Go to ride! No, that you shall not, until you can learn to have your wits a little more about you. So, content yourself to stay at home, miss."

"O, father,—— " began Helen.

"Hush, Helen, I have settled it. I wont have her riding about; it is not safe; she will have her neck broken, next,—she is so careless. If she ever learns to be like other folks, I shall be glad."

Tears, scalding tears, started to Laura's eyes. She took up her cup to hide them, and swallowed them down with her hot tea; but they burnt to her heart's core. No one spoke, and before long, all rose to leave the table.

"Come," said Mr. Clay, who was now quite good-humored, "who wants to go and rake hay with me?"

"I, I," said Helen; "come, Laura, it is good fun. Why do n't you come, Laura? Where are you going?"

"To my room to get my lessons. I do n't want to turn hay."

"Come, come, Helen, Laura is sullen; let her alone. I do n't want any sullen girls with me."

Still the child kept back the tears, until she was fairly in her room, and had locked her door; then the lacerated feelings found vent. The flood-gates once opened, all control became impossible; she threw herself upon the bed, buried her face in the pillow, to stifle the convulsive sobs which she could no longer command. A deep darkness seemed to rest upon all the world; she saw no ray of joy; she had no consciousness but of misery. Now and then, through the still summer air, came up Helen's merry voice, as she frolicked with her father in the newly-made hay. Laura heard it with feelings perhaps not unlike those with which the lost hear the angels sing, and it added much to her woe. Childhood *does* shed bitter tears. The happy voices at last ceased; darkness crept on. Some one tapped gently at the door, once, twice, thrice. "Laura! Laura! it is *me* — only *me*. The folks are all gone away. Let *me* in."

"Is it you, dear Amy?" said the child, unbarring the door, and throwing her arms about the old nurse's neck, while her sobs broke forth afresh.

"La! now, I thought as much. What upon arth have they been a-saying to you now, to make you take on so. But there, Laura, do n't mind none of 'em." Amy seated herself in the rocking chair, and drew Laura to her, and rested the little throbbing head upon her bosom. "What has happened now, dearie?"

"O Amy," said the child, in a tone of the deepest woe, "nobody loves me, Amy, in this wide world. I wish I was dead, I wish I was dead and buried, Amy."

The good old nurse wiped away her own fast-flowing tears with a corner of her apron, and tried to steady her trembling voice. "Not love you, Laura? — nobody *love* you? Bless your little heart, do n't *I* love you better than my own soul and body? How can you talk so? I guess some folks that scold some folks will have something to answer for, one of these days."

"They cannot help it," said Laura; "no one can love me. I am not like other people. Helen is good, and pretty, and happy. Mother loves her, and father loves her, — everybody loves her, and likes to have her about. But they do n't love me, and they can't. I wish I was out of their way — in my grave, and then no one would have the trouble of me, — yes I do!"

"There — there — do n't talk so any more," said Amy, coming to her better self — "they do n't know they hurt your feelins so much. They do n't know you 've got any feelins; you never say nothing. If you only cried, like Helen, they would n't scold you. Why 't was no more nor day afore yesterday, I heard your father say to Helen, 'What a great cry-baby you are; I wish you would behave more like Laura; she does n't make such a baby of herself.' There now, darling, — everybody loves you that knows you, so do n't cry any more. Bless me, how your temples beat; and how hot your little head is! Does n't it ache?"

"O Amy, it aches very — *very* hard!"

"Well, there — there — do n't cry any more, — everything will be right to-morrow." So she smoothed the damp hair from the child's burning forehead, and rocked her to and fro, like an infant;

and soothed her with homely words,—but they were those of love, and they were grateful as the gentle dew. The tears of her little charge ceased to flow; the head became more heavy on the nurse's arm; the sobs changed to heavy sighs—then into occasional convulsive starts. She seemed to be listening to the old nursery songs, which Amy was softly singing to her as she rocked her there in the dark. Amy ceased at last, and bent over her,—she had fallen into an uneasy sleep. Gently, as a mother dresses her first-born, Amy prepared her darling for bed, put her head upon the smooth, cool pillow, waited awhile to see if she would awake—then kissed her burning cheek, and wiping her own eyes softly left the room. And all this suffering was for a few hasty, cutting words, which her father, twice blind, thought had fallen on stony ground. What can release a parent from the *duty* of knowing his own child?

"HELEN," said her mother one day, "I think you need a new trimming to your hat; this never was very becoming, and now it is faded."

"Why can't I have one, too? I had mine just when Helen did," said Laura.

"Well, that is no matter,—that is becoming enough to you, and I can't trim but one at present."

"That must be Helen's, of course," thought Laura,—"she is pretty, and I am not." She did not speak, howêver, and her eyes returned to her book. It so chanced, for once, that her father observed the flush on her cheek.

"How is this?" said he, putting down his paper; "mother, what is all this?"

"Nothing, only I think it best to retrim Helen's bonnet, and Laura is sullen about it; just as she always is. It is n't best to take any notice of her."

"I am not sullen now, mother," said Laura, trying to smile. Her father detected the tremor in her voice. "Now, Mrs. Clay," said he, "I wont have any partiality shown; if you get Helen a new bonnet, you must get one for Laura."

"Why Mr. Clay, I tell you her's will do very well for the present, well enough for her. If she is not contented with that, let her go without."

"Aye, aye! if that's the case, Miss Helen may go without too." Helen put up her beautiful lips. "Hush up there, now," said her father; "I'll have none of that. You are a great cry-baby. I'll see if I can't put a stop to it!"

"Well, if Helen does cry, it's all over with and she is pleasant — and does n't go moping about all day, as some other little folks do."

Laura bit her lips, choked, and then turned over the leaves of her book very rapidly, but her father's eye was now upon her. "Well, the long and the short is, Mrs. Clay, that I'll not have any partiality shown. I do n't think you do right to find quite so much fault with Laura."

"*I!* I am not finding fault, I am sure; I was only speaking of the bonnet."

"Laura, my daughter, come and let father see what you are reading." The unusually kind and gentle tones in which this was said cut their way to the child's heart. "Come, my dear, father will see that his little daughters share alike." He drew her to him, placed her on his knee, caressingly parted her smooth hair, and kissed her. They might have scolded her from morning to night, without drawing forth a word or a tear; but the heart had no armor that was proof against kindness, — neither has that of any child. Laura threw her arms around her father's neck, and sobbed aloud. He was surprised — more, astonished. He could not comprehend it. It was a new and strange development. He understood about as much of the delicate net-work of that young heart, as he who slaughters for the shambles understands the mechanism of the human eye. Yet his feelings were touched, and something like self-reproach arose. He soothed her as well as he knew how, and wiped away her tears.

"What is all this about?" exclaimed Mrs. Clay,

in wonder. "Why Laura, who would ever have thought of your making such a fuss about a bonnet-ribbon?"

"I tell you, Mrs. Clay, I'll not have Laura blamed any more."

"I am sure I had no thoughts of blaming her, Mr. Clay. I should be very glad to fix her hat too, if you think best. Laura, what color will you have, green or cherry?"

"My dear," said Mr. Clay, after the children had left the room; "it wont do to speak to Laura so; the child has more feeling than we think for."

"I always knew she had feeling enough," was the reply; "but she is a strange child. I do n't know what she will make in the world, I 'm sure; not much, I 'm afraid. Her teacher says she is dull at her books."

"I do n't believe that — I do n't believe that; she has as good a mind as Helen's, and you are spoiling Helen. The gypsy is getting very vain. You flatter her too much."

"*I* flatter, Mr. Clay? I never told her she was pretty in my life; it is you who tell her that. Besides, she must find it out some time or other, and we cannot help it; a few months earlier or later will make no difference."

WITH such influences around her in her childhood, it is not surprising that Laura, as she passed into her teens, became sober, thoughtful, reserved, silent, unintelligible. Such was her character when, at the age of fifteen, she entered Miss Merton's boarding-school.

"What do you think of our new scholar?" said one of the group of school-girls who were collected around the fire before breakfast.

"Who, that Miss Clay?"

"Yes."

"Oh! she is very homely, is n't she?"

"Yes; very, very!" echoed several voices.

"Now, I do n't think so," said Mary Hale; "she has a sensible face, and most beautiful hair, I am sure."

"But she fixes it so out of all manner of taste — so countrified."

"That may be the fashion where she came from; she looks like a good solid girl."

"Why, Mary Hale, how can you say so? I never saw a more solemn face on any one. She looks as if she had lost every friend she had in the world. I do n't believe she knows how to laugh!"

"She has left all her friends, and I dare say the poor girl is homesick. Do not you recollect how you felt when you came among us a perfect stranger?"

"But," interrupted another, "you did not look so proud and haughty."

"How can you call her so?" persisted the good Mary Hale; "I cannot see anything about her that looks like pride."

"O, Mary, Mary, there you are wrong," exclaimed several voices at once. "She never looks up," continued one; "and she goes about as if she did not care to know us, and thought herself better than any one else. Here is Miss Merton, let us ask her. If Miss Clay is not proud and haughty, then I lose *my* guess."

"Now, do tell me the difference."

"Why, proud — is proud — "

"And haughty is haughty," added another."

"What is all this, young ladies?"

"We are discussing Miss Clay, and all of us think her proud and haughty, but Mary Hale, who thinks every one perfection. Wont you tell us what you think, Miss Merton?"

"I think it would be a piece of injustice to pass an opinion on a poor girl who has come among us an entire stranger, and is depressed with home-sickness."

"Well, do not you think she *appears* so?"

"Diffidence and reserve are very often mistaken for pride, by those who look only on the surface of things."

"I am sure she is cold-hearted," said a little miss, who stood with each arm over a neighbor's neck.

"And I know she has a bad disposition," whispered another.

We look for cheerfulness and good-humor in youth, as much as we look for buds in May, — and we have a right to do so. Woe to you, parent, if you have brought a blight over life's springtime.

Laura was perfectly unconscious what an unhappy expression had become habitual to her, and how little there was that was really attractive in her appearance. Neither had the thought ever come into her mind, that she had any power over the muscles of her face.

"I hope," said Miss Merton, "that you will do all you can to make Miss Clay forget that she is a stranger among us."

"I know I never shall like her," said a lively, prating girl, with a toss of her head. "But, hush! here she comes." The little mimic drew her hand over her face, and extended it with a most woful expression. She, of course, did not wish Laura to see it, for she had turned her back to the door. But Laura did see it and at once drew back, that she might not enter a circle where she was an object of ridicule. That little mimic would have gone a great while without her laugh, if she had known the pain it gave. Poor Laura's heart swelled almost to bursting; she would at once have returned to her room, if Miss Merton had not spoken to her.

"Good morning," said Miss Merton, cheerfully, holding out her hand, "wont you come to the fire?" Laura timidly obeyed. She scarcely dared to raise her eyes; she felt that she was an object of dislike to the girls, — that they had been making fun at her expense; and if it had not been for her long-practised habits of self-command, she would have answered the kind voice of Miss Merton with a flood of tears.

When once more alone in her own room, she leaned her arm on the table, rested her head on her hands, and tears dropped fast over her open book. Thus she thought, "So it is always, so it has been, and so it must be. I *am* a doomed thing. How foolish I was for a single minute to wish to leave home, or to indulge a hope that if I came among strangers, I might find some one to like me. I will write, and ask to be taken back again. Helen loves me, I think, and father and mother too, sometimes. And Amy — dear, good old Amy — if I could only put my arms around her neck, it would do my soul good. Dear heart! she, I know, misses me." Thus her home came up before her as the only spot in the wide world, where the light of love, feeble as it was, could shine upon her; and her heart yearned for it. She had left it with joy, to seek some better land; but, with the cold chill of disappointment, she turned back to it with fast-flowing tears. What else could she do? The present was miserable, — the future, full of gloom, — so ingenious had she become at the age of fifteen, in making herself miserable. Father, mother! this character was one of thine own forming.

Long had she indulged in this painful reverie, — her lesson still unlearned. At last, some one tapped gently at her door. She started, gave a hasty glance in the mirror; her eyes were red and swollen. She kept perfectly quiet. They tapped again; still, no reply. The sound of retreating footsteps left her again in solitude.

AFTER Laura had been for some time at school, she made the discovery that there were two persons who had won, by a most judicious course of kind treatment, both her confidence and love. These were Miss Merton and Mary Hale. One day, Miss Merton told her that she should be happy to see her in her room, after tea. Though this was said with a winning smile, yet it brought the color to Laura's cheek, and made her heart beat like that of a little culprit. All day long, she worried herself with the most anxious and foolish conjectures about the object of this private interview, and at the appointed time, she knocked tremblingly at Miss Merton's door.

"Come in, my dear," said she, looking up from a table covered with papers. "I am very busy just now, and should be glad of a little of your assistance. Will you look over a few of these compositions? Where you find three words misspelt, put a cross, and place it in that pile. They worked awhile in silence, and at length, the business over, Miss Merton closed her desk, drew her chair nearer the fire, and placed an ottoman at her feet for Laura.

"Laura," said she, playfully weaving her fingers through Laura's glossy ringlets, "if I am not mistaken in your character, you are one who likes plain speaking; you can take a reproof for a fault without its being so spiced with flattery as to lose its taste."

"Yes, I am sure I can," said Laura, a little proudly. "You, you, — I was going to say, — that you know me better than most people" — and her voice slightly trembled.

"I thought I was right, Laura. Now I have no serious fault to find, but I have been wishing for some time to speak with you about your studies."

Laura's brow clouded. A deep blush crimsoned her cheek. "Miss Merton," said she, hesitatingly, "I *cannot* study as the other girls do; they have better talents than I have."

"That is the very thing I was going to speak of, my dear. A great many people in this world overrate their talents; you, I am convinced, underrate yours."

"Indeed, I do not, Miss Merton," and the tears were fairly started.

"I think you do. You set it down at the outset, that you must fail in everything you undertake; and you expect, as a matter of necessity, to have the worst recitation in the class. Your mind never will act vigorously under such a pressure. A sure way of obtaining a defeat is to prepare for one. Your natural abilities are good, and you may take a stand with any girl in school, if you would only think so. You can accomplish anything which you will determine to accomplish."

"I can never make a scholar; my teachers always said so, and father and mother think so;" and Laura sighed deeply.

"Then show them all, my dear, that they are mistaken. Remember, 'Those who would shoot high, must aim at the sun.' I wish to put you into the first class of Intellectual Philosophy. Now, will you promise me to feel that you can do as well as the others, and give the experiment a fair trial?"

Laura remained lost in thought for a few minutes. Such words fell like the voice of a trumpet on her ear. Ambition started at the sound. Her face lighted up with an expression full of meaning, and her eye sparkled with an honest pride that had long been a stranger to it: "*I will try*," said she, drawing herself to her full height, and standing erect for a moment, as if breathing the atmosphere of the mountains.

"That is all I ask, and it is the signal of victory!" said Miss Merton, affectionately kissing her cheek. Laura, forgetting all difference of station, threw her arms around her teacher's neck, and returned the caress ten-fold. From this moment might have been dated a new era in her intellectual world. She determined to deserve the first words of praise which she had ever heard; and with a heart made light by so slight an attention, her mind took off its garment of sackcloth. Hitherto, her life had all been one of feeling; now she began to think, to reason. She seemed like a new creature; she surprised herself and every one else; her self-respect daily increased, and her whole manner showed the change. Yet there were rocks, and snares, and pit-falls in her new path. One day Miss Merton entered the school-room, and found her sitting alone, apparently thinking very intently with her eyes fixed on the grate. "Why, my dear," exclaimed she, "what a 'brown study!' Do you find any familiar face in the coals? Why are you here in play-time? 'A penny for your thoughts.'"

"They are not worth a penny," said Laura, coloring, and taking up her book.

"'Mind is that part of our being which thinks, wills, remembers, and reasons'—is that what puzzles you so, Laura?"

"O, no—but—"

"What?"

"Why, I really do n't know, exactly, what I want to say. But after I have been studying, I get to thinking, and thinking, and thinking, and everything seems so strange and all mixed up."

"What is mixed up, child?"

"I know you will think me silly; if I were more like other girls, I could understand better; but I do n't see what *matter* is, nor what *mind* is. I was just thinking there is no world.—Here is the fire—what is it, a picture on the retina of the eye? I am all in a puzzle. What are you? and What am I? It is confused and strange; I feel sometimes as if there were an iron chain around me,—the farther I go, the more tightly it is drawn. I am afraid I shall never make a scholar, until this is in some way broken."

"That is an iron chain, my child, whose pressure

we all feel when we attempt to cross the boundaries of human knowledge. This union of mind and matter — this 'What am I?' is a mystery, which you can never solve here. In another state of being, —in heaven, Laura, if we get there, — we can explore the whole ocean of truth without feeling these shackles. Do not make yourself unhappy because you do not know what God did not design that you should know, here. You are by no means singular in these thoughts and feelings; all have them when they first wake to a real consciousness of existence."

"Well, — but Miss Merton," said Laura, who having once opened her heart seemed determined to bring forth all that had been troubling her there, "I do not know what good it does to study. Here we spend day after day, year after year learning books; at last we must die and be buried up, and there is the end of it; and what good has it all done us?"

"Is that the end of all things, Laura?"

"Well, but in heaven I thought they sung psalms, and played on golden harps. I never thought much else about it. We could sing as well without studying all this Philosophy and Algebra — ".

"Laura! Laura Clay! where are you?" shouted a pleasant voice in the entry. "Oh, here, I protest, in the school-room, over your books, when we are all at play. We want you to see our snow-house; come, they sent me for you!"

"You had better go, my dear," said Miss Merton, gently taking her book from her hand.

TWILIGHT is the hour sacred to thought. It was the hour our night-shade loved; the one in which she often stole away to be alone in her room, or with her friend Mary Hale. Once, she was sitting at her window watching the beautiful sunset clouds, with eyes filled with tears.

"Dear Laura," said Mary, seating herself by her, "what is the matter now?"

"I am a foolish girl, Mary, and I am ashamed of myself; but I will tell you all about it. I was sitting here looking out, and before I knew it almost, I was thinking of home and had imagined that father and Helen were dead. I was in our large drawing-room; it was dark; on one table there was a long coffin and on another there a shorter one. Mother, dressed in deep mourning, pale as marble, called me to come and give the last kiss to the dead. A rough man was standing near me; as soon as I had kissed one, he shut down the lid and was screwing it down — I could not help crying, I wish that I could hear from home."

"Why, Laura! are you superstitious?"

"No, I am not."

"Well, I never saw a girl so ingenious in making herself miserable in my life."

"Do n't you ever get thinking so, Mary?"

"No, indeed, dear Laura; I should think it very wrong to allow myself to do so. It is distrusting the watchful love of God. I believe Him when he tells me, that He will not suffer us to be tempted above what we are able to bear; 'As your day is, so shall your strength be!' And if I did not, a little observation as to how things really go in this world, would prevent my being so unmercifully wretched, — for it has passed into a proverb that the evils we most dread never come, while those we least think of are the ones at hand. Why should we embitter a short life with imaginary evils? We need all the energy of feeling which we throw away so, to meet the real calls of life."

"Well, it is my nature, and I cannot help it," sighed Laura.

"Cannot help it! Will you allow that you have no power over your thoughts?"

"No, but —"

"But, dear Laura, you have not the resolution to be happy; with everything in the world to make you so, you still prefer the *excitement* of these melancholy feelings; you voluntarily choose the bitter waters."

"Why, Mary, it is my *nature.* You know nothing at all of what such a person as I, has to suffer. Excepting my love for you, — and I do love you dearly, Mary, — life seems to me a dreary waste. I am every hour oppressed with the feeling that it is slipping away. I put my head upon my pillow, not for pleasant dreams, but to think, think, think that I am one day nearer the grave and the judgment. You cannot know anything of this, Mary. Life has been to you, one long summer-day —

> 'And all that you wish, and all that you love,
> Come smiling around your sunny way!'"

"I have seen trouble," said Mary, a shade passing over her sweet face, as she thought of that hour in the early morning of her life which left her motherless; "and yet I have been very happy thus far. In 'to-day' I always find something to enjoy, and I always look for a bright to-morrow. I feel that I shall be taken care of, for the young ravens and the lilies are, and why should not I be? This is a pleasant world, and it seems to me ungrateful not to enjoy it. If I lose one friend, some one else comes in to take her place. If I am disappointed in one thing, another, as pleasant, turns up."

"Well, Mary, everybody loves you. I wonder why it is?"

"I do n't know, I am sure; I cannot tell. I never thought whether they did or not. But it may be, as the girl in the story said, because I love everybody, — it seems to me I do."

"So do I, Mary, every one who loves me; but those are very, very few. I can count them all over on three fingers."

"Well, Laura, one trouble with you is in your manner. You feel that those you meet will of course not like you, and so you draw back, and your manner seems to say, 'I will be beforehand with you, and show you that I do n't care for you.' This will not make friends."

"Do you always expect people to like you?"

"I never, somehow, think anything about it," said Mary, laughing, "but it so happens that I almost always find something to like in every one."

"Well, you are so social and open-hearted and kind, no one can help loving you, Mary."

"I do n't know about that; but I am sure, Laura, if you would be more social and open, you would be much happier. You are so reserved; you keep your real feelings so much to yourself, that it seems to say to others, 'Keep your distance; I do not wish to be meddled with." Now, girls will not take the trouble to force their friendship upon any one, particularly if she stands aloof, and seems to say, 'I do not care for it.' It touches their pride and self-respect,—'I will give as good as I receive,' they say. Now, a hundred times I have known the girls to say things which hurt your feelings very much; yet, you looked so perfectly calm and composed, they thought of course that you did not mind it at all. This provokes them to repeat the attack, and all the time they think they are striking on granite. O, if you would only be honest, and show what you feel—let people know you as I do—they could not help *loving* you as I do, dear Laura."

Laura shook her head, and sighed deeply. "I cannot do it, Mary. When my heart is full almost to bursting with deep, intense feeling, I cannot speak,—I cannot explain; they would not understand me, if I did; they would not like me, if I could. It is my fate; I was born so; I am an unfortunate child; my mother would tell you so."

"There—there it is again," said Mary, kissing the tears from Laura's eyes. "Now, why will you cherish such fancies? Why, darling, you are overshadowing the brightest part of your life. You can, you must, you ought to be happy; you have everything in life to make you so. Laura, it is a great thing to have a mother; mine is dead."

She paused a moment. "And you have a great many other friends to love you. It was but yesterday I heard two of the girls talking about you."

"What did they say?" inquired Laura, very quickly, for she was remarkably anxious always to know just what was said of her.

"I will tell you. One said, 'There is that Miss Clay, — she always looks just so, sober as the grave, as if she had not a friend in the wide world.' 'Not always,' said the other; 'sometimes she brightens up wonderfully.' 'That may be,' was the reply, 'but it is like the flash of lightning in a dark night, — it makes everything ten times blacker for it; and when you speak to her, she always answers in just the same tone, whether it is about the Bible, or a shuttlecock. There is no *sunshine* in her presence; it is like going into the frigid zone. I could never love such a girl.' Dear Laura, I tell you this only to convince you that you yourself are your worst enemy. They could not help loving you, if you would act out your own heart, and be happy among them."

Not long after this, there was a great noise one morning in the school-room. The girls were all talking together in loud voices, — 'I will have this, and you that.' 'No, I want that, and you may have this.' There was a perfect Babel for a little time, until the various characters in a tableau which was to come off at Christmas, had been decided upon. "Here is Laura Clay," exclaimed one at length, "standing as mute as a hearth-stone. What shall she be?" Some said one thing, and some said another.

"O do not give me anything," said Laura. "I could not act, if you did; I should spoil the whole. Pray do not give me anything."

"There," said one, "she is vexed because you did not ask her before, — that's the reason." Laura gave Mary a look, which said, 'Did not I tell you so? You see I am right; they cannot understand me.' Laura might have read Mary's reply, 'But you did not say the right thing.'

"No, no," said another, who observed that Laura was moving away to another part of the room, which she did to hide her tears, "she does not get vexed, but she is in her heroics and moral sublimities. She loves dearly to make a great heroine of herself. I suppose now she will go to her room, and think she is the greatest martyr since Nero's time."

"You to be Nero?" said a child, looking up from a pile of engravings, "Who may I be?"

"Me, Nero? No, I hope not. I was talking of the poor, persecuted Miss Clay."

"Jane — Jane, I would not," said Mary Hale. "You do not understand Laura. There!" said she, as the door closed upon the retreating girl, "You have wounded her more than you can imagine. She is the most sensitive creature I ever knew."

"Well, why does she behave so strangely, then? Why could not she join our play, and appear at least interested in somebody besides herself? How can she expect us to like her, when she does so, and does not seem to care a pin for us? Feelings? I am sorry if I hurt them, but why does not she let us see sometimes, that she has feelings. I am sure it is not my fault."

Laura was again sitting alone with Miss Merton. It was only a short time before her leaving school. She sighed deeply, and seemed to have sad thoughts.

"You must write often to me, Laura," said Miss Merton.

"O yes, I am very sure that I shall; it will be almost the only pleasant thing left for me to do, then. How quickly these last happy years have gone! They have been to me the happiest in all my life; and now I must leave you, Miss Merton, and Mary," and her voice trembled, and her lip quivered. She covered her eyes with her hands.

"But, my dear Laura, you are going back to

your home,— to your father and mother and sister. That home must be made brighter and happier by your return."

"O, Miss Merton," Laura would have said, had she not felt it too much to speak, "I can never make that home happy. If I thought I could, my heart would leap for joy." There was a pause, and Laura said, "What is there now worth living for? Life is to me a bitter drug, — I mean, when I am away from you, Miss Merton; there will be no one to —— understand me." She was about to add, 'no one to love me,' but she stopped, startled to find that she had almost said the very thing which she most feared to say. "What have I to do, — what object in life? I have no school, no studies. It is, get up in the morning, eat, drink, sew, and sleep again."

"My dear Laura, I am sorry to hear you speak so; there is a great deal for you to do in this world. You must be *useful* here, — you must make some one better and happier by what you do, and by what you *are*. If you have the wish to do this, strong in your heart, you will easily find the way to do it. It is for this purpose you have been cultivating yourself, — that you may be fitted for usefulness. You must keep before you the highest standard of perfection, and aim daily to make your own character nearer and nearer like it.

Those around you must be made better for your influence. You have enough, and more than enough, to do."

"Then," said Laura, upon whom this speech had evidently made little impression, "when away from you both, what shall I do with my sad and lonely hours?"

"You must not have any such hours, Laura."

"I cannot help it, Miss Merton, indeed I cannot. They come over me like a spell in my gayest moods, — like sudden night at noonday. Sometimes — often, when I think I am happy, all at once my heart seems to become heavy as lead. I want to go away alone and weep, I cannot tell why, either."

Mother! want of early care has done this for your child.

"Laura," said Miss Merton, after a few minutes' silence, "solitude is a bad friend for you, and one which you must shun. Throw yourself as much as you can into society; be with those who are around you; do something for them. Discipline your thoughts perseveringly to dwell upon others, and not on *yourself*. Do this with real energy and decision of character. I would not give this advice to a weak-minded girl, but you are capable of the effort. Determine to live happily, and to some purpose, and not waste your life, because you are too indolent to improve it."

"But, dear Miss Merton, I do have such *lonely* hours. You cannot know how at times my heart pines for something to love, and that would love me, and how then this world seems to me almost a desert."

"Laura, we can make our own deserts, and walk in them, if we choose."

"But, I do not choose, Miss Merton. I *cannot help it.* My path has been marked out here, — right here, and nowhere else, — this is my nature."

"*Nature*, again, Laura. Do you know upon whom you throw the blame, when you charge it upon your nature?"

"But how *can* I help it? I *was* born so. To long forever for friends, and never find them; or, if I do, to love them with all my heart, and then feel that they do not love me as much, and that they *cannot.* Sometimes, even when I am happy, and always when I am sad, I feel such a void here, — I seek for sympathy, — I do not find it, and my heart aches."

"Laura, you say that you love Mary and myself. You know and feel that we love you. Now tell me, honestly, since you have known us, has this filled that void in your heart? Has it supplied that craving for a deeper sympathy?"

Laura confessed that it had not.

"Neither can it do so, nor can any other earthly love, my child. You may go this world over, and with your serious, reflecting nature, you will never find the friend to *satisfy* the wants of your soul. You must go to a different, a higher, purer fountain, before you will ever feel pure happiness."

Laura did not raise her eyes; she replied only by a shake of the head. Miss Merton, perceiving the expression, forbore to press the point; but said to her soon after, as she was leaving the room, —"I 've something more to tell you, Laura, but I will defer it until I write to you. Good-night—pleasant dreams to you."

Laura left school with many tears, and returned with a heavy heart to her not very attractive home. It seemed to her that she could live contentedly, forever, with her teacher. Not long after her return she received a long, affectionate letter from Miss Merton, the object of which was to urge her again to seek happiness at that only source where it could be found. A short extract from this letter follows:—

"Here am I, my dear Laura, writing in my little study. The room you know well, for I believe you learned to love it almost as much as I do, while you were with me. I have been thinking of you — of the last evening that you spent here— of the expression of your countenance — of the tone of voice in which you said to me, 'There is a void in my heart.' I wish I could make you feel as I do, that there is but one Friend who can fill this void; — that which you need to satisfy the wants of your soul is to love your Saviour with all your soul. This void will never be filled until you come and link your heart to *His*. Then, all your plans and purposes will be changed. Your vision will be no longer bounded by the dark and narrow grave; it will stretch on into a region of unclouded light, where dwell those blessed ones 'who die in the Lord.' And for this world, you have enough and more than enough, to do — to obey your Saviour — to follow where he leads — to 'go about doing good,' as he did, and to prepare yourself, and all around you, to meet Him in heaven. Laura, this Friend is calling you, and you are searching for Him, though you do not know it. That you may hear His voice, and see His face, and one day be 'satisfied' with 'His likeness,' is the earnest prayer of one who remains,

Very affectionately, Yours,

L. Merton."

The remainder of Laura's history is, for the most part, unwritten. But another short extract from a letter which she wrote to her friend, Mary Hale, about a year after her return from school, will show that, though now fast coming to womanhood, yet her position at home was not essentially different from what it had been in her childhood. She was still almost a stranger to her parents; their intercourse with her was such as to forbid anything like intimacy between them. They never made the attempt to win her confidence. They never made a *friend* of her. They did not know how to do it. They had not *studied* her character in her early years, and now it was too late. She writes to her friend, Mary, as follows:—

"You are happy, Mary, because you are a Christian. I do not doubt it; I, too, love my Bible,—I love my Sabbaths, and the hour of secret prayer as I never used to. Some of the happiest hours I know are spent in my closet; and sometimes my heart trembles with joy at the thought that, perhaps, even *I* am a child of God. I wish I could come out openly and say to the world, 'As for me, I will serve the Lord.' Then, why do I not? you ask. Because, Mary, I do not dare to do it. I have not the courage to break the thing to my parents. Would they oppose it? O no! They are both of them Christians. I dare say it would make them happy. But they have never in all my life taken me away alone, and gently encouraged me to speak to them of my religious feelings—not once. I cannot tell why it is, but I am somehow *ashamed* to let them know how deeply I do feel on these matters. My father prays night and morning at the family altar, that we may become the children of God; but then he never speaks to me about it, and my heart shrinks from going to him, and telling him all I feel. I cannot get the courage. I cannot first break the ice. These feelings are so sacred, I cannot voluntarily expose them. I am sometimes very unhappy about it, Mary. I wish that, like you, I were a professing Christian. But you see how it is. Good night.

Your friend,

LAURA."

THE COUNTRY COUSINS.

A PLAIN TALK WITH GIRLS WHO "LIVE OUT," IN THE CITY.

I.

THE START.

ONE pleasant Monday morning, Deacon Jones, the farmer, his wife, his daughter Ruth, and some three or four boys, were seen standing in the yard; rather, the elderly members of the group were standing, — the boys were pitching themselves over the low fence, and trying to see who could walk the farthest on his head. From between their hands they cast many glances up the road, each one being anxious to spy out first the old stage-coach. The farmer stood whittling a lilac bush.

"You will remember what I tell you about dressing warm in cold weather, Ruth," said her mother. "You must not think you can be careless because you are living in a city. Many a poor girl has caught her death, that way."

"I will be careful, mother, I promise you," said Ruth.

"You must write often, Ruth," said the farmer. "We shall want to know all how you get on. If you are steady and industrious, you wont have to live out always. As soon as these youngsters are a little older, we can get along and keep you at home, I hope."

"Coming, coming, coming!" shouted the boys, all together.

"Hush, boys; do n't be so noisy," said their father, clearing his throat. "Well, good bye, my child; keep up good heart. May God bless you, and keep you from the snares of that great city." He kissed her fast-falling tears.

"Good bye, mother;" and saying this, she threw both arms about her mother's neck.

"I can carry Ruth's trunk, Mr. Driver; let me," said little John.

"No, you can't begin to; let it alone, I tell you," said George, the eldest. "I can carry it in one hand." Then John began to cry.

"You sha'n't any of you carry it, if you quarrel. I'll carry it myself," said Mr. Driver. In this uproar, the boys almost forgot to bid Ruth good bye.

"Are *you* there, Lucy?" said the farmer, looking in at the stage window."

"I am here, large as life," said Lucy. "Come,

Ruth; if you are going to Boston, you must leave your baby-skin at home."

Ruth looked up, and tried to smile, as she took her seat by her cousin. At the first glance, she saw how much Lucy was dressed, and a momentary feeling of shame at her own simple attire, came over her. Her father also noticed it; but his good sense told him that Ruth had the advantage.

Lucy was pretty, had bright black eyes, with good features. She had this day curled her hair in long ringlets, and put on bows and laces, a white veil, and light kid gloves, and also wore short sleeves, — all this, to ride in a dirty stage-coach, on a dusty summer day.

Ruth's hair was brushed back plainly under her simple straw bonnet, and she wore a new calico dress, with long sleeves and cape to match, and neat cotton gloves. Her countenance was ruddy and good-humored. She need not have felt ashamed for a minute. The farmer was right in his opinion that she looked much the better of the two.

Mr. Driver cracked his whip over the heads of the boys, bringing it rather nearer Master George's ears than was strictly agreeable, — and he was rewarded by a thundering word, which, however, did not make noise enough to reach him.

Our two adventurers had the coach all to themselves, after the first ten miles, and talked freely about their plans and prospects.

"My father says, if I do well," said Ruth, "for a year or two, till the boys get able to earn something, that I shall not need to work out longer."

"I need not now, if I a'nt a mind to," said Lucy; "but it is so stupid and dull here in the country, I am glad to go. Besides, if I stay at home, I can't have anything to dress on. I have to do as the rest of them do."

"I do n't mind that," said Ruth.

"Well, I do. 'Go it while you 're young,' I say; 'when you 're old, you can't.'"

Ruth laughed; she was used to Lucy's ways. "You wrote to Aunt Baily, and told her we should come to-day, did n't you?"

"Yes," said Lucy. "The driver knows where she lives. I feel sort of strange about going there, I never saw her."

"I do n't know as I do exactly," said Ruth. "I have heard my mother talk about her so much, that I feel acquainted with her. I suppose we shall not have to stay with her long."

"No, indeed," said Lucy. "We can have as many places as we want. Down East girls are in great demand, they say, and they will give almost any price for them."

The girls had so much to talk about, that all the beautiful places through which their road lay, passed unnoticed. The deep, dark woods, the bold rocks, the picturesque waterfall, the tumbling brook, the pretty farm-houses, and the honeysuckles, and violets, and birds, — these were country sights, and they had seen them all their lives, and thought them scarcely worth the minding, now they were on their way to Boston.

II.

THE ARRIVAL.

Dusty and tired, — just on the edge of evening, our travellers entered Washington street. It fully answered all their expectations. Carts and coaches, and cabs and omnibuses, rattled by them; water-carriers were laying the dust in the streets; men, women and children thronged the side-walks. This was quite a new world.

"I know I never shall like it," said Ruth; for a feeling of homesickness came over her, as she looked from the window on these strange sights.

"O, it is first-rate," said Lucy, fairly clapping her hands; "we shall have grand good fun here."

Soon they turned out of Washington street, — and winding around through some quiet places, they stopped at length before a neatly painted wooden house. They entered, by a side-gate, into a very small yard. A board walk led to the door, and a lilac tree, in full bloom, shaded the windows. Lucy lifted the knocker, — "Girls, is it you?" said Mrs. Baily — peeping through the lilac branches.

"Yes; here we are," said Lucy. Their aunt

met them cordially. Tea was ready, and the table all set; so they knew they were expected.

"You must make yourselves at home, girls," said aunt Baily. "Put away your things, and get ready to sit down."

Our travellers felt a little strange. They found they had no correct idea of their aunt; indeed, many years had passed since they last saw her. She appeared older than they had expected; and while she was very kind, there was a decided tone and manner about her, different from what they had been accustomed to. She urged them to eat, and filled their plates with good things, and asked many questions about 'the home folks;' questions which were easily answered,—and by degrees the strangeness wore off, and they began to feel acquainted with her.

After tea, it seemed very natural to Ruth to offer to help her aunt in her work. She took the towel for this purpose, but her aunt declined, and advised them both to go to bed. "They had had a long day's ride of it," she said. "The next morning, if they would get up early, she would go with them to a couple of places which she had in view. One was a place where a girl was wanted for a chamber-maid, and the other where one was wanted for the nursery. She would see then whether they would suit the ladies."

"I do n't believe there is much doubt of that," said Lucy. "I hear these city-folks are glad enough to get country girls, any way."

"Not if they do n't understand their business," said aunt Baily.

Lucy thought her aunt was rather cross. Ruth had some misgivings, lest after all she should not suit city people. Another attack of homesickness came over her, and she sat at the open window quite still, looking out upon the houses.

"Would you like to go to bed?" said aunt Baily, by and by.

"I should," said Ruth; "I feel very tired."

"Well, I guess I will, then," said Lucy.

Aunt Baily had arranged her own chamber for the girls, and she herself was to sleep upon the sofa-bed. They were soon alone.

"She is cross!" said Lucy in a half whisper to Ruth. "I do n't like her at all."

"I do n't think so," said Ruth, warmly. "I think she is right kind to us. Look! this is her room, and she has turned herself out."

"What a hurry she is in, to get us off her hands! For my part, I mean to take my own time. I do n't want to go to a place to-morrow; I want to look around and see Boston; — what 's the use, when we 've come to see the world!"

Ruth attempted to convince her that this was

not wise. They should go when their aunt could best spare the time to take them, — and must go also at the time engaged, lest they should lose their places. Lucy was not convinced, and went to bed in ill-humor. Ruth extinguished the light, and raising the white curtain, sat down by the open window. In the house opposite to where she sat, women were bustling about with huge frilled-caps, and coarse men sat puffing away at their pipes. Scarcely a breath of air was stirring. Brick before, stones below, and a narrow strip of sky above, — she could scarcely see the stars. How unlike the scene from her own little window at the farm-house — in her mind's eye, it was still before her, — the old well-curb, which threw such huge shadows by moon-light, — the large green yard, with the old apple-tree, in the corner, now bending with age and splintered by storms. She loved that old apple-tree. With tiny fingers she had made nosegays from its blushing blossoms in spring, and had eaten its golden fruit every autumn, as far back as she could remember. So different was the scene from this pent up city, that Ruth began to weep, she was so homesick.

"Why do n't you come to bed," said Lucy, petulantly, — "I would n't sit there all night looking at the dark!"

"I 'm coming," said Ruth; but here, now, was

a difficulty. This was the first time in her life she had ever passed a night away from home. It was her habit always to kneel at night, to pray. She had been brought up to do this from very early childhood. How could she manage it now, with Lucy there talking to her, and ready to laugh at her? She felt very anxious to do so, because it would seem like home, and her feelings were much softened. She knelt, hoping to catch a few minutes unobserved. When she was partly through her prayer, Lucy raised her head.

"Ruth, what *are* you about, you silly fuss; why do n't you come?"

"Coming," said Ruth.

Now she hoped to finish her prayers in bed; but when her head was fairly on her pillow, and Lucy had ceased talking nonsense to her, she was much too weary to pray. She dropped asleep, thinking — "Well, when I go to my new place, I can do as I wish to."

Thus passed their first night in Boston.

III.

THE NEXT MORNING.

Early the next morning, the girls heard aunt Baily. " Come," said she, " it is time to get up; I shall soon have breakfast ready. The neighbors are all stirring; keep your curtains down, if you do n't want them to see you dress."

As soon, however, as she properly could, Ruth took a peep. The neighbor's house was not improved by the sunlight, nor were the neighbors either. The windows and blinds were dirty ; here and there, a geranium or pink growing in a broken tea-pot, were the only green things visible, for the lilac bush was out of sight. Then there was such a din from the streets — milk-carts, bakers' wagons, trucks, and hacks, all rattling over the rough pavement together, and seeming as if they must run into each other as they rushed by with their noisy drivers and restless horses. It seemed to Ruth as if everything was on fire, people were in such a hurry. She thought even the sun appeared to get along faster over the chimney-tops, than it did at home over her father's barn. She began to look forl-

"I do n't think I shall like Boston," said she.

"Pooh! Nonsense!" said Lucy; "you can't see anything here; wait a bit, till we get out of this hole, and we shall find it 's like a great muster-day all the time. Besides, if we do n't like it, we can go back again, and be no worse off than we were before."

"I should not feel as if that would be right," said Ruth, "after they have been at all the expense of sending me."

"Breakfast ready, girls, all hot and smoking, and the sun is getting hotter," cried aunt Baily, at the foot of the stairs.

Lucy hurried; Ruth lingered. The truth was, she wanted an opportunity to offer her morning prayer.

"I 'll come in a minute; do n't wait," said she to Lucy. But Lucy would not go without her; and Ruth reluctantly followed.

Things looked much more cheerful down stairs. Aunt Baily had her room in nice order; her windows were open, and the lilac-blossoms were fragrant. A few pots of thriving geraniums, well watered, stood there. Hot cakes and coffee served in the "best dishes," invited them. Ruth waited as if she expected aunt Baily to ask a blessing. Her mother did so when her father was away, but such was not the custom here.

The conversation naturally fell on the business of the day.

"These places which I have in view for you," said aunt Baily, "seem to be in first rate families; and they give good wages for beginners, — seven-and-six a week."

"Is that all?" exclaimed Lucy. "You do n't catch me going out under two dollars!"

"You must find your own place, then," said her aunt, coolly. "You can't earn that money; you are young and inexperienced. I would not recommend you to any such situation."

Ruth was satisfied. It was even more than she had expected to earn. "My father told me again and again," said she, "that he cared a great deal more for the place than the wages. He wants to have me in a good pious family, where they will take some interest in me. He is dreadfully afraid of these great cities for young folks."

Lucy laughed loudly. "Well, I am glad," said she, "my father is not so notional; he thinks I can take care of myself, and it 's a pity if I can't. All I want is money. I do n't much care where I go, or what I do. I am willing to work for it."

"I can tell you, Lucy," said her aunt, "that money is only half of it. There are a great many things of more consequence to a young woman, than a few shillings more or less, a week. Brother

Hiram has the right on't. He and I always used to think alike. If I was sending a daughter of mine into the city to live out, I should tell her just as he did. Get into a good pious family, if you can, — at any rate, among the good sort of folks. Place first, and wages second. A young girl coming for the first time into such a city as this, wants a home — that 's what she wants. She needs to be looked after and cared for, and to have some one to tell her where to go, and when to stay, and how to spend her money. It is not half the poor girls that can get this. They come down and go to the Intelligence Office, and wait and wait, — boarding all the time, — till at last their money 's gone, and they are driven to take up the first offer they get."

"I suppose they can't help it," said Ruth.

"No, a great many of them can't," said aunt Baily; "but for a young girl who comes to the city for the first time, it is a pretty dangerous experiment; it has been the ruin of many a one. If they have relations in the city, the best way is to ask them to look out before they come, or to have an eye on them at least, after they do come; and if they have n't, their father, or somebody from home, had better make a sacrifice and come down with them and see, at least, that they are in safe places."

"It is not very often they can afford this," said Ruth.

"I know that," said her aunt, "and more's the pity. Then if 'worst comes to the worst,' a girl must make all the inquiries she can, of people who know about these things, and go to the best office, and best boarding-house she can hear about; and have her eyes open, and not be afraid to ask questions; and have a distinct idea in her mind of the situation she wants, and the work she can do. She must not mind a dollar or two, more or less, in getting a start. She should not come alone, without money enough to take care of herself properly until she is provided for. But it is high time we were off; you get ready, girls, while I clear away."

This "getting ready" was an important affair to Lucy. She opened her trunk, and took out her best. When fully rigged, therefore, she had on a slimsy silk dress, a lace cape, blue kid gloves, and carried a pink parasol, and a pocket handkerchief trimmed with wide cotton lace. She intended to make an impression. She thought 'genteel places would want genteel girls.'

Ruth, also, wore her best; but this was a pretty gingham, ironed without wrinkle, of a neat color, with cotton gloves to match, and her plain straw bonnet. Aunt Baily saw at a glance how much advantage Ruth's simple and neat appearance gave her. Her first thought was to advise Lucy to dress in the same way; but she looked into her pretty, bright face, and concluded to let the girls take their own course in the matter. She was ready, and they started without delay.

IV.

SEEKING PLACES.

Our party called first on Mrs. Fay. She was the lady who wished for a nursery maid. As the cousins entered her handsomely furnished parlors, they were somewhat awestruck. They had never seen so much splendor. "Why, the Squire's house in their village, would not begin to compare with it." Even Lucy began to think she never should be genteel enough for such a place. They seated themselves by the window, and awaited in some trepidation Mrs. Fay's appearance.

Mrs. Fay was a very pleasant lady. She knew aunt Baily, and aunt Baily seemed to feel at home with her. She inquired which of the two girls wished to live with her — looking at Ruth all the time. Ruth colored, and did not know what to say at first. Her aunt answered for her. Mrs. Fay wished to have her come on the Monday following, and make a trial; and she spoke so simply and pleasantly, and right to the point about the work, — telling just what was to be done, and what was to be paid, that Ruth felt there was a perfect understanding between them; and she took leave, well satisfied.

"I shall like her, I know," said Ruth, as soon as they were alone. "I do n't believe I could have found a better place; and I like to take care of children."

"More fool you," said Lucy; "you never know when that work is done up."

"I do n't care," said Ruth, "if it is harder, sometimes; it is pleasanter. It pays its way better, because the children love you, and you love them."

"I guess you will be a pretty good hand at it," said aunt Baily.

After a short walk in another direction, they called on Mrs. Roberts. Lucy's eye brightened, when she entered parlors which were even more magnificent than those they had just seen. Here were velvet couches, and chandeliers, and crimson curtains, and mirrors, and pictures, — and many things of which they knew neither the name nor the use.

"How elegant!" said Ruth; "it is handsomer than our pulpit, Lucy. It reminds me of the Bible story about Solomon's temple. I did not know as anybody lived so in our country."

"Nor I, either," said Lucy, who began to have many fears lest she should not suit city people. Perhaps she was too 'countrified.' She would have looked more stylish if she had known how.

Mrs. Roberts asked more questions than Mrs. Fay had done. She did not seem too well pleased with Lucy's appearance. She asked if Ruth was engaged; and looked disappointed on hearing that she was. Being, however, in immediate want, she told Lucy she might come on trial; but wished her to come immediately after dinner. "She could return," she said, "and put on a suitable dress, and her trunk should be sent for in the evening."

Lucy was much downcast. "I do not believe I shall like her," said she; "she is one of your particular folks. I do n't want to go to-day, either. It is too bad. I wish I had not told her I'd come."

"I know of no other place for you," said aunt Baily, "and I have n't time to look up another. If you do not meet your engagement, you must go to the Intelligence Office and try your luck. You will have chance enough to see Boston. Mrs. Roberts's girls all speak well of her."

Lucy saw that it would not answer for her not to keep her appointment. They crossed the common, and walked through the mall under the arching elms. Countless numbers of nurses and frolicking children were there, — the common seemed alive with them.

"You will probably have to walk here every pleasant day, Ruth," said aunt Baily.

Ruth looked much pleased; indeed, she felt so;

and for the first time her city life seemed attractive to her.

"See what I shall get by taking care of children," said she to Lucy. Lucy was silent. She was not well pleased with her own prospects; however, she made no more objection to them. After dinner, she dressed herself more simply and went to her new place.

Ruth felt lonesome at first; but she occupied herself with sewing until her aunt returned from her work, and was ready to sit down and talk with her. The evening passed in friendly conversation. Ruth began to like her aunt; and to feel a sense of home and relationship, which quite compensated for the loss of Lucy. She also had her room to herself. She could now read and pray, as was her custom. She felt self-satisfied after she had performed these duties, and slept peacefully.

The next day was the Sabbath. Ruth rose at the usual time; but aunt Baily was not up. She therefore took her Bible out of her trunk, and sat down by the window to look over the lesson which her class had for the day. She had a vague feeling of seriousness, and a general impression that she must not think of everything, because it was Sunday. The good deacon, her father, had brought up his family to be very strict in the observance of the Sabbath. Good habits formed under his strict religious training, were now to be Ruth's great safeguard,—for she had no better experience of true piety.

Much later than usual, her aunt called her down to breakfast. Ruth did not know exactly what to talk about. Soon, she found that aunt Baily made no great difference, in the subjects of conversation, between this and any other morning. Ruth was surprised. She began to think it possible that she might have misunderstood her father, and that her aunt was not a professor of religion. Ruth had never been away from home before; she had yet to learn, that there are many professing Christians who make no change in their conversation for the Sabbath.

Ruth went to church all day. It seemed to her like some great holiday. She asked, with surprise, 'if it was always so, on a Sunday?' She also now heard an organ, for the first time. She was bewildered and astonished by everything she saw and heard,—the frescoed ceiling—the marble pulpit—the carpeted church—the gorgeously dressed assembly;—she felt as if she were very meanly clad,—she thought people noticed her. At night, she was weary with excitement. Aunt Baily never went to a third service, and Ruth was glad to stay at home. She read, or tried to do so, until tea-time. After tea, they talked again, until sunset. As soon as it was dark, Ruth went up and brought down her knitting-work.

"Dear me!" said aunt Baily, "do you knit Sunday nights?"

"Why, yes; we always do, — we keep Saturday night."

"Why, I do n't know as I have seen any one do it, these dozen years."

"It is not the fashion, then, in Boston," said Ruth.

"No, indeed!" replied her aunt. "They would not know what to make of you here, to see you knitting! However, I do n't know as it makes much difference."

Ruth rolled up her work; but this little circumstance increased the strangeness of the day to her, — she again felt cheerless and homesick. It was growing dark; she suffered the tears to roll down her cheeks, for she knew they were not seen.

Ruth retired, dissatisfied. She had experienced nothing of the calm and tranquillizing influence of a Sabbath at home. She was now to find out how much of her religious enjoyment she owed to the influences around her, and what share her own heart really had in it.

V.

RUTH'S INTRODUCTION.

On Monday morning, Ruth went to her new home. She was already neatly attired in a working dress, and was soon installed in the nursery. Here, she made so good a use of her time that by noon she had quite won the hearts of her little charge. At dinner, Robert and Alice were loud in her praises.

"She has cut me horses all the morning, father," said Robert.

"She is a beautiful girl," chimed in Alice. Their father smiled, and made some remark about 'new brooms sweeping clean.'

It was not long, however, before father and mother were quite as well pleased as the children. Ruth had been exceedingly well brought up, and she soon showed her good, industrious habits. Mrs. Fay, after telling her what she wanted done, left her at first to take her own way of doing it, — in order to see how much she knew about her work. Ruth had been accustomed to rise as soon as she was awake, and always woke early. It was a great comfort to Mrs. Fay not to be obliged to call her every morning, as she had her predecessor; and it was an advantage to Ruth, also; since she gained in this way a short, uninterrupted time to herself. This she devoted strictly to reading her Bible, and prayer: for she knew that if she did not secure this time for her religious duties, she could not find a quiet moment through the day. These seasons also she enjoyed, to a certain degree, for there was something in the freshness of morning air, and rest of mind and body, which made enjoyment easy. Besides, she was always satisfied with herself when she had gone through her daily forms of prayer, — and troubled in her conscience if she neglected them. Thus, invariably good-humored, and very tidy in her dress, she went to the children. Sometimes, "they got out of bed the wrong way," as she would tell them, and were fretful, and troublesome to manage; — "yes, fretful" — Ruth would have said, "if you have a mind to be fretted by them." But she felt that this was a part of her business — to take them just as they were, and make them good-humored, and have them dressed for breakfast if she could. "Children will be children," she had heard her mother say a thousand times, as she, — a perfect model of patience, — bore with her boisterous boys. O, these good mothers! God bless them! Are they not everything to us?

Mrs. Fay often went into her servants' rooms. Ruth's room was always in order; her clothes were hung up; her brushes in their places; everything was neat and comfortable, just as it was in the nursery, — and her mistress began to like her so much, that a visitor gave her a caution, one day, to be careful lest she should spoil her by too much attention and familiarity. Perhaps there was not much danger of this; for Ruth was really very modest in her deportment. She never made any improper advances towards intimacy with Mrs. Fay, — and yet when she came to sit down to talk with her she was very free and social, for she early began to look upon her as the best friend and adviser she had in Boston. True, she was a Yankee girl — the daughter of a Yankee farmer, and it is not easy to get the idea of *service* into a Yankee mind. Yet her father was a man of good sense, and he had given her some good advice on this point.

"Now, my child," said he, "do n't you go with any notions in your head about not being made a servant of, because you have never lived out; you need n't let folks abuse you, — they sha'n't do it; but you must do everything that properly belongs to your office. This is what you are paid for, and if you feel above it the only way is to quit it, and take one you are not too good for. For my part, I had rather you would be a good servant in a good family, where you will be looked after, than to have you go to a trade. I think it is more healthy. And as to a factory, you never shall go into one with my consent." Ruth remembered this, and remembered how her father chucked her under the chin, when he had said it.

Some of my readers, by this time, may be thinking to themselves, — "Why, this Ruth looks very well in a book, but one does not often meet with her in real life. Pray, had she no faults?" In reply to this I have to say, that I knew one such Ruth, at least; and that I believe there are many more. Perhaps she had faults — we shall see.

One Saturday night, Ruth showed Mrs. Fay her week's work completely finished, at which Mrs. Fay expressed surprise. "Why Ruth, how in the world is it, that you manage to accomplish so much, when you are not a *quick* worker?"

Ruth laughed. "I do not know, I am sure," she said in reply, "unless it is because I use up all my odds and ends of time. I used to think I never could do anything unless I sat right down to it; but I have learned since I had babies to take care of, that one gets along by catching up when one can. I always calculate to have my work handy, — so I can sew, if I have n't more than five minutes." Ruth liked to be praised when she had done a thing well, and Mrs. Fay liked to praise her.

"This knowledge will be worth something to you, if you ever have a family of your own," said Mrs. Fay.

Ruth blushed, and looked rather foolish, and "guessed that would never come to pass."

Much as she accomplished by this policy, her time was not wholly occupied with sewing and taking care of children. She had leisure for reading, and was fond of it. She read every story-book and novel that fell in her way; and they were not a few. Kate, the cook, had a brother who used frequently to bring in there worthless. cheap stories; Lucy, also, found them in great numbers, at Mrs. Roberts's. Mrs. Fay saw, with pain, one succeed another in Ruth's work-basket; and thought, so far as they made any impression at all, it was an injurious one. Ruth lost her relish entirely for more sober and profitable reading. Sometimes she would be so interested over a love-story that she could not leave it in the morning, except for a very formal, short, hurried prayer. She became moody, and often lost her cheerful expression. Her imagination and feelings were excited by sickly sentiment; and her conscience troubled her. She had never read novels before, in all her life. Ruth was now in some danger. It was well for her, that she was with kind Mrs. Fay, who felt interested in her improvement. After a little time she talked with Ruth, and told her that such reading would do her far more harm than good, besides taking up her time which might be much better employed on other things. She talked earnestly, and Ruth listened to her and made her a promise that she would read no more such trash. Mrs. Fay, after this, took much pains to provide for her interesting and instructive books. Some of these were of a directly religious character. Ruth's conscience and heart became again tender. The dust no longer settled on that Bible which her father had given her. She became strict, again, in the observance of all her religious duties; but still, alas! with much secret self-satisfaction.

VI.

MISS DARLING.

KATE, the cook in Mrs. Fay's family was an Irish woman, and a Roman Catholic; of course, she never attended family prayers. Ruth could not attend, unless the baby was asleep; and she soon fell into the habit of staying away, and making no effort to attend. On the Sabbath, also, she wandered about from one church to another; sometimes from curiosity, and sometimes by accident, dropping into all sorts of places of worship; and in this way the day was quite lost to her. She had a feeling at heart which she would never have expressed in words, 'that girls who lived out and worked hard, could not be very religious; that if she ever had her time at her own command and could read her Bible and pray regularly, and attend prayer-meetings often, then she would become a child of God and serve Him very faithfully.' Mrs. Fay offered to procure her a seat in the church which she herself attended; but Ruth for some time declined, saying, "she would rather look around a little, before she settled down anywhere."

Not long after she came into this family, she became acquainted with a mantuamaker, Miss Darling,—whose acquaintance was of great importance to her. Miss Darling was a most excellent woman, —quiet, unpretending, modest in her demeanor, but intelligent, and a very Christian. It was wonderful how much good she accomplished; though she did it as silently as the dew falls. She never left her little room for her day's work, without a sincere prayer that God would give her the heart and the opportunity to do something for Him; and though she said comparatively little, and was busy all through the day with silks and satins, yet at evening, there remained among those who had been with her, a silent but deep impression of the value and dignity of a pious life.

Ruth and she sat and sewed together several days; and almost before she was aware of it, Ruth had told her "all the things that ever she did," and what an excellent home she had left; and, also, how she was now spending her Sabbaths; and she acknowledged that her father would not be pleased with her Sunday roamings. But she said that her aunt Baily was a Methodist; and she did not care to go there, for she had never been used to their ways, and that she felt timid about going with Mrs. Fay, because she knew no one there.

Miss Darling told her that, if she would only

settle down in one place, and join a Sabbath-school, she would be happier. "I think," said Miss Darling, "that if we lose our Sundays, nothing goes right through the whole week. It is all topsy-turvy; and besides, this gadding about in our religion is not profitable. We need to belong to some one church, and to feel that it is *ours*, and that the preacher is *our* minister; and that we have *our* meetings, and sewing-circles, and societies. If you will only promise me to do so, I will call for you next Sabbath and go with you, and introduce you to some of the girls whom I know."

This was just what Ruth needed, to be taken by the hand in this way. She thanked Miss Darling, and told her she would go; though she was much afraid she could not keep up with the city girls in studying, and she felt almost ashamed to go because of her ignorance.

Good as her word, Miss Darling called for Ruth on the following Sabbath. She was ready to go; at least she was dressed, but her mind was somewhat out of tune. The baby had been troublesome, and the necessary work of the day had fallen behind-hand. This disturbed her; she would have preferred to put off joining a Sabbath-school class until another time; but did not like to propose it, as Miss Darling had taken the trouble to call for her. This good friend, by quiet and pleasant conversation, led her soul into stiller waters, so that by the time she reached the church she was tranquil and happy.

She now joined Mr. Clark's class, which consisted of several young girls near her own age; and in a very short time she became acquainted with them, and attached to her teacher. He had acquired a great deal of influence over his class. Ruth never had a teacher whom she liked so much. She would quote his opinions, and repeat his remarks on all important occasions, as if there could be no appeal from them — so much power had he over her. Often, when she could be spared for an hour, she would slip in to have a talk with Miss Darling about the Sabbath School. Not a day passed in which she did not find a few minutes to devote to her lesson. Mrs. Fay provided her from her own library with all the help she needed, and often a light might be seen in her attic-window till late in the night. She would study a while then, if it had happened so that she had not been able to do it through the day, — for she was very ambitious to go into her class well prepared. If she met with difficulties which Mrs. Fay could not solve, Miss Darling seldon failed to explain them for her. Now this studying, aside from its moral bearing, was worth a great deal to Ruth for its intellectual discipline. She must read, and think, and compare, and reason, and remember, and often her teacher required her to write her thoughts. All this, it is true, was secondary to the main object of Mr. Clark's teaching, but still it was valuable to Ruth; it was all the schooling that she now had.

Mr. Clark talked to his class a great deal about "asking questions." He told them that it added so much to the interest of the recitations, he wished they would do it freely. Ruth soon found that one must know something, even to ask a question. She therefore made it a part of her preparation, to notice the thoughts and feelings excited by the passage she was studying, and frame them into such questions as she would feel willing to ask before the class. This was a good plan; she knew what she was about, and could be self-possessed when she came to speak.

Much other good, also, came from her joining a Sabbath School. She formed acquaintances among an excellent class of girls. This gave her the society which she needed, and that of just the right kind. They often had pleasant social meetings in the evening; sometimes to study a difficult lesson; sometimes giving an evening to refit old clothing for destitute children. As Ruth now never asked to go out except on some such occasion, or to see Miss Darling, and was really moderate in these requests, Mrs. Fay made an effort to gratify her if possible. Sometimes, however, it so happened that she could not be spared. She bore the disappointment very pleasantly, I am glad to say, — feeling that she must accommodate herself to the comfort of the family of which she was now a happy member.

'Cousin Lucy' could not be persuaded to join this Sabbath School; and from a variety of causes, which we may by and by notice, had not succeeded very well. Ruth had never spent a happier or more profitable winter. She wrote home regularly, and her letters were a great source of comfort to her parents and amusement to the boys; her wages, also, were accumulating, to be ready for her father's use in the spring.

Perhaps I leave the impression that Ruth was very happy. I ought to qualify it; there was one burden on her conscience. She felt that she was not really a child of God; and yet she thought she was in earnest in wishing that she could be one; and she would comfort herself by hoping that at some future time she should be.

VII.

MONEY AND DRESS.

We have nearly lost sight of cousin Lucy; indeed, it is not so pleasant to keep trace of her. Perhaps a call, which she made on Ruth in the spring, may let us a little into the secret of her progress.

Ruth was sitting at the nursery window, busily doing up the week's mending. Her Question-book was on the window-sill open, and occasionally she looked into it, for a single minute. The children were playing around her, on the floor, very contentedly. They liked to be with Ruth, for she never scolded them. The door opened, and a richly-dressed person entered. Ruth looked twice, before she recognized Lucy, and when she did, she exclaimed: —

"What in the world have you got on?"

"My own clothes," said Lucy; "what makes you so astonished?"

"Why, how could you afford to buy such a shawl as that?"

"Easy enough," said Lucy. "I'll tell you all about it, if you will ask me to sit down."

When she was seated to her satisfaction, and had made some inquiries after Ruth's welfare, she took off her shawl and hat and began to talk.

"What do you think of *this?*" said she, turning the brightest side of the shawl out, and throwing it over Ruth's shoulders; "is n't it elegant?"

"Yes, indeed!" said Ruth; "but where is your blanket-shawl? That was nicer than mine."

"La! that is nothing but an old dud; nobody wears such things now!"

"Do n't they?" said Ruth; "why Mrs. Fay told me, mine would answer nicely."

"They a'nt genteel — that, I know. No genteel people wear them. This is all the-go; for Fanny and Mary Roberts have them, and I heard them say where they were bought, and that the price was ten dollars; and I went and beat the man down to eight — wa'n't that a bargain? And my bonnet, too, is n't it splendid? Only put it on! — I declare, Ruth, it makes a different girl of you! I should not know you! You must have one! I'll tell you how cheap I got it; I asked Mary Roberts where hers came from, and I knew it was eight dollars, — and I went to the milliner's and got one almost exactly like it, and made her let me have it for five. I 'll get you one, if you want me to."

Ruth had been standing before the glass, admiring her improved appearance. She had never worn anything so costly; the articles were, indeed, exceedingly becoming. She wished she had some like them, — "and why not? was she not earning as much money as Lucy? Then, why should she wear '*old duds*,' when Lucy dressed so handsomely?" Very soon, however, this feeling left her; — she turned away from the mirror, and laying the finery carefully down on the bed, went back to her darning-needle with a pleasant smile on her face.

"Well, what do you say?" said Lucy, a little disappointed.

"They are very handsome, but not suitable for me," said Ruth; "in my situation, if I dress neatly and prettily now, it is all I can do; I can't afford to be genteel. I want my money more than I do fine clothes."

"Who has been filling your head with such prim notions, pray, Ruth?"

"I do not know as they are prim, Lucy. Mrs. Fay often talks with me about spending money; and she advised me, when I first came here, to put by just such a proportion of my wages as I thought I ought to spend on dress; and then spend that, and no more. If I had to buy a heavy article one quarter, and exceeded my allowance, — spend just so much less next quarter, and make it up. This has been a grand plan for me; for I never had money before, and did not know how to spend it, nor what I needed. I set down everything now, as fast as I buy; and when I see any pretty thing I want, I run and look in my little book, to see if I can afford to buy it; and if I can't, I have made up my mind not to think more of it. I have already laid by more money for father than he expected I would."

"Dear me! Ruth, I think you are a great fool! For my part, I mean to take the comfort of my money as I go along. I a'nt going to slave myself to death for nothing, I know; and I'll not wear anything that looks mean; my things shall be genteel. We must be up to the ways of the world, Ruth, if we mean to have the good of living in it."

Ruth laughed. "You think a good deal more of that than I do, Lucy. Everybody who knows anything about me, knows that I am a poor girl, and work out; and if I try to cut a dash, all they can say, is — 'See, she puts all her wages on her back!' If they do n't know me, I do n't care what they think. I do n't want to spend my money on something handsome for them to look at, as they walk along. 'Nothing looks well that is not suitable,' Mrs. Fay told me once; and the more I think of it, the more I believe it. Now it seems to me, that I should really look better in my nice blanket-shawl than in one like yours, which would not correspond with anything else I can wear."

"O Ruth, I do love you dearly," said little Alice, who was tired of sewing, and had a sudden love-fit.

"What will you do when she goes off," said Lucy.

"Mamma said last morning, she never should go off; she is going to live here all the time; she is my Ruth."

"She will go one of these days, before you know it," said Lucy.

The child began to get into an angry dispute about her proprietorship in Ruth; this excited the baby till he began to strike up his tune.

"So much for taking care of young ones," said Lucy.

"It is work *I* like," mildly replied her cousin, as she pacified the children. When peace was restored, the girls resumed their conversation.

"There was something I wanted to say to you, Lucy — what was it? oh! now I remember, — about buying things like the young ladies; do they like to have you do it?"

"I do n't know — I never asked them. I can dress as I have a mind to, I hope; my money is my own, — what business is it of theirs?"

"Well, I was going to tell you, — when I first

came here, Mrs. Fay wore a morning dress, which I thought was very handsome; and I wanted to have one just like it; and one day I asked Miss Darling if she would cut it for me, if I bought it? She told me very kindly, that perhaps I had better ask Mrs. Fay, before I purchased, for it was not customary here for the girls to dress like the ladies with whom they live, without asking them beforehand."

"You wa'n't such a goose as to mind her?"

"Yes I was; and I was glad of it, too. I asked her one morning, if she would care if I bought a dress like that? And she told me that we should both of us be likely to get tired of it, to see it about so much; and if I would like to have her, she would buy me something a little different, but just as pretty; and she bought that one you like so much."

"Mrs. Roberts never would take that trouble for me, if I went without clothes; and I do n't want her to. She would n't get the fashionable ones. I have to work like a dog, and I mean to take some comfort out of it."

"Do n't you like your place?"

"No; they do n't pay me wages enough. I am going to leave, and do n't mean to go out a cent under two dollars!"

"You know what aunt Baily told us about running round for higher wages."

"No, — I've forgotten."

"She said, it reminded her of the huckleberry-parties in the country; those who ran round the most after thick spots, came home with baskets half-filled, while those who kept in one place that was good enough, filled both basket and dipper."

"I guess I must be going," said Lucy — arranging the elegant shawl; "when are you coming to see me?"

"I'll come to-morrow-noon, if you'll do as I want you to!"

"No, I should n't like to be tied down to one church, — and I walk Sunday noons; it is about all the time I *do* get to dress up and go out."

Ruth tried to persuade her; and told her what right pleasant times they had at their class-meetings and sewing circles, — but she could not influence her at all, — her head was full of her new finery.

"Perhaps you will think better of it, and want me to buy you something decent, Ruth; if you do, let me know."

"When my ship comes in," said Ruth, smiling, — and they parted.

VIII.

A CHAPTER OF TROUBLES.

Matters had gone on for many months in Mrs. Fay's family with little change, and thus far Ruth had had smooth travelling; but towards spring she met with up-hill work. The baby took cold, and was very ill for a time. He was contented with no one excepting his mother and Ruth, and they shared the labor of nursing him. Before he was well, and while still very fretful, Mrs. Fay was taken sick, and for a few weeks was alarmingly ill. Watchers and a nurse were provided; and Ruth was kept with the children, who by this time were all of them ailing. It was when all excitement from danger was past, that the hardest time came for Ruth. She was worn down by broken nights and anxious days; the children hung round her continually, now their mother was out of the way; and if anything needed setting to rights in the house, she was called upon. Additional work had made Kate, the cook, very cross; so that Ruth felt glad to keep out of her way. One day Kate came into the nursery to give her a scolding, because she had left her saucepan and glasses in the kitchen without washing them.

"You know I could not, Kate, for the baby cried and I had to run!"

"That's what you always say," said Kate; "and I've made up my mind to get another place. I wont hire where I have to do all the second girl's work."

"I think you had better wait till Mrs. Fay gets well," said Ruth.

Kate made no reply, but went out, slamming the door after her. Baby was asleep, and Ruth sat by his cradle, with her head upon her hand, — and the tears began to flow. It seemed to her, that she could not stand it any longer; 'take it all round, she had more than she could bear.' She thought of her home, and her father and mother, with real heart-yearnings. A few hours' ride, and she might be there! She thought she would go home; she was tired of living out. She had laid up money, and could go now with a good conscience. She began to imagine just where they would be when she entered the house, and how surprised they would look, — and how the boys would spring, and what they would say to her. And then she fell to counting how many days it would probably be before Mrs. Fay would be well enough to spare her. The nursery door softly opened, and Miss Darling's pleasant face peeped in:—

"You here, Ruth," said she, in a whisper, "and baby asleep?"

"Yes," said Ruth, wiping her eyes quickly,—"do come in—O, I am so glad to see you!"

Miss Darling stepped gently in, and closed the door. She had a large bundle under her arm. "What do you think this is?" said she, laughing. "It's my work, and now I am going to take care of the children all the evening, and I want you to get ready to go to your sewing-society. They all want you; and Mr. Fay is going to help me about the baby, if he worries."

Ruth's feelings were all afloat,—and at this unexpected kindness she burst into tears again.

"I do believe I am a fool," said she the next minute—half laughing and half crying. "But I had got clear discouraged, and I was just thinking I would n't live out any more,—I would go home as soon as Mrs. Fay was well enough to spare me."

"Hoity toity!" said Miss Darling. "You must take life as it comes,—hard and easy, up and down, light and dark,—go where you will."

"I know that," said Ruth; "but somehow, you can stand it better to take care of your own sick folks."

"O well! sickness does n't last forever; and besides, when we go to live in a family, it is best to think they are 'our folks,' is n't it, and take life with them as it comes? You have not had any extra trouble before, since you have been here, have you?"

"No, I have n't had any to speak of, excepting Kate. She has been very cross since Mrs. Fay began to get better. Just before you came in, she was in here giving me a real blowing up because a sauce-pan was n't washed. I sometimes think I cannot get along with her, and I wont try," said Ruth, warming up a little; "she says she is going off, and I do n't care if she does!"

Miss Darling had by this time laid aside her things, and sat down to her work. She laughed a little at Ruth's earnest voice.

"Come!" said she, "go and dress before dark; you are tired out; a little change will make the whole world look brighter to you. Kate's temper is the last thing to be unhappy about. Let her blow; just take in sail, and lie on your oars. Have nothing to say to her when she 's cross. She hurts herself a hundred fold more than she does you. I feel sorry for these poor girls who let their tempers get the upper-hand so; it is a great misfortune to them."

Ruth had never thought of such a thing as being

sorry for Kate, but she had been provoked many a time, and she was not now in a mood to be very charitable.

"It is pretty hard," said she, in a martyr-like voice, "to bear it quietly always. Girls who live out have to put up with a good deal."

"And so do those who do n't live out," said Miss Darling. "We all must have our trials in this world; the girls in the kitchen must have just the the ones they will feel; and the ladies in the parlor, just such as they feel. You may think theirs would be no trial to you, and perhaps they would n't; and that is the reason you do n't have them; and they may think just so of your troubles, —but that does not make them any the less troubles to you. Now, my little Ruth, let me tell you; if you had n't Kate's temper to put up with, you certainly would have something else; and all that we can do with our trials, is just to watch our own hearts and see that we get all the good from them which God meant we should; do n't you think so?"

"Yes, I suppose I do," said Ruth, looking a little brighter.

"Well, then, on the strength of that, run and get dressed; we are using the daylight all up with our talk."

Just as Ruth had finished braiding her hair, her

eye fell upon her Bible. She felt as if she would like to read a few verses, and pray before she went out; she hardly knew why! She softly drew the bolt to the door and did so. The truth was, she had recently had many serious thoughts on life and death, as she sat by the sick beds; and, somehow or other, Miss Darling always made her feel as if "she wished she was a child of God."

She went to the sewing-circle and had a delightful time. Mr. Clark came in, the latter part of the evening; and this added much to the enjoyment of his class. He closed the meeting with an appropriate prayer, to every word of which Ruth listened, — and unobserved by any one, the softened state of her heart made the tears come.

Some of her companions walked home with her, and as she entered the nursery her bright countenance showed how much she had enjoyed.

"You look fifty-per-cent better," said Miss Darling; "and we have had a fine time of it; baby has been up with his father here, most all the evening, wide awake, and in a great frolic. I think we have cured him for you!"

IX.

A CHANGE.

THE baby and the baby's mother rapidly recovered. Kate made a few inquiries about a new place; and, probably, finding none to suit her, said no more about leaving. Brighter days had dawned, which all the household seemed to feel excepting Ruth. She was unusually silent, and frequently sad. Mrs. Fay often inquired, "if she were quite well?" She would answer somewhat hastily—"Yes." Now it was observed, that she came in much oftener to prayer—and "Philip's Guides" were found in her work-basket. Sometimes, Kate teased her about her red eyes, and would have it that she had been crying!

If the truth must be told, Kate was right. Ruth wept often in secret, for she was deeply anxious about the salvation of her soul. She realized that all this saying her prayers, and reading her Bible night and morning, and wishing she was, and determining she some time would be, a Christian, would not make her one.

Either by her teacher or friend, she had been led to think much of God, and of His character; — when all at once, suddenly, as it were in an instant, such a view of His infinite holiness opened upon her — and of what He required of her — and how sinful she was, that she was overwhelmed with terror! These few words, "My heart is at enmity with God," which she felt now in her inmost soul, plunged her into despair. Her past life was so full of sin, and the future seemed so full of woe, she often wished that she had never been born. If God had only made her to be a little canary bird, like the one that mocked her with his blithe notes, in aunt Baily's cage, she thought she should have been happy.

In this wretched state of mind, she went one evening to see Miss Darling.

"Why Ruth!" said she, as soon as she looked at her, "what is the matter with you?"

Ruth made no reply, — but sinking down into a chair, burst into tears. Miss Darling kindly soothed her, took off her things, and led her to speak calmly. She soon knew the whole truth: "I am so great a sinner, I cannot come to God, and love Him — I dare not! It seems to me, I cannot live so, — and yet, *how can I die?*"

Miss Darling, with a tremulous voice and a heart full of feeling, spoke to her of the Saviour, — but it was all dark to Ruth — "My heart is full of enmity, and I cannot come to Him."

Miss Darling put aside her evening's work, and opened her Bible. With much discrimination she selected a few passages, which she read. Ruth listened, — those were very precious words; but still, all was dark — she, somehow, could not feel them!

"We are alone, Miss Darling," said Ruth at length, — "and I wish you would pray with me."

Miss Darling did so. She was a praying Christian; and she expressed, in fervent language, Ruth's wants.

Ruth rose somewhat comforted. She saw now, what she had not seen before, just what she needed to pray for.

Before they separated, Miss Darling advised her to go the next evening to a private inquiry meeting, at her pastor's house. Ruth had for some time wished to do this, but had felt afraid. Miss Darling pressed it, and she promised that she would do so if she could be spared.

To make this easy for her, Miss Darling slipped in, on her way to her work, at breakfast time, to give Mrs. Fay an intimation of Ruth's object in asking to go out again so soon. So that when evening came,— and she asked with evident embarrassment if she could be spared a little while, after the children were asleep,— Mrs. Fay told her with an expressive look — "Certainly, I am very glad to have you go."

It seemed to poor Ruth as if everybody were kind to her now, and took an unusual degree of interest in her; and she felt so unworthy of it she could scarcely bear it.

Baby was early asleep; and Alice and Robert had leave to sit up awhile. Ruth retired to her little room before going out. She knelt alone to pray — alone with God.

"O God," prayed she, — "I cannot save myself, — can I find a Saviour? He who died for guilty sinners, can it be that He died for me? Dear Christ! wilt Thou take me just as I am, so sinful and wicked, and make me fit to love Thee? *Wilt thou* take me?" said she, with a choking voice and a flood of tears. Light began to break in upon her. She went hastily out, and walked with a quick step to the pastor's house. It was a bright moonlight evening; she forgot she was alone; and, also, her dread of this meeting.

She was the first one there. The pastor met her very kindly, though she was a stranger to him. He sat down by her, and led her into conversation. She felt no fear of him: she was herself surprised to see how freely she talked with him. She told him how she had felt—"And how is it now?" he asked. Then, in simple language she gave utterance to feelings which had seemed to be all in commotion, since she left her room. He heard her with deep interest. "You have then given yourself to Christ, have you? Do you look to Him as your only Saviour? Do you believe that He is able and willing to save you, and are you willing to let Him do it in His own way? Is that the feeling you have about it?

"O if he will only *take me!*" said she; "it seems to me, that I love Him now, with all my soul!"

Soon, others entered, and the pastor could not converse longer with her, then. "Keep near to God," said he in a low and solemn tone, as he left her.

She went out, and shut the door hastily; she could not say 'good evening.' "Had Christ, then, accepted her? 'Keep near to God!'—Was she then a Christian? and if so, O, could she live away from Him, who had forgiven her sins?"

Ruth felt inexpressibly calm and happy. She looked up on the beautiful moon half-wistfully, as if she thought somewhere round in that region of light might be seen this dear Saviour whom she had now found.

X.

FRUITS.

AND this was a new birth. Ruth was greatly changed, — as she expressed it, "Such a load was gone!" The burden of her sins was laid upon "one who is mighty to save;" and like poor Pilgrim, she now went on her way rejoicing. For some days, her face seemed almost radiant with an expression of deep, calm joy. The tones of her voice were softened and musical; — she was living those blissful hours which succeed the change from death to life, — which in the heart of the new-born soul leave their memory forever.

Ruth had now just as much work as ever to do, and rather more than formerly, for the spring opened; but she found she had time to love God, and to think of Him, and to serve Him. She found that true piety consists in the habits of thought and feeling which we cherish, more than in anything we are doing. She looked back upon her past life with surprise; she did not see how she could have been happy when she was loving herself more than God. Then, she was quite satisfied if she laid by money for her father, and pleased Mrs. Fay. All this was right; but her heart beat quickly when thinking of these things now; because she felt as if she now had so much more to live for. Her common round of duties became dignified and important, in her view; true, it was a very little thing to do them faithfully and well; but when she did so, because she thought it would please Christ to see her 'diligent in business, fervent in spirit,' — it was to her no longer a trifle.

From the pure fountain, flow sweet waters. Ruth had always been so good, Mrs. Fay did not think piety would make much change in her. But in this she was mistaken. In all her conduct, holy motive silently made itself felt.

Ruth found now, that as in other things, so in the matter of attending family prayers, where there is a will there is generally a way; and at night, also, by a little good calculation, she could lay by her sewing in season to study her Bible awhile. She found by experience that, though often tired, yet on the whole she could study a little, even if but a verse or two, with more profit to herself than in the morning; for then her thoughts were disturbed and hurried by her work.

Let Kate, the cook, have had ever so hard a day of it, she always found time to repeat long prayers before she went to bed; and this first led Ruth to think that she also might redeem a few precious moments for her religious duties, either from her sleep or her sewing.

It distressed Ruth very much to hear Kate repeating long prayers of which she understood nothing. At first it seemed to her, that she must persuade Kate to come for the pardoning of her sins to that Saviour whom she had found, "who alone is able to forgive." Full of zeal, and warmly anxious to persuade Kate, she one day attempted to convince her that she was wrong; but she found that she did not understand the subject at all. She could not begin to reason with her; Kate got angry, and quite overwhelmed her with proofs that a good Roman Catholic was sure of heaven.

"You believe what your priest tells you, and I believe what my priest tells me," said she.

Ruth left the kitchen much disheartened.

"You had better not try to argue with her," said Mrs. Fay. "Avoid all discussion; but let her see that yours is a religion of the heart, and not of form. Live the Christian, and pray for her. This is all you can do for her, and God may bless these means to her conversion."

This change in Ruth was seen in her intercourse with the children. She told them as many stories, and played with them as much as ever; but now, she was so often thinking of God, that almost unconsciously she very frequently gave a religious turn to what was going on ; and this she did in a simple, natural and happy manner, which surprised Mrs. Fay. If she had known Ruth's mother, however, and how she had managed with her family, she would have ceased to wonder.

Ruth wrote home, in the fullness of her joy, to tell of her hope in Christ. She received in reply a joint letter from father and mother ; good, and full of comfort and good advice. On her mother's page, now and then tears had dropped ; and Ruth shed more over it. She carried her letter in her bosom, and read it so often that at length it was quite worn out.

They wished her to come home in August and make a visit. She mentioned this to Mrs. Fay, and found that it would be sadly inconvenient for her to spare her then, as she needed her more than through any other summer month. Ruth at once decided not to go, and wrote saying, "that all things considered, she thought it would be best for her to defer her visit till another year." Mrs. Fay was much pleased with this considerateness, and at once carried into effect a plan which she had for some time had in mind, by which she could raise Ruth's wages.

XI.

A TEA VISIT.

In the spring the two cousins were invited to take tea with aunt Baily. Ruth went early, and took Alice with her. She was received by her kind aunt in the same little room where she first went on coming to Boston. It was now as then, neat and cheerful; and the thriving geraniums in the window almost supplied the place of the lilac-tree. Ruth took her seat by them, and soon unfolded her sewing. Aunt Baily gave Alice bright bits of paper, and taught her how to make fly-catchers.

Before long, the conversation seemed to fall into a serious vein. Ruth spoke to her aunt freely of the change which had taken place in her feelings, and that she was hoping soon to make a public profession of her faith in Christ. Her aunt sat and wiped her eyes. "She was thinking," she said, "how glad her father and mother would be; and how her father, good old man, would pray when he heard the news. Brother Hiram never could keep anything to himself, — but if he was happy, he must go right away and tell God all about it, and thank Him for it."

Thus talking, an hour slipped quickly away, and both began to wonder why Lucy did not come. At length she made her appearance, slowly walking up the yard with another girl, who was gaudily dressed and had a bold look about her. They seemed to be talking very busily, for they stood some time on the steps before parting.

"Who is that girl, Lucy ?" was aunt Baily's first question.

"Nancy Everett, a friend of mine," was the reply, in a tone which seemed to say, "It is none of your business."

Though Lucy's friends were glad to see her, yet there was something in her manner and appearance which threw a damper over them. She wore, to be sure, her best finery, but it was tumbled and worn, and gave her a neglected air which increased her depressed expression. She did not enter very heartily into conversation, had brought no work, and at first made some ineffectual efforts to amuse herself with Alice; the child, however, took no great liking to her.

"How are you getting on, Lucy?" said Ruth at length, kindly.

"Well enough," was the short reply.

"Now I a'nt a-going to have a bit of this," said

her aunt; "something or other don't go straight, so out with it, and let us know the whole story. There is nobody in Boston cares as much for you as we do."

"Do n't know about that," said Lucy, with a peculiar toss of her head.

Aunt Baily eyed her keenly; "I have it," said she to herself.

"Do you like where you are now, better than you did at Mrs. Roberts's?" asked Ruth.

"I am going to leave," said Lucy.

"Going to leave!" said her aunt; "what 's that for, pray, when you are getting ten-and-six a week?"

"Can't help that, — I go to-morrow."

"And now," said aunt Baily, "I must know all about it; it wont do to be running about in this manner, and changing your places every month; you will lose your character by and by, and wont be able to get a good situation anywhere."

"Mrs. Mason says I do n't suit," said Lucy, bursting into a flood of tears, which she had been vainly trying to brave out; "and I am sure I cannot tell any body what the reason is. I have done my best to try to please her. She finds no fault, — she only tells me I must go. I would leave to-night, if you would take me to board until I can get a place."

Mrs. Baily looked very sober. This would make the third time, within a few months, that she had given Lucy a home until she could find a place.

"I am a going to look into this, Lucy," said she, "and I must go now; I sha'n't have any more time this week; if one of you will put on the tea-kettle, I will run up before tea."

Lucy did not say whether she wished she would, or would not; so aunt Baily took her own way. When she returned, the girls had the tea all ready, and they sat down at once to the table. Lucy colored a little when she entered, but made no inquiries.

Ruth thought her aunt seemed waiting for some one to ask a question; so she ventured at length to say, "Did you see Mrs. Mason?"

"Yes," replied she; "I had a long talk with her about it; and now, Lucy, I am going to tell you just what she said, good and bad. I think it will be best all round. She said you were a strong, capable girl; could do everything she required of you, and do it well, if you only had a mind to; but the trouble was, you had n't a mind to. Your head was full of other things; you took no interest in your work, and were careless and forgetful; and that it gave her so much trouble to look after you, she must change hands."

"She meant to tell her own side of it, I guess," said Lucy, in rather an irritated tone.

Aunt Baily took no notice of her, but went straight on with her story.

"She says your passion for dress is a great injury to you. That you commonly hurry through your morning work, so as to spend an hour or so before dinner fixing you up; and then you have so much to do in making and altering your dresses, and rigging out something or other, that every minute you can catch, down you sit to your sewing; that you sit up late at night, and it gives them a great deal of trouble to get you up in the morning."

"She lies, there," said Lucy, in an under tone.

Perhaps aunt Baily did n't hear, — she took no notice of the remark, but proceeded — "She says that she never can send you out on an errand in the morning, because you will stop to dress all up in your best, and keep her waiting so long."

"Well, who 's a going into the street looking like a scarecrow? Not I, I can tell her, if she does have to wait."

"And she says," continued aunt Baily, "that you are troublesome to the young ladies; that you are always talking to them about their dress, and asking the price of everything, and where it was bought; and when you can buy anything like theirs, you do; and she thinks it would be better for you to live in a place where there are no young ladies, and where you will not have so much temptation to spend your money foolishly."

"My money is my own, and I guess I can do as I 've a mind to with it," said Lucy.

"Then she spoke about the manner in which you spend your Sabbaths. She said it had tried her exceedingly, for she could not persuade you to do differently, and to go to church. She says you go out then, and at other times, with a young man, and a girl whom he calls his sister; and that you spend your time strolling about the streets with them; that you have twice, lately, been to the theatre with him, and she had not found it out until day before yesterday. She thinks you have fallen into bad company and bad habits; and *I am afraid she is right about it!*"

"It is none of her business what company I keep," said Lucy.

"Well, it is some of mine, if it is n't hers," said her aunt. "I do n't want to see my brother's gray hairs brought down with sorrow to the grave. You are on the road to ruin and if you do n't mend your courses you 'll be there, and no mistake. Mind what I tell you now; there's no two ways about it."

Ruth and her aunt were both alarmed by this account of Lucy. They pleaded with her earnestly, to promise them she would never again go to the theatre; and this she at length did.

No entreaties, however, would prevail upon her to promise to attend church on the Sabbath. "She worked all the week," she said, "and she would have that day to enjoy herself in."

As soon as they began to speak about her breaking off her acquaintance with that young man, of whom she acknowledged she knew nothing except what he himself had told her, she rose to go.

It was now dark, and near Alice's bed-time. Ruth, therefore, said she would walk along with her.

"I mean to have you come here, Lucy," said aunt Baily. "Come right back here, and stay until you get a place. This is the only proper home for you. I never will desert my brother's child, if she do n't do right."

Ruth tried again to persuade Lucy to join their Sabbath School, and enter that circle where were so many excellent girls, and where she had found so much profit and enjoyment. But Lucy would not listen to it, and thus the cousins parted.

XII.

HOW MUCH OUGHT I TO DO?

RUTH did not find that everything in the world was to go smoothly with her because she was a Christian. The more she thought about herself, and looked into her own heart and scrutinized her motives, the more sin it seemed to her she found there. And now, if strict obedience to God's holy law would alone ensure salvation,— how, with such a heart, could she be saved!

"O I could not," she would sometimes say, "if I had not the Saviour to come to,— I should perish." Her faith in Christ, and love for him never wavered; but she realized more and more, day by day, that the Christian's course here must be a conflict. It was not always easy to do just what she knew was right,— and to feel what was right. Sometimes she would quite lose her temper with Kate; then she would go away and mourn; she felt that she had brought a reproach upon the name of Christ. Sometimes fretful thoughts would rise in her mind, when things went crookedly around her, and she would often seem to have lost the light of God's countenance, and be walking in darkness.

Then she would seek Him with tears, and make fresh promises of a new obedience; yet in these very struggles there was a deep, settled satisfaction, in the conviction that she had, as she said, "got hold of the right thing to live for," and that she was steadily pursuing that object for which she had been born. There was a self-sustaining power in this conviction which, amid all her trials, gave to her a certain elevation of character.

At one time, Ruth was sorely troubled to know just what was her duty in reference to the various objects of Christian benevolence and effort. One of her class-mates, named Caroline, was very forward and active in all these matters. She gave her hand to every good work, — thinking she would, as she was often saying, "spend and be spent for the Lord." Caroline attended all the church-meetings; she was a Tract-distributer, a Collector for one or two Societies; she was on the Committee for visiting poor families in a certain district, for finding out the children, and their various necessities, and having them brought into the Sabbath School. She seemed to be 'on the go' the whole time; she had good health, and was for the most part at liberty to do as she pleased.

She felt a great deal of interest in Ruth, and was constantly urging her to take hold of some of these benevolent enterprises. Ruth did not know exactly what to tell her; she did not quite see her way clear to do so, and yet did not like to refuse, lest it might seem to Caroline as if she were not sufficiently interested in these good things.

One evening at their sewing circle, Caroline urged her very much to take her Tract district; for she had been requested to enter a larger one. "You do n't know," said she, "how much satisfaction there is in distributing these good books."

"I know there must be," said Ruth musingly.

"We must do all the good we can, while we are in the world," said Caroline.

"I know that," said Ruth. "Well, I'll think about it, and let you know before the next meeting."

Before Ruth had considered this matter, Caroline called on her. "I have come," said she, laughing, — "I want to know if you will do my collecting for the Jews Society for the next month. Mary Paul is sick, and I must take her part of it. Here is a list of all the names to be called on."

"O dear! How long will it take," said Ruth.

"Why not more than two afternoons."

"But I have n't got the two afternoons to spare; I really cannot."

Caroline did not seem much pleased. "She was sure," she said, "she did n't know what to do."

"Well, what about the Tracts?" she inquired —

"I have not yet had time to decide," said Ruth.

When left alone, Ruth thought, and thought,—but the path of duty did not appear. It was a subject which she had frequently prayed about; and to tell the truth, she was expecting that some clear conviction would be sent in answer to prayer.

Finding that she could conveniently be spared in the evening, she ran in to have a conversation with Miss Darling about her perplexities.

"I have sought to know what is my duty," said she, in a disappointed tone; "but I am just as much in the dark as ever."

"God had given us our wits to find out our duty with," said Miss Darling; "and if we do n't use them, we have no right to expect that he will take any other way of teaching us. Now let us look at this matter just as it is. See what it is you are asked to do, and wish to do. Here, to begin with, is church all day, and Sabbath School, and lecture in the evening."

"Yes;" said Ruth, "only I can't be spared to go in the morning."

"Friday evening," continued Miss Darling,—"Church meeting; Thursday evening, Sabbath school prayer-meeting; and every other Wednesday, your sewing circle. Once a month, comes the Missionary concert. Now add to these Tract-distributing and Jew-collecting, and how much time would you have left to earn your living in?"

"Not much, to be sure;" said Ruth, laughing, in spite of her troubles, at the odd medley Miss Darling made of it all.

"Then, even if you could consistently do all this, you would find just as much more around you to be done,—so that you would have to come to a definite understanding of your duty at some point on your way."

"That is a fact—I see it now," said Ruth.

"Now I feel," said Miss Darling, changing her tone a little, "that God has placed us all in just those situations in life, which are best for us. I work with my needle, and must work. You are hired by a family; you give your time and labor for your money, and this is your lawful calling. Now certainly, it would not be right to take all your time, or half of it for other purposes, and yet receive your wages; that is all plain enough, you know."

"Yes, I know that," said Ruth.

"Suppose now that Mrs. Fay should think,—'Well, it is all for good objects; I'll try and get along;' and by and by she finds that she had hired only the help she needed, and that she cannot do without it; and then decides that what she does for benevolent purposes, she must do in some other way than giving up the time of her girl, and tells you that you cannot be spared,—she would be doing perfectly right, would she not?"

"Certainly," said Ruth.

"Then — is it your duty to undertake any good work which you must do with time which does not belong to you?"

"No, I do n't see how it can be; I must be honest any how," said Ruth.

"So far then, it is all clear," said Miss Darling; "and now the next question is, what portion of your time does properly belong to you, and what shall you do with that?"

"Why I have my evenings generally, after the children are asleep; sometimes I have a stitch or two to take, that has broken in the course of the day; and occasionally there is company or something that takes up my time; but I can depend upon one or two good hours every evening, on the average. When it does so happen, for several days, that I am kept occupied longer than usual, Mrs. Fay seems to know it, and generally takes the nursery herself and gives me an afternoon to run out in; and then I am out every day with the children."

"Precisely as you are situated," said Miss Darling, "I do not see how you can take the work of collecting or distributing upon you without taking time for it which does not belong to you. That certainly would not be right. It seems to me you may set your heart at rest on that matter, if you are really conscious that you are ready and willing to do everything in your power for the good others. Here now are two ways which are urged upon you; you pray that you may have a right spirit in the matter; and then sit down calmly and judiciously to see if you can meet their claims, and find you cannot, and at the same time properly discharge all your other duties. Now I think it is right to dismiss them from your mind, and feel easy and happy about them. If God has given us one set of duties, he certainly will not be pleased if we neglect them, and go to hunting up others for ourselves."

"Well, but," said Ruth, "then cannot I do anything for good objects?"

"I'll tell you what I do," said Miss Darling,—"I have very little time which I can call my own, but I have some;—now, every new claim that comes up, I pray over and think about, and turn it round this way and that, and look at it all about, and arrange and rearrange it till I understand what I ought to do. If I find I can meet it, I give it its day and hour, and keep to it, unless something comes up in which I think I can be more useful still; if so, I make another deliberate change. This I find is the best way for me. I keep my mind clear and quiet; I am not disturbed by every new object; I know what I ought to do, and whether I am doing it or not; I must do a little at a time and keep at it; I can't give up, now and then, a whole week, and then do nothing for a month."

"It seems to me," said Ruth, "now you talk about it, and set it all out so clear, that I might spend a part of my time in sewing for charity."

"Well, you do, do n't you?"

"Why yes, I go to sewing-circle."

"And is not that as much as you ought to do?"

"When I bring work home to finish, I think it is."

"You have to do all your own plain sewing."

"I know it," said Ruth — stopping a little, "and that I ought to do, I suppose, as much as I can; but sometimes it seems to me I might leave out a line of stitching, or a little extra frilling, and be doing something for charity."

Miss Darling looked much pleased; she found that Ruth's heart was in the matter. "But," continued Ruth, "I do not always have anything to do."

"Suppose you estimate your time at so much an hour, say six, eight, or ten cents," said Miss Darling, "and sew for yourself and put that by in money; if you really feel that this is one of the ways in which you can conscientiously work."

"I do n't know but that would be a good plan for me," said Ruth, with a brightening countenance; "I'll think about it. Then, when I do have an afternoon, it seems to me I might visit now and then some poor families, if I knew where to go."

"You had better think over this," said Miss Darling, "and plan it all out; how long it will take to go and come, and how much time you would like to spend there; and just what you want to do when you get there;—and if it is one of the ways you decide on, you can have it in view, and make inquiries of the girls,—and keep a list of those you hear about who need visiting. I am telling you things," said Miss Darling, "which have helped me along. Now you may find out better ways than these for yourself. If you have given yourself wholly to Christ, and are in earnest to work where he would have you work, you have the right spirit, and wont be long in the dark after you set yourself to thinking about it."

"It has sometimes troubled me," said Ruth, "because Caroline was doing so much, and I so little."

"I find it wont do to measure our duties by other folks' lines," said Miss Darling; "Caroline does n't have to live out."

"I know that," said Ruth, "and as soon as we get the boys along a little, I sha'n't have to."

"Well, perhaps you never will be placed in a situation where you have more opportunities of doing good than you have in living out."

"What do you mean?" said Ruth.

"I've seen a great deal of hired girls in my day," said Miss Darling. "When I am sewing alone, or down stairs pressing, I somehow make friends among them, and they talk to me freely, — and the mistress talks to me, and I see just how things work."

"Well, how do they work?" said Ruth.

"I'll tell you how it is. I have made up my mind, from all I have seen and heard, that a hired girl is a very important member of society; that she really holds a very responsible office; and that if she fills it well, there are few situations where she can exert more influence."

"Why, how you talk!" said Ruth.

"Perhaps you do not think so now," said Miss Darling; "but you will, if you live long enough, and view the matter rightly. I sometimes think a hired girl has a great deal to keep her in the Christian life. In the first place she has a regular routine of duty and responsibility; she knows generally where they begin, and where they end; and a regular busy life is a great help to her; she finds in her calling what many a young lady just from school is really suffering for."

"I think that is true," said Ruth; "I know Lucy used to say the Miss Roberts never seemed to know what to do with themselves."

"O it is a great thing to have some regular work, in this world, which you must do," said Miss Darling; "it keeps the mind active, and saves it from falling into listless ways, which are a great hindrance to prayer and serious thought. Then being faithful in the service of their employers, seems to lead their minds easily into the idea of being faithful in the service of God, and gives them a practical notion about it, which those who have no employers or employments, do not seem fully to get at always."

"I never thought of that," said Ruth; "but there is one thing, — girls who live out have a great many little things to fret and vex them."

"Not any more than they need, to keep them good-tempered," said Miss Darling; "and if they meet them rightly, in a gentle, forgiving, charitable spirit, and live on, day by day, like Christians who pray much, — they somehow seem to affect a whole household for good; I can hardly describe how. It is the little leaven. I can tell you, Ruth, these hired girls are a very important part of our families over this great city."

"I do n't know but they are," said Ruth.

"You may depend upon it," said Miss Darling. "O, how many times have I seen a whole house, from garret to cellar, disturbed by one solitary fretful, unprincipled servant. They can manage to produce as much general discomfort, if they have the mind, as anybody in the ordinary walks of life, — and on the other hand, as much comfort."

"It is n't every girl, if she is ever so good, who gets into a religious family, as I have," said Ruth.

"I know that," said Miss Darling; "you have been much favored. But if a Christian falls into an irreligious family, there is so much the more reason why she should be watchful, and seek to exhibit the spirit of Christ, by walking humbly and softly before God. How does she know but that she was sent there for that very purpose? I can recall now three or four instances of persons who were first led to serious reflection, by seeing that their domestic possessed some source of enjoyment and high motive, and peace of heart which they had not."

The clock struck nine. Ruth started — it was much later than she had supposed; later than she liked to be out alone, and she hurried home.

XIII.

HOW MUCH SHALL I GIVE?

ONE pleasant morning Ruth's little charge, ready for their walk, were waiting on the steps, while baby was packed into his waggon. They were in great glee, for they were going to aunt Baily's to see the singing-birds.

Before baby was accommodated to his entire satisfaction, Mrs. Fay came out, and seeing her little folks so bright and pleasant, she felt inclined to change the direction of her walk, and join them.

"O mamma," said Alice, "do go to aunt Baily's to see the singing-bird — yellow, Ruth says.'"

"No, Canaries — Alice; are not they Canaries, Ruth? — you had better go, mamma."

Mamma could not refuse these invitations. "I think I must go too," said she. Ruth looked pleased, and all being in good spirits, they had a very pleasant walk of it.

Aunt Baily was at home, and received the party very cordially, — and opened a fresh bottle of ginger beer for them; and Canary did his best to entertain them. Ruth felt proud and happy, as if she were showing off her own family to her aunt.

While they were waiting there, Mrs. Fay observed, with much interest, a pale-faced young woman, sewing at an attic window in the opposite house. Steadily and swiftly went her needle in and out — in and out; and she never raised her eyes except to reach for the thread. At length Mrs. Fay inquired about her, and aunt Baily had a long story to tell, the substance of which was this: —

"Those two attic rooms were occupied by an old man, and this his daughter. He was very infirm — had been bed-ridden for six months; she supported herself and him by taking in slop-shop work. For the past few months their doctor had 'come down upon them pretty hard for his pay;' and there the poor girl had toiled for half, and often two-thirds, of the night. Provisions, too, had been dear, and she had had a hard time of it to live, for these slop-shops do n't pay nothing for their work."

Aunt Baily did not tell how many nice and wholesome bits they had received from her table; nor how she sometimes staid at home on a Sunday, to let the poor girl run out, and get a bit of fresh air.

Mrs. Fay was touched by this story, and she put a bill in aunt Baily's hands, which she begged her to use for their benefit. Ruth, with the tears in her eyes, turned quickly round and, with a look at her aunt which meant — "don't speak," placed by it half a dollar.

"Take that back," said the blunt, straightforward aunt, "you have n't money enough to be giving away so."

"Yes I have, I am rich," said Ruth hastily, at the same time making herself busy with the baby.

"I know better than all that," said her aunt; "I know how many ways you have for your money to go. I do n't believe Mrs. Fay knows how much you give away; and what 's more, I do n't believe you do, either."

"I do not know that we have ever had any conversation about it, have we, Ruth?" asked Mrs. Fay.

"I guess not," replied Ruth; "and sometimes I *am* puzzled as to just what my duty is."

"I wish you would give her some right notions," said aunt Baily; "she is so quick-feeling she gives before she knows it, a'most, and that a'nt the right way."

"No, that is not the best way," said Mrs. Fay; "what we give should be from principle, and not from impulse. We must have in our own minds some settled convictions of what we ought to do, and do it; whether we feel like it at the time or not. It wont do to trust our Christian charities to the chances of excited feeling."

"That's just what I think," said aunt Baily; "our feelings carry us out to sea sometimes, when we've neither chart nor compass on board; and we are in danger of getting swamped. I wish Ruth would settle her mind on just the right thing. I think it would be a comfort to her."

"Some people," said Ruth, "give us the rule that we must give to the poor one tenth of what we have."

"I know it," said Mrs. Fay; "but it is easy to see that that will not answer for all; and that you cannot make one rule for all. For instance, here is a person with an income of seventy thousand dollars a year; and here is this poor girl over the way, earning scarcely one hundred. What would the rich man's tenth be to him, in comparison with hers to her?"

"Just nothing at all," said aunt Baily;" and it a'nt that poor girl's duty to give anything, according to my notion."

"No, certainly not," said Mrs. Fay; "for she can but scantily provide the bare necessities of life for herself and her aged father."

"I want to give a great many times," said Ruth, "when I do not feel quite sure that I ought; for I know that my father needs all I can spare; and yet, earning what I do, it seems to me I might manage to save a little for charity."

"According to my way of thinking," said aunt Baily, "charity begins at home; if you do n't take care of those of your own household, you are worse than an infidel."

"This is a doctrine which has been much abused," said Mrs. Fay; "and we must practise on it, it seems to me, prayerfully and watchfully; though it is all true. On this subject, we need particularly to have an enlightened conscience."

"I wish I knew just what I ought to give," said Ruth.

"Well, Ruth," said Mrs. Fay; "you know precisely what your income is a year, — and you know what your dress costs you, do n't you?"

"Yes 'm," said Ruth, "I have kept an exact account of everything, ever since I have been with you. I always set it down at night; it has been a great help to me."

"Then you know what you want to send your father — does this take every dollar, after you have deducted what you need for dress?"

"No, ma'am," said Ruth; "he wishes me to send him only what he thinks, at any rate, I ought to lay by for a wet day. He says, while I am young and have my health, I ought to live so that I can put by something."

"That is just as it should be, I think," said Mrs. Fay. "Now, from your regular income you can deduct what is required for dress and for your father; two expenditures which it is right you should meet; so much of your money then, is employed, and does not properly belong to you to distribute in charities."

"I think that is clear," said Ruth.

"A girl ought to lay by a little every year, if it's nothing but a five-dollar bill, I think," said aunt Baily. "'She is born, but she is n't buried,' and how does she know what will happen to her! She had better make sure of her money while it's in her hands. That's a part of brother Hiram's notion, I know; one of these days Ruth will get it back again out of the farm, with interest, I'm a thinking."

"Very likely," said Mrs. Fay. "I see she has had a good father. Now, Ruth, deducting these two, what have you left of your wages, for leeway, as we say?"

"About ten dollars a year," said Ruth, after a few minutes' thought.

"This, then, is really your only available money; it is all which you have a right to reckon on. From this fund you must make up for all your mistakes and miscalculation. If you run over your allowance for dress, it is from here you must meet it; if you wish to go home or to a dentist's, you must take it from here; and from here, also, must come your charities. Now, have you any regular plan about giving, or do you know how much of your money goes in this way ?"

"Not exactly," said Ruth; "but at our Communion I generally put in a little, perhaps twelve and a half cents; and about the same at Sabbath-school concert; and this winter they made an effort to enlarge the library, and I gave fifty cents. Then I give to about six of the objects which are presented annually, the same."

"Anything more ?" said Mrs. Fay, who sat with pencil in hand.

"My tax at the sewing-circle is fifty cents; and this winter we came to a pinch for a poor family, and I gave twenty-five more — and — and I do n't exactly remember —"

"I guess you have told enough," said aunt Baily.

"Well," said Mrs. Fay, "reckoning some things which I know you have forgotten, you have probably given away in these small sums over five dollars this past year."

"I did not know it was so much as that," said Ruth, — "but I think I can do that."

"It leaves you pretty short for extras," said aunt Baily.

"Well," said Ruth, "I can't expect to do all I want to with my money, and not come short somewhere.

"It strikes me," said Mrs. Fay, "that you would find it an assistance to put by just what you conscientiously feel you can give away. I do not mean, now, what you *conveniently* can."

"No need of telling her of that," said aunt Baily.

"I know it," said Mrs. Fay; "but I want to have her understand just my view of it. Then, divide this among the objects which seem to you most worthy; and give to them, whether you happen to be particularly interested in them at the time or not; give it, or send it as a matter of principle. Your mind will be clear then, and your conscience at rest as to your duty. Then I would not exceed my limit."

"But suppose something comes up suddenly which I could not expect, and I want very much to give a little?"

"You had better make provision for this very contingency. In portioning out your charity money, leave a part for an unlooked-for call."

"That would be a good plan," said Ruth; "it seems to me I have a good many."

"And always will," said aunt Baily; "but I am glad you love to give. Hiram was always just so; he'd take the victuals out of his mouth if he thought anybody wanted them."

"What if I should want more than I had?" said Ruth.

"You have no resource then, but to cut down your clothing. Now, here this morning, you have given away half a dollar, and exceeded perhaps by twenty-five cents your allowance in this department. If so, you must contrive to make it up, or take it from some other benevolent object."

"'That would be robbing Peter to pay Paul,'" said aunt Baily.

"Just so," said Mrs. Fay, — "unless the dress comes short; perhaps she could contrive to make it up in that way, — say, get one yard less of ribbon for your summer hat, and give up the bow, and wear it plain."

"You do not think bows are wicked, do you?" said aunt Baily. "It seems to me, it would n't hurt Ruth to feel that it is right for her to dress just as pretty as she can."

"I do not think it would," says Mrs. Fay; "and after a girl has laid by just what she conscientiously thinks she ought to spend on her dress, it is worth time and trouble to select just as pretty things for her money as she can get. It is an innocent exercise of taste. What I mean is this. That, with limited means, a girl cannot do everything she wants to do, of course; and if she prefers the pleasure of giving to some unexpected call a sum exceeding her charity allowance, she must sacrifice to it the pleasure of wearing some innocent ornament, like a bow on a bonnet, — both of which she might do if she were richer. It is only in the matter of mere ornamental parts of dress, that I should think it proper for her to retrench. It is not good economy, in the long run, to buy cheap goods."

"That is just so," said aunt Baily. "It costs as much to make up a slazy frock as a good one, and it do n't wear half as long. A girl who is living out, wears clothes faster than she does at home, and she ought to buy what is good, and strong, and suitable; she 'd better have less of them, and have them the right sort."

"That is very true," said Mrs. Fay.

"And besides this, get them as pretty as she can, — do you hear that, Ruth?" said aunt Baily. "I would n't preach that doctrine to Lucy, but it wont hurt you a bit. Poor Lucy! Everything she gets goes on to her back; and she does n't now, after all, look as well as Ruth does."

"Nothing looks more shabby than cheap finery," said Mrs. Fay, rising to go; "we have made you a long call this morning, Mrs. Baily."

"O mamma," said Alice, "do let me stay all day, — see this fly-catcher I made one time when I come — I want to stay and make some more fly-catchers."

"Not now," said her mother; "you shall come again."

"Here, Ruth," said aunt Baily, handing her back her half-dollar; "You have gone over your charity money, this year, I know, — take it back."

Ruth cast her eye up to the attic-window. The pale-faced woman seemed not to have moved; it was still sew — sew — sew, — in and out — in and out.

"O, I cannot," said Ruth — thinking about the bow on the bonnet. "I will make it up somehow, and I will plan better another time, so I need n't get into trouble. I see now just what I can do."

Aunt Baily ceased to urge her, — and the little party bidding her good-morning, took their leave.

On her way home, Ruth was thinking whether in some of her sewing times, she could not give the pale-faced woman a little lift on her slop-shop work.

XIV.

ANOTHER CHANGE.

Five or six months passed away at one time, and neither Ruth nor aunt Baily heard or saw anything of Lucy. She was so frequently changing places, that they could not keep trace of her, unless she reported herself. One Sabbath morning she suddenly made her appearance before Ruth, dressed in a thin white muslin, which was gaudily trimmed with lace.

"Why, you look like a bride!" was Ruth's first exclamation.

"And so I am!" said Lucy, "or am to be to-night; and I want you to go with me, at six o'clock, to the Universalist church, to be my bridesmaid!"

"Whom are you going to marry, — that Mr. Hale?"

"Not he, indeed! — We quarrelled long ago. I am going to marry John Thompson; he is a right handsome fellow. — I want to have you see him!"

Ruth begged Lucy to stop awhile, and tell her all about it. She sat down reluctantly, declared she had not five minutes to stay, — she had everything to do. There was not really much to tell. "She had known John Thompson about six weeks; the only account which she could give of him was, that he was a 'travelled gentleman.' He had no profession nor trade nor employment of any kind; but he said he had a rich old uncle, who was going to leave him a fortune when he died. He dressed well, seemed to have plenty of money, and wore black whiskers!"

"But what will you live on?" asked Ruth — quite in distress.

"I do n't know!" said Lucy, hastily. "That is his look-out and not mine. He manages to pick up a living somewhere; I rather think his uncle helps him. We are going to travel for a little while."

Ruth burst into tears. She saw at a glance all the hazard which her cousin was incurring; and she did not know what to say to dissuade her, now matters had gone so far.

"Dear me!" said Lucy, "I can't stop to see folks crying. Ruth, there's nothing to cry about; your turn will come next. You wont have to live out always, — so keep up good-heart about it. We will call for you at six, and — wear your white veil now, mind you."

Ruth had tried to persuade her to go home, and

ask the consent of her parents,—but it was all in vain. Thinking they would not forgive her if she deserted her cousin now, she reluctantly promised to be ready.

Ruth was not at all pleased with Mr. Thompson's appearance, and it was with a voice choking with emotion that she bade Lucy good-bye upon the church steps, and resigned her to his care. Poor Lucy! She had put her last sixpence upon her bridal-veil!—and yet, with all her faults, she deserved a better fate. Aunt Baily would not come to see her married. She said, "she had done the best she could for her; and Lucy never would take her advice, and now she must go her own ways."

XV.

THE RETURN HOME.

About the time in the second year when Ruth had planned to go home, another child was added to Mr. Fay's family, and the young infant was put into her arms, — and on the whole, she did not feel like leaving her charge. Three years therefore passed by before Ruth made the long-anticipated visit home. Her trunk was well loaded with presents, for all the little folks must needs put in something for "Ruth's brothers."

Ruth was now quite ready to go; she was well clothed, and had already sent her father one hundred dollars; and thirty more she had to carry with her.

The ride was pleasant, but saddened somewhat by recollections of Lucy. When she entered her native village, tree and rock and hill greeted her like early friends; — she was excited, but yet happy, — for she was now very conscious that there had been a change in her. When she used to dwell among them she was living a selfish life, — now, she felt that she had higher motives, and that

God was her friend, — and silently she expressed to him her gratitude and love.

By and by the road turned, — and there was the roof of the old farm-house just peeping through the trees. Ruth leaned out of the window — her heart beat quickly, — she strained her eyes to peer through the trees, — but her sight was dim! — another turn, and the farm-house door and the old stone-step came to view! — and there stood the same party watching the lumbering old coach, which had stood there three years before — not one was missing!

Ruth saw first her father and mother, — they had not changed. But the "little brothers" she would scarcely have known; there they stood, a row of great sun-burnt boys, half-men, feeling strange and acting awkwardly; yet, when she fairly came down among them, they welcomed her with a shout not a whit less noisy than the one with which they had helped her off!

That was a great day at the farm-house — when Ruth came back. A looker-on would have smiled to see how the old people tried to set the young ones an example of moderation, and how poorly they succeeded.

Ruth's mother, good old lady, must soon call the tall boy to put on the tea-kettle, — and call the other, whose white crown was only a trifle lower down, to put on fresh logs; and she must stir up a fire-cake which she remembered Ruth loved, that they might have an early tea to rest the traveller. — And after tea, the father must stop in his walk up and down the room, — as soon as he saw things were cleared up a little and say: "Well, mother, shall we have prayers now, because the boys are all here, and it's the first night Ruth has come?" — And mother accedes most heartily, and they all seat themselves in the old kitchen — an unbroken family circle; — then, after reading from the well-worn Bible, the father kneels in prayer, and acknowledges God's great mercy to them in keeping their dear child from the snares of the wicked city, and bringing her to a saving knowledge of the truth as it is in Jesus; and restoring her to them in due season. Aunt Baily was right about it. "Brother Hiram could never keep anything to himself; if he was happy, he must go right away and tell God all about it, and thank Him for it."

Ruth had a delightful visit home, — and then the question of returning was agitated. Her father said "that it was not necessary; the money which she had advanced had relieved him from embarrassment." Ruth was inclined to think, that 'until the boys were able to be bringing in ready money, she had better keep at work, — she was not really needed at home.' Her mother favored this idea,—saying, "Ruth might now put by in the Savings Bank, and thus have a little for a wet day." Ruth therefore returned. Mrs. Fay and the children had missed her very much. She found friends almost as glad to see her at this end of the journey as the other.

Lucy's return to her native village a year or two later than this, was in sad contrast. As might have been expected, her husband turned out to be a worthless fellow, and he soon deserted her. She struggled on awhile alone, until broken down in body and mind, with two sickly children, she sought a refuge in her father's house.

THE NIGHT AFTER CHRISTMAS.

"DRAW the shades, Rose." A fair young girl stepped lightly within the damask curtains,—and, with soft, jewelled hands, drew the shades.

"Shall I ring for lights, mother?"

"Not yet," replied her mother; "fire-light will be pleasant awhile."

The Liverpool coal, as if hearing its praises, began immediately to play pranks. It shot up pyramids of flame;—whirled them round in circling eddies,—darted them forth at the jolly fire-set,—and even went so far as to shoot its glances through the half-opened closet-door and crack its jokes at the shining silver. Indeed, it seemed to have set out to make itself as agreeable as possible,—which was its business, as the furnace did the labor for it,—making those large drawing-rooms like summer, this cold December evening.

Rose tried to finish the point of a carnation leaf by the ruddy light,—but soon gave it up, and sunk into the velvet couch to build air-castles!

Mrs. M— also dropped her knitting of rich worsteds, and gave herself up to the comfort of her luxurious chair.

A violent gust of wind shook the blinds, and made the windows rattle.

"We shall have a cold night of it," said Mrs. M——.

"Yes," said Rose, — what difference could cold make with her? — "Is it not almost tea-time, mother?"

"Your father has not come yet. — Well, Peter, what is wanted?"

"There is a woman down stairs, ma'am, who wishes to see you."

"What is her business? — Do you know?"

"No, ma'am, — she did not say."

"You may ask her up; but stop, I dare say it is a beggar! I will go down."

She stepped quickly over her velvet carpet, and bidding Peter light up, she went to the kitchen. Near the door a woman was standing. She was poorly dressed in a faded calico, and a thin shawl — for so cold a night, it was very thin.

"Have you any business with me?" asked Mrs. M——, in a very business-like manner.

The woman hesitated; attempted to clear her voice; then replied, — "I was told you were rich here, and was advised to come and see if you could help me a little; I am in trouble."

"Well, I have had nothing but beggars here for the past week, it seems to me," said Mrs. M—, not at all pleased; "I have given away, all I have to give. Why do n't you work? You look pretty hearty, it's enough better than begging. How many children have you?"

"One, and she is sick!"

"Well, you are well enough, I dare say. I cannot give any more; I believe it only encourages idleness."

As the woman turned to go, the light fell on her sorrowful and care-worn face; but she either could not, or would not, speak.

"What is the matter with your daughter?" said Mrs. M——, in a gentler tone. She was touched a little by that speaking face.

"*Consumption*," was the reply, in a sharp tone which made the lady start. "I declare," said she, as she heard the outer door open, "how mad she is. I do not believe a word she says. Now, Ann, understand, I am not to be called down to see any more beggars. Tell them I've nothing to give, and send them off; it's the only way."

Mrs. M—— returned to her parlor. Under the brilliant chandelier sat *her* only child. Rose was again busy with her carnation leaf; and one rounded arm, bare to the elbow, supported the embroidery-frame. Her golden hair lay in ringlets on cheeks which, among its other pranks, the Liverpool coal had painted,—and she was, indeed, a very sweet object to look upon.

"Rose, you are beautiful!" thought her mother. "I really wish I knew whether there were a word of truth, or not, in that woman's story!" She sunk back into her easy-chair and tried to knit, but she was not successful. "An only child dying of consumption! Well, the worst of it is, one never knows what to believe. I dare say I have done more harm than good in my life-time, by giving away to poor folks. There! I am glad Mr. M—— has come,—now we will have tea." The still-small-voice was effectually silenced by two cups of Orange Pecco.

The poor woman, who had been turned away from this lady's door on a cold December night, went away with a heart filled with bitter feelings. A sharp blast blew aside her shawl, penetrating her through and through. The change from a hot kitchen into such an atmosphere for a moment made her feel sick and faint. She sunk down upon the covered granite steps of a house near by;—she wished she could die,—she almost forgot to care for her child, or thought of her with despair—"We shall both die, the sooner the better!" This faintness, however, passed off, and she rose to go; but as she rose the cheerful light from the windows, near where she had been sitting, fell upon her and almost seemed to warm her. She looked in at the windows though with angry looks and words,—"Yes, comfortable enough, *you* are—you rich and hard-hearted! May I die in the streets, before I ever beg at your doors again!"

Still, she lingered, as if the fire could really warm her. A lady sat there by the grate, and at her feet, surrounded by costly and expensive toys, sat a little girl. While the poor woman was looking, the lady smiled on the child, and pointed with her finger to the elegant time-piece. A shade passed like a cloud over the sunny face of the little one, and it was gone. Then she dropped her pretty playthings, and shaking back her long ringlets, she came directly and knelt at her mother's knee. Folding her little hands and closing her eyes, she began to pray. As her lips moved, the poor woman thought she could hear her.

"Dear Father, who art in heaven," was a part of the prayer, "if there are any people to-night out in the cold, without anything to eat or drink or keep them warm, wilt *Thou* take care of them. Make somebody kind to them; make somebody give them a fire, and things to eat, that they may be warm and happy, for Christ's sake. Amen."

Did she really hear that prayer? — or why was it then that her angry feelings all vanished in a moment, and that with streaming eyes she stood riveted to the spot? She forgot her angry resolution; she even placed her hand on the bell-handle — she would go in and beg here; — but the little child gathered up her toys, kissed her mother, sprang into the nurse's arms, and was carried to bed; and the lady sat there alone. The poor woman's heart failed her; she gave up her half-formed plan, and left the house.

Now she walked rapidly through the half-darkened streets. Lamps were already lighted. People hurried past her. Standing hackmen rubbed their hands and beat their breasts, — it was very cold. On she went; it was a long way, from Beacon street quite to the South End—a weary way after a hard day's work.

It was very dark when she entered her cold and dismal room.

"Is that you, mother?" said a feeble voice.

"Yes, it's me."

"O, I am so glad you've come; I've had a hard time of it, coughing; and I feel very weak; it is lonesome, too, when you are gone."

"Well, don't try to talk; how long has the fire been out?"

"'Most ever since you went away. I've had a hot spell and didn't mind it, but I begin to be chilly now."

Her mother felt her way to the shelf, and striking a match, lighted a candle. She then took up a bit of rug, which was before the stove, and threw it on the bed, — tucking it in around the shoulders of the sick girl. She did this without speaking, kindled a fire in the stove and sat down by it, with her head on her hands.

"Did you get my arrow-root?" was asked in a feeble voice.

"No, I did n't; I never thought a word on't."

"That's too bad," was the fretful reply. "I've felt all gone, ever since I coughed so;" — and the poor girl wept.

"You would n't say a word if you knew what I had to go through with; you would n't complain of me."

"I a'n't complaining," said the child, — touched by the unusual sadness of her mother's tone. "Did n't you get anything?"

"Get anything? No, not I. — But it was not that I minded so much; it was the way she spoke to me. It cut me somehow right in two!"

"I would n't care about it, mother; it's no matter; I shall be off your hands pretty soon, and then you'll get along easier. If you will warm over the water-gruel, I'll drink that."

"No, you sha'n't; I'll go and get you arrow-root, Susan, — if you can make out on a little porridge till I come back."

Susan said that would do, and took the porridge, — but without knowing that she was taking all her mother's supper, — or that the small peice of money now going for her arrow-root, was the very last of the week's earnings.

It was some distance to the grocer's, and this time the widow walked with weary step and slow. She was completely worn out; she could only drag herself there and back. When she returned and opened her door, there was a great change in her room: a fire now burned cheerfully in the stove; candles were on a table which had been placed by Susan's bed, and which seemed to be covered with parcels; and she, bolstered up, her eyes brilliant with expression, half-laughing, half-crying, held up before her astonished mother a bunch of white grapes.

"See! see! *she* brought them; and she has got more washing for you, too."

"Who?" said her mother, sinking into a chair.

"I do not know: a kind lady somebody sent here; she did not tell me her name."

"*Who* sent her?"

"She did not tell me, mother; it is no matter. Make haste and get you a cup of tea — real tea, only think, — do, mother, and give me some of it."

"I know who sent her."

"Who was it?"

Her mother did not reply. She was not yet quite clear enough in her knowledge; she was putting this and that together, in her mind. In her heart she could not help feeling that that little child had prayed for her, and that God had sent her aid in answer to that prayer; but she did not like to say so. She was not used to expressing religious feeling, though, having been religiously brought up, she had it.

"God bless her, whoever she is," was her reply.

Yes, God bless her, who would go herself to look up the suffering. How those grapes cooled the parched lips of that dying girl! and that cup of tea, — how much it comforted and strengthened the worn out mother.

For some days after this, Susan gradually failed. The neighbors who helped her mother at night were the first to notice the change. Her mother felt that she must die, but still regarded it as a distant thing.

One Monday night it was her turn to watch. From two o'clock in the morning until late in the day, she had been over her wash-tub; for her work had very much increased since that mysterious visit. She sat before the stove, thinking she might catch short naps in her chair, when Susan did not need anything. An old comforter had been hung before the bed, through the day, in order to keep off the steam as much as possible. She did not take it down, for the room was a little chilly.

"Here's your drink and your grapes, Susan," said she; "if I should have a nap and not wake when you want your drops, you must call me."

"Well," said her child faintly, opening her very large dark eyes and fixing them upon her mother; "go to sleep and I'll call."

"How much she looks as her father did afore he died!" thought her mother; "she reminds me of him every minute."

The night wore away. The tired washer-woman sank from her chair in a deep sleep, and lay on the bare floor. When she awoke she felt quite stiff; the fire was out and the room was very cold. She pinned back the curtain to let in the grey light of morning, and then went hastily to the bed. Susan lay on her side, her face buried in the pillows—one hand was stretched out as if reaching for grapes. Her mother spoke to her — spoke again — touched her arm — shook her gently — she gave no sign!

The lady and child, of whom we have already had a glimpse through a window, were sitting in their cheerful dining-room on the evening of the day on which Susan died. The door-bell rang; it was Susan's mother who rang it.

"Can I see the lady of the house?"

"Well, I believe she is very much engaged now," said John.

"I want to see her, very much," said the woman, stepping into the entry.

Just then the door opened, and the sweet face of the little girl peeped out.

"Yes, mamma is here, come in."

"Wipe your feet, then," said John.

"How do you do," said the lady kindly, as she entered. "It is a very cold night, — you look cold, — come to the fire; Kitty, dear, bring a chair. Sit down, will you?"

"Thank you, I will," said the woman, "for I am 'most beat out."

"Have you walked far?"

"From the South End, ma'am."

"It is cold, is it not?"

"Very cold, ma'am, but it was colder one night, the night arter Christmas, if you remember it. That 's the time I want to tell you about. You see I had one daughter, about sixteen. My husband has been dead these many years, and my daughter took his consumption, I suppose: she was very sick. I managed to keep soul and body together by taking in washing; but about Christmas, in that cold snap, my coal gin out, and my rent-bill came in, and my washing fell off, and I was hard put to 't. I could n't stand it very well, to see my poor sick girl a' lying there without anything to comfort her aching body. I was clear down, and says a neighbor to me, says she, 'why do n't you go to some of the great folk in Beacon street, who roll in gold and live in great houses, and you could ask for a little something which they throw away, and it would make you both comfortable.' Now, as I told you, ma'am, I never begged in all my life; but it came tough to see my poor one a' lying there with nothing to comfort her, and I made up my mind to it. So I came up here. It was a bitter night. I walked by these big houses, and I looked up first to one and then to another, but I had n't the heart to go in. Pretty soon, close to here, I saw a pretty young girl, I should think she was just about as old as my Susan, I saw her come to the window and draw the shades. Think 's I, if I must beg, I'd rather beg of that young girl's mother; she will be the most likely to feel for me; so I went into the kitchen and sent for her. The servants were cross, but it was n't that I minded, but it was the lady herself; for when she came down she told me I was a beggar, and I might go to work; and as I shut the kitchen door I heard her say, how mad I was. I do n't know but I was mad, I was clean cut up, some how; I suppose it was this and coming out of a hot room into such cold, made me faint like; so I sat down on your steps a minute, to get over it. I looked into that window, ma'am, over the screen. You had just such a bright fire as that, and sat where you do now, and your little girl on the floor by you, with a plenty of playthings. How comfortable you looked! Then says I to myself: 'You rich and hard-hearted, may I die in the streets, before I ever beg at your doors again!' Just then you pointed up to that clock, and what did the child do but come and kneel down and fold her little hands and pray. God bless her. I do believe she prayed for me; seemed to me I heard her. My anger went away, and I stood stock-still on the steps, a' crying like a baby; for my mother used to make me pray once to her.

"But, to make my long story short, I was a' coming in, but she went to bed and I felt afraid to when you were alone; so I went away home. And what do you think, ma'am? why that very night God sent somebody to help us, and I could n't help the feeling that it was because that child prayed for us; for I never have found out who it came from, and I do n't know to this day, so I cannot go to her, but we were helped in a good many ways, and got along nicely till now. Now my poor girl is dead. I found her dead this morning. What I determined I never would do to keep her alive, I have made up my mind to do, — come once more a-begging, that I may give her a decent burying."

Kitty and her mother were both in tears, and Kitty took a sparkling purse from her pocket and whispered eagerly to her mother.

"Yes," said she, "you may."

"Ah! my little dear," said the poor woman as the child approached her, "you were playing with that very purse that night. I saw it shining on the floor."

"Yes," said Kitty, "so I was; papa gave it to me Christmas day; and this money, too, and you shall have the money, I do n't want it: here, take it, I do n't want it."

It was a five-dollar piece. The widow hesitated; she felt that it was too much.

"Take it," said the lady, "and expend it on yourself; I will see to the funeral expenses. Where would you like to have your child buried?"

"Her father lies in the burying-yard in our native town," said the woman, after some hesitation; "it is about thirty miles up country."

"On the rail-road?" inquired the lady.

"Yes, ma'am."

"You would like, then, to take your child there?"

"It would be a great comfort," said the widow, "but I suppose it would cost too much, and perhaps it is n't much matter where these bodies lie; yet it would be a great comfort; if I could get there myself, I would stay. I might earn a little among them that know me. It wont be very long, I am a-thinking, that I shall want anything, and it would be a comfort to feel that I could be buried by them both."

"I will come to-morrow morning early, and see you myself," said the lady, "and have these arrangements made. You must have some supper before you go. Kitty, dear, touch the bell. John, will you tell Bridget to give this woman some supper, and send a carriage here, John, to have her taken home. She looks quite too much worn out to walk. Yes, Kitty, you may go and show her the way, and pour out her tea, if you wish to."

The poor woman could not speak; she tried to, but only her lip quivered, her heart was too full for words; so placing her hand in Kitty's, she went silently out. Dear little Kitty! how much good she had been the means of doing. O, teach your little ones to pray and to pray for the poor. God loves their simple prayers, we are assured, and will answer them, though we may never know when or where.

www.ingramcontent.com/pod-product-compliance
Lightning Source LLC
LaVergne TN
LVHW010208110826
845151LV00002B/637